Win We Shall

K'Luma Book 2

Heidi Alert

Summary: In the K'Luma Empire, a new power rises with a mysterious shadow dragon fueled by the dark realm. Charlotte and Sonos, now the Empire's most wanted rebels, must rescue their loved ones amidst emerging enemies and deepening shadows. As they navigate unseen realms and test their limits, their journey in "Win We Shall" is a values-based fantasy adventure with Caribbean and Samoan cultural influences.

Cover by Grayson Alert

www.behance.com/graysonalert

Editing by Shala Alert

www.linkedin.com/in/shala-alert

First Edition

ISBN: 979-8-9866267-1-0 (paperback)

BOOKS BY HEIDI ALERT

<u>K'Luma Series</u>
Fight We Must
Win We Shall

Praise for *Fight We Must*

Amazon reviews

"A great read and story about hope and destiny in the face of darkness."

"Strong themes of trust, faith, and friendship. Excellent for teens and young adults."

"If you're looking for something to read that is uplifting and thought provoking, but still engaging and action packed, this is the perfect choice."

"This book was an absolute delight! The storyline was captivating, the message uplifting, the characters well developed."

For Mosaic, my fellow authors and writing group.
Your fingerprints are all over this story.

Contents

Chapter 1

“THEY VANISHED. YOU CAN ask me a thousand times, but there's no other explanation.” Wylder's words hung in the air as he fixed a deadpan stare on Baku's spindly figure.

Ade sighed in frustration, drumming his fingers on the Emperor's desk. The ornate room adjacent to the throne felt stifling to him as his patience wore thin witnessing the fruitless exchange. Something needed to change—the entire Empire hung in the balance.

Days had passed since the Mountain Kingdom debacle, and Sonos and the rebel girl from Jamroq still eluded their grasp. They had apparently *vanished*, as Wylder kept insisting. Why couldn't Baku figure out what had happened on the battlefield? Ade narrowed his eyes towards the man who had been his father's most trusted advisor: the keeper of all secrets and intelligence. Was it that he couldn't figure it out, or was he holding something back?

“Perhaps applying your famed inquisition tactics to Sonos' bodyguard would yield better results than endlessly questioning me.” Wylder crossed his arms and attempted to shift the questions back to Baku.

Baku's jaw ticked—a rare glimpse of emotion from the head of the Imperial Guard. “Rest assured; we will break Taine soon enough. But I had presumed that a merchant of your caliber would possess keener observation skills. You are the last one to have seen Sonos and Charlotte before they disappeared."

The room grew heavy with tension. A shadow in the corner seemed to move and Ade cocked his head. Was something in the room with them?

"Perhaps your Elites need better observation skills," Wylder retorted. "It seems the Emperor has remained elusive as well…"

The memory of Sonos' curse on the Emperor echoed in Ade's mind like a haunting refrain. *"For seven years, you will be confined to live in the Badlands as a wild beast…"* Afterward, the Emperor had transformed into some hairy monster. *How had Sonos learned to harness the unseen realm?*

"Enough!" Ade's voice reverberated with a pitch higher than he intended. He took a moment to regain his composure. A flicker of opportunity ignited in his mind—an idea he had suppressed for the last few days. The Emperor was missing without a trace.

The shadow in the corner was pulsing, as if tracking his thoughts. Ade was vaguely aware of the other two men staring at him, but there was something else in the room. Maybe it was the Emperor trying to communicate with him somehow.

He was taught never to allow weakness. His father would never approve of an empty throne. This was his opportunity.

He decided to take it.

"On Feast Day, my father declared this to be the year of the dragon. With his undefeated army, he set out to claim the Mountain Kingdom for K'Luma. And now, the nobles want their spoils of war."

Before leaving the aborted battlefield, Ade had put Commander Uzoma in charge of the continued assault on Noiz, with the additional mission to extract the fabled gold buried somewhere in the bowels of stone. But thus far, the gold had proved as elusive as Sonos and the Emperor. Ade shifted his gaze between the two men. Someone would need to take the brunt of the nobles' anger.

"The Empire has never tolerated failure and will not start now!" Ade slammed his fists on the desk.

Wylder flinched, but Baku didn't shift.

Ade hardened his voice and continued. He needed to spin the right narrative. It was the Emperor who had taught him that history is written by the victor. He was determined to come out on top of this story. "On the eve of our grand assault against the Mountain Kingdom, the Emperor transformed into a Shadow Dragon, a level of power never witnessed before in the unseen realm. He embodies this year of conquest." Ade paused; his following statement would change the course of the future. "As his son, I now step forward to carry out his will and desires for the glory of K'Luma."

"Highness..." Baku's patronizing tone and title grated on Ade's nerves.

Ade stood in a flash. "You will address me as Emperor!"

Wylder's head bowed immediately, but Baku remained unchanging. "The Emperor is resilient and powerful. When we find him—"

"My father hasn't gone anywhere," Ade interjected, his voice low and deliberate.

Baku frowned.

"He is here, with me, giving me power from the darkness." Ade's gaze shifted to the shadowy corner of the room, where he could faintly discern the outline of a dragon. His heart raced with anticipation. Maybe Sonos was not the only one. Maybe Ade could command the unseen realm, too... from a different side—the dark realm.

Baku followed Ade's gaze, shifting uncomfortably in his seat, disbelief covering his face.

"I can speak for the merchants, Emperor Ade. We are eager to forge a partnership with you for a prosperous future." Wylder spoke with a newfound deference, his voice brimming with respect that was notably absent from Baku's demeanor.

He is a threat that needs to go. The thought formed in Ade's mind as he looked at Baku.

"It's the dawn of a new era," Ade told Wylder. He could work with the merchants. "Strength forever." He formed the symbol of K'Luma over his heart with two fingers and the stub of his thumb in between.

"Strength forever," Wylder echoed, bowing his head and returning the symbol.

Baku muttered the same, but it was too late for pretense.

"I will meet with you later to discuss how we will address the nobles," Ade told Wylder. They would also find a way to deal with Commander Uzoma and the elusive gold.

Wylder stood, nodding solemnly. "I shall be ready at your command, Emperor." He perched his floppy hat atop his head and exited the room, his dark trench coat billowing behind him as he went.

Baku stayed seated, observing Ade with a watchful gaze. He wisely kept his mouth shut, but his earlier words had already shown where his loyalties lay—firmly with Ade's father.

Defiance of any form was intolerable, a lesson his father had taught him well. Moreover, if the Elites were able to find the Emperor in the Badlands, the sorcerers might yet be able to unravel Sonos' lucky curse. His brother was weak, too much like their mother. He realized the Empress would also need to be dealt with, permanently and swiftly. But first, Baku.

Ade walked around the desk, eyes fixed on Baku's back. He knew what needed to be done. The shadow in the corner seemed to solidify in agreement.

Determination gleamed in Ade's eyes as he pulled the dagger from his belt.

Chapter 2

AIMANI'S ANGUISHED CRIES FILLED the air, echoing through the chamber of the temporal portal. "*Ou te le tuua lava lo'u uso!*" The warrior lifted her head. Tears shimmered in her eyes. "I cannot leave my brother!" she shouted, her gaze fixed on the blurry wall they had unknowingly jumped through leaving a paralyzed Taine at the mercy of Wylder.

Charlotte's heart sank. She knew the pain of losing family to the Empire. Her sisters had been kidnapped three years ago from before her very eyes.

"I'm sorry," Sonos whispered, his voice hoarse. He glanced over his shoulder as if willing the cave where Taine had been to reappear.

Charlotte swallowed around the lump in her throat, replaying the jump in her mind, and wondering if it could have played out differently. She glanced up and caught Sonos' gaze for a fleeting moment. There was a flicker of vulnerability in his eyes as if he carried a similar weight of uncertainty.

Taimani waved her hand dismissively at Sonos. "He was trying to keep his oath to protect you. *I* should have been able to do both—get you to safety *and* return to save him." Her words were filled with anger and frustration.

Charlotte knew how fiercely Taimani had fought and how much she had sacrificed, driven by her love for her brother.

"Taine is already gone." Rapha's mellow voice broke through the moment. He sat on his haunches with his long simian arms crossed over his furry chest. "We must keep our eyes on the future."

Taimani bristled. "Gone? Gone where? I won't just forget my brother and keep moving forward!"

Even Charlotte was a little shocked by Rapha's insensitivity. She was equally surprised that Taimani and Sonos weren't reacting to hearing the monkey speak for the first time. She had told them before about the first time Rapha had spoken to her and Jax in Jamroq, but hearing it for themselves had to be surreal. Perhaps their fascination was overshadowed by Taine's capture.

"Who said anything about forgetting?" Rapha asked. "Quite the opposite; Taine is immensely valuable. But he must find his way on a different path."

"You're using him," Taimani spat.

The commander of *El*'s army shifted against a wall behind Rapha. The obsidian tip of his spear glimmered in a ray of light coming through a crack in the ceiling.

Rapha clasped his tiny hands behind his back, his black eyes intense against the white fur of his face. "The heart has eyes that the mind cannot see. You must open yourselves up to a more powerful reality at play."

Charlotte remembered Princess Lenora from the Mountain Kingdom speaking the same words about the heart having eyes.

"You speak in riddles," Taimani said, her face flushed, but her anger was fading.

Memories of Ava and Lily, her mom, her dad, and Gran flashed in Charlotte's mind. Her family would never be the same, even when she rescued her sisters from the Legacy Towers. Her mom was gone forever. She wiped a tear from her eye. She was here, trying to save her sisters so they could be safe again.

"He speaks the truth," Charlotte said after a moment, steeling herself. "We have to keep going," she continued, her determination growing. "We will destroy the Legacy Towers and set those prisoners free. We'll save my sisters and your brother, Mani." She reached out a hand to touch the tall warrior's shoulder.

"You will," Rapha confirmed. "But you must follow the way carefully and operate from a different realm."

"You mean we will be based in this temporal portal?" Sonos asked.

"No. You'll be in K'Luma as normal, but you will get direction and resource from the unseen realm," Rapha answered.

Sonos frowned, looking around the empty room.

Charlotte instinctively rubbed her wrist, missing her gazer—the banned tech she had worn for years. She and Taimani had used it to destroy the chemical dragon meant to decimate Noiz, but now she felt lost.

Eyes forward, she reminded herself. They needed to get moving. The scene they had left on the battlefield had been chaotic, and the Emperor was gone. They needed to get to her sisters and Taine as quickly as possible. She forced herself to focus, determined to be the strong, resilient leader her sisters needed. She didn't ask or expect to be in this position, but she wouldn't shrink back now.

"What's the plan?" she asked Rapha.

Rapha gestured towards the commander.

The imposing warrior stepped forward, reaching into the jacket of his midnight black uniform. The stripes of the Mountain Kingdom colors on his sleeves caught the light. *Or maybe the Mountain Kingdom got their colors from* El's *army,* Charlotte thought.

"This is not a Sahemy gazer," the commander said, handing her a ring made from obsidian.

She turned the object over in her hands, feeling the familiar hum of technology. She slipped it onto her finger, her heart racing with excitement.

"It's made by the technology core at Noiz, and it communicates using a frequency developed by the Mountain Kingdom. It's completely undetectable to the Sahemy," Rapha said, pride spilling through his words.

"Can I communicate with Jax?" Charlotte asked, thinking immediately of her best friend who had to stay back in Noiz with a broken ankle.

Sonos stiffened near her.

Is it technology or Jax that's making him tense? she wondered.

"To make sure he's okay and the dragon's chemicals didn't reach anyone inside the mountain," Charlotte added quickly.

"I promised they're safe in the Inner Sanctum," Rapha said. "But, yes, you can communicate with him once you're back in K'Luma."

Charlotte fidgeted with the ring for a moment and found a small button on it. She gasped when she pressed it and the ring emitted a beautiful, complex holographic dashboard. She started swiping the air, but most functionality was locked—probably because they were in the strange portal.

"These darts are loaded with specific concoctions," Rapha told Taimani as the commander handed her a pack of darts and a sleek-looking blowgun. "The red ones will render victims unconscious, the blue will cause temporary blindness, and the green will cause hallucinations."

The corners of Taimani's mouth turned up as she accepted the weapons.

Sonos looked with expectant eyes towards the commander.

The commander held out a thin writing instrument to Sonos.

His face contorted in confusion as he spun the device in his hand as if looking for something more. "A pencil?"

"Observation and listening skills are necessary for the journey," Rapha said. "This pencil will never break or run out of lead. You have your journal. Use it wisely and be very brave and courageous in the coming season."

"Brave and courageous," Charlotte repeated under her breath. Those were the exact words she had found written in the journal back in the hollow of the samaan tree in Jamroq —the moment when everything had changed.

Sonos didn't look convinced at Rapha's words, but he shoved the pencil into a pocket of his cloak.

"While we're here where you can talk— I mean, where we can hear you..." Charlotte corrected herself. "Can we go through the plan to save our siblings and destroy the towers? Knowing the details in advance would be much more helpful."

"It is the glory of *El* to hide a matter, and it is the glory of kings to seek it out," Rapha said. "The way will be made clear at the right time, but remember that it is the journey that will make you strong for the finish."

"I see what you mean about him not speaking straightforwardly," Sonos muttered as he leaned toward Charlotte.

"Ent?" Charlotte agreed with a frown, slipping into the casual dialect of home. When Sonos raised an eyebrow, she explained. "It means I agree. And it looks like we won't get any more details." She fought not to roll her eyes.

They needed to get going. Charlotte walked over to Taimani and clasped her forearm, as she'd seen Taine do with his sister before. "We will get Taine back. We will save my sisters. And we will burn those towers to the ground."

Taimani met her gaze, dark eyes shining. She had been a prisoner of the Emperor's Legacy Towers just like Charlotte's sisters.

Sonos joined them, laying a hand on Charlotte's shoulder. "I've lost my whole family and my best friend." His eyes dropped to the ground. "It's time to stop losing."

Charlotte reached her hand to cover his and waited for him to lift his gaze. His eyes were the blue-gray of a stormy ocean.

"Fight we must," Charlotte said, enunciating each word.

"Win we shall." Taimani finished the expression they had learned on the journey to save the Mountain Kingdom.

Sonos bit his bottom lip and nodded. "Win we shall."

Rapha slipped a piece of folded paper into Charlotte's hand.

"A poem written many years ago," he explained.

Charlotte turned the paper over in her hand. *Unconquerable* was written in bold letters on the outside page.

"*Win we shall* is not just something to say; it's a declaration. It's a reality. It's a promise. It's truth. Remember that, especially when things get dark," Rapha said.

Charlotte wanted to ask more questions, but Rapha turned and started humming as he and the commander walked towards a shining crevice that appeared on the wall.

"Wait." Charlotte held out her arms to stop Sonos and Taimani from following. "I want to read this first," she said, unfolding the paper. She remembered how Jax had only been able to read the words of an ancient scroll inside the other portal they had found in Jamroq. The letters had turned illegible outside the portal.

Sonos leaned in close, reading over her shoulder. Something squeezed her heart at his proximity, but she took a breath and read the words aloud.

To the deep darkness of night,
To the crushing flames of fire,
You have threatened and roared,
You have promised defeat,
but

You have no sight of who I am.
You have come as a thief in the night,
Creeping in and out through slivers,
You have claimed and screamed victory,
Yet you slither on evermore,
because
You have no sight of Truth.
Your fight is futile,
You come against eternity with time,
Your roar is harmless,
You come against truth with lies,
Your mammoth shows of power are no more than wisps,
for
You come against El with humanness.
So, fight on, my giants,
Make your show, my foes,
Plan your ways,
Mark your path,
Set your sights.
But hear this—
Hear it loud,
Ringing clear,
The shout of a king is among us!
Hear the mighty thunder of Noiz,
See the numbers who stand in Truth,
Feel the tremble as El arises,
You have touched one who is unconquerable.

CHAPTER 3

A SHIVER COURSED THROUGH Sonos' body as he emerged from the temporal portal. The transition from the otherworldly crevice of light to the vast expanse of a flat, green field left him feeling disoriented and vulnerable.

"Where are we?" Charlotte's voice trembled slightly.

Taimani's hands twitched toward the darts strapped to her thigh, her eyes scanning the area with unease.

Sonos couldn't help but envy her possession of a weapon or advanced technology like Charlotte, contrasting sharply with his fancy pencil. He frowned but reminded himself of their mission. They were here to rescue Taine and Charlotte's sisters.

Charlotte shifted next to him as Rapha chittered and scrambled up to perch on her shoulder.

The commander was gone.

The field was bathed in the dim glow of the late afternoon sun.

Rapha pointed ahead in the direction opposite the setting sun. The vague outline of a village could be seen.

"I will secure the area while you figure out the plan." Taimani jogged off, making silent, wide circles of the area.

Sonos felt the sharp absence of Taine. Usually, the two warriors would flow like a river working together to protect their charges. What was Wylder doing with his bodyguard, his friend? He prayed that they would rescue Taine before Baku had a chance to—

Charlotte yelped, interrupting his thoughts, and stared at her hand. "The gazer... it's vibrating." She fumbled with the ring, pressing a button and causing the holographic dashboard to pop up. Her eyes lit up at the same time.

Despite the unease, Sonos smiled at her unabashed love for tech.

She tapped the air with one hand while holding the gazer before her.

Rapha shifted on her shoulder.

A flicker of hope appeared on Charlotte's face as Jax's image materialized on the screen. His dark eyes held a sense of urgency as he peered into the camera.

"Char! Where are you? It's been a week since the attack, and I haven't heard a peep." Jax's anxious tone reverberated through the air.

"A week?" Sonos gasped, incredulous. The passage of time had felt like hours at most within the portal.

"Jax!" Charlotte had a big grin on her face. She was clearly more concerned with connecting to her friend than worrying about time.

But Jax continued as if he didn't hear Charlotte. "I hope you get this message. I'm getting worried."

Charlotte allowed the video to play for a moment before her fingers swiped across the dashboard, navigating through various images and prompts. Her initial joy at connecting with her friend waned, replaced by a furrowed brow.

Jax's voice continued to echo across the silent plain. "Princess Leonora promised that you were supposed to get your gazer-ring from Rapha. I have no doubt you can figure it out..." He paused and brought the camera closer to his face—really close and dropped his voice. "You better not be so smitten with Prince Sonny that you've forgotten me."

Sonos picked up on Charlotte's frown, and his stomach dropped slightly.

Jax gave a lopsided grin as he repositioned the camera. "Nah, don't worry, I dun know yuh wouldn't forget me jus' so." Jax may have laid the Jamroq accent on thick, but the message was clear. He wasn't worried about Charlotte forgetting him.

The teasing tone, tinged with a touch of possessiveness, evoked a mix of emotions within Sonos—amusement, concern, and a pang of guilt. He shook his head, trying to clear his mind.

"Anyways, connection in the Inner Sanctum is horrible. I can only make and receive calls when I convince Tuvo and Malachi to let me join them for scout reporting. Otherwise, I'm stuck with hovering healers. Lenora has been wonderful, but I'm getting restless."

"Wonderful?" Charlotte muttered under her breath, repeating the word after Jax. *Was that a hint of jealousy?* Sonos wondered.

In the video, Jax cast a wary glance over his shoulder, his voice lowered again to a hushed tone. "Okay, I need to go. But please leave a message when you get this. Let me know if you're all right. And don't go having all the fun without me, okay? Remember, we're saving Ava and Lily together." Jax's image faded with a wink, leaving Charlotte sighing in its wake.

"It looks like this was sent through yesterday," Charlotte murmured, her mouth drawn in a tight line.

Taimani jogged over. "A week since my brother's capture?" Her gaze bore into Rapha, accusatory.

Sonos could sense the weight of her emotions, the deep concern, and the rawness of her frustration. He remembered Charlotte's explanation that they were only able to hear, or rather understand, Rapha inside the portal.

"Sorry, Mani." Charlotte's voice broke through the tension, bearing an apology they all seemed to carry. "I didn't know that would happen when we jumped," she whispered.

Taimani's fiery eyes darted between Sonos and Charlotte, then back to Rapha, her silence full of unspoken questions. She sucked her teeth in annoyance and stalked off without saying anything further, heading in the direction of the village.

Rapha scampered down Charlotte's side and ran after Taimani.

"Do you think she's...?" Charlotte's voice trailed off.

"She'll be okay. It's... Let's focus on finding Taine and your sisters," Sonos added quickly.

"I need to call Jax back," Charlotte said, swiping through controls and typing codes Sonos couldn't understand.

"Can you type and walk at the same time?" Sonos asked. "I don't think we should let Mani get too far ahead."

Charlotte glanced up and nodded. She walked absently beside Sonos, tapping the dashboard with one hand while the other extended in front of her, holding up the gazer-ring.

Sonos placed a hand on her back to guide her around a rivet in the field before she tripped. As they walked silently, his mind flashed back to the battlefield where he had confronted his father. *"Your pride, lust for conquest, and oppression of others stand in judgment against you. El has seen and now speaks. For seven years, you will be confined to live in the Badlands as if a wild beast until you raise your eyes and acknowledge El as sovereign over all the kingdoms and all the empires of the entire earth."* Sonos remembered the curse perfectly as if he had just spoken them, as if the words had been written on his mind.

"Ah! I got it," Charlotte exclaimed, returning his focus to the present. He reached out to catch her as she stumbled in her excitement.

She hardly noticed, then frowned. "Never mind, I thought I had it."

"You'll get it," Sonos said, trying to offer some encouragement. "I have yet to see tech that you can't master."

Charlotte turned her head to look at him.

"What? It's true. And I mean it as a compliment," Sonos explained as they resumed walking. He kept his hand on her back to keep her moving in the right direction. His heart thrummed a little faster with the protective touch he offered, but he didn't allow his thoughts to wander. They had a long road ahead, and he wasn't sure how Charlotte felt about him. Truth be told, he was still trying to sort through his feelings, while staying alive.

"I know. It's not that. It's just... that sounds like something Jax would say," Charlotte said.

Jax, again, Sonos thought with a frown.

She distractedly flipped through a screen on the hologram, then looked at Sonos again, her eyes filled suddenly with tears. "I know losing Taine and what happened with the Emperor and Ade must hurt. I'm sorry things have gone so sideways."

Sonos knew the guilt that flooded her words all too well. "Char, you did the right thing, jumping over that chasm towards Rapha."

"I wish doing the right thing didn't feel so terrible sometimes," Charlotte muttered.

"Don't always trust what you feel," Sonos said. "Sah Timur used to tell me that."

Since being on the run, words or phrases that his former tutor used to share came to life in a very real way.

Charlotte looked up again, her green eyes softened with gratitude.

Sonos resisted the sudden urge to tuck an errant curl behind her ear.

A video feed popped up on her holographic screen, and her gaze shifted. The moment was broken. "Oh! I think I got it!" Charlotte said. A video of her face appeared in a holographic square frame.

Sonos leaned his head closer. "I don't see Jax, just us."

She pointed to a red flashing dot on the screen. "I think that means it's recording. I'm still getting used to the Mountain Kingdom protocols." She shook her head. "Jax, if you get this message, know we're all okay. We followed Rapha into a temporal portal. Do you remember how it treated time differently for each of us back in that samaan tree? Well, the same thing happened with this one. We just got out. And now we're..." She turned towards Sonos. "Where are we?"

"Uhm, we can't see the mountains. The temperature is warm, but the breeze still has a bit of a bite. Lots of fields and what looks to be a village up ahead," Sonos said. "But honestly, we could be almost anywhere in K'Luma."

Charlotte frowned. "Very helpful."

"I suggest we call him back after we get to the village," Sonos said, ignoring Charlotte's sarcasm.

"Okay, yes," Charlotte spoke back to the video. "Taimani and Raph ran ahead, so let me call you back after we catch up with them. We should have more information then." She sighed, then added in a somber tone, "And hey, you know Wylder, the merchant who was chasing Sonos and the warriors before? Well, he captured Taine. Maybe you can ask King Mason if he could help get him back. I have no idea where he is, but Mani is distraught. We need help." Charlotte paused, then ended with, "Walk good." The video cut off.

"Walk good?" Sonos asked.

"It's a way to say goodbye in Jamroq. It means, take care, and I wish you good fortune... that kind of thing," Charlotte answered.

Sonos smiled. "Walk good. I like it. I suppose it holds a double meaning for Jax with his broken foot."

"I forgot to ask how his foot was!" Charlotte tapped her gazer on again.

"Hey," Sonos laid a hand on her arm. "Why don't we wait until we have the update from the village and a little more information? Then we can do another video."

Charlotte nodded. "Okay. Let's go find Mani."

"Speaking of Mani..." Sonos gestured towards a figure running at them across the field.

When Mani reached them, she was barely out of breath from the sprint. Rapha jumped from Taimani and scurried to his usual place on Charlotte's shoulder.

"Come quickly," the warrior said. "They're playing a video from Pergamum, and it sounds like a big announcement will be coming through soon."

CHAPTER 4

T HE MAIN SQUARE OF the small village teemed with a mass of people, each jostling for a view of the platform where a large screen had been erected.

Amid the chaos, Taimani found a pocket of space against a weathered building on the border of the square.

Charlotte sucked in a deep breath, trying to recover from the sprint across the field.

Rapha was tucked securely in her jacket.

"What is it?" she asked Sonos, who was staring at the shop behind them where a quaint wooden sign swung gently above the door. It depicted a steaming loaf of bread.

"It reminds me of the bakery in Portemore, where we first met Miss Gemma," Sonos answered. He had the hood of his cloak drawn up so he wouldn't be recognized.

Taimani's head snapped up to the sign. "We're not in Portemore."

"I know, it's just... something feels familiar." His voice grew more distant.

Everywhere on the mainland of K'Luma still felt foreign to Charlotte. A pang of homesickness for her family and the scents and sounds of Jamroq grew, and she pulled her cloak, which was over her jacket, tighter, trying to keep the warmth inside. The sun never seemed to work hard enough on the mainland.

Rapha hummed softly, bringing her back to the present. She needed to stay focused.

The blaring of trumpets abruptly shattered the buzzing chatter, signaling the start of the broadcast. Members of the Imperial Guard were stationed at every exit, their watchful gazes scanning for any hint of disturbance. A captain, bedecked in the red and gold trim signifying his rank, stood proudly on the platform before the towering screen.

The whole scene and feel in the square brought back stark memories from Feast Day back in Jamroq, when everything had fallen apart—the image of Jax and her dad strapped to a block about to be whipped. She closed her eyes and focused on her breathing, trying to avert the heavy feeling in her chest that was beginning to weigh her down.

"This must be something big," Sonos whispered. "Did you catch any clue about what's happening?" he asked Taimani.

Taimani shook her head, her eyes continuing to scan the crowd. "The moment I saw the gathering, I knew I had to find you both," she said, her mouth drawn in a tight line.

In a sudden burst of light and sound, the screen flickered to life, revealing a regal image of Ade, seated upon the throne. He had the Emperor's crown on his head.

Charlotte's breath caught in her throat, her eyes widening in disbelief. "It's your brother..."

"What is Ade doing?" The question slipped from Sonos at the same time, laden with apprehension.

The camera panned across the throne room and broadcast images of nobles dressed in all their splendor. Charlotte thought she caught a glimpse of Wylder with his tech-infused dark cloak among them, and her heart dropped. He was the one who had captured Taine.

"Where is the Empress? I'm not seeing Baku either," Sonos muttered as he tensed beside her.

Ade straightened on the throne, emanating an aura of authority. "Citizens and servants of K'Luma, my father declared this year to be the year of the dragon, and his words have never faltered," Ade declared, his voice filled with triumph. "I am thrilled to announce the utter annihilation of the Mountain Kingdom and its defenders."

"What?" Charlotte instinctively covered her mouth, eyes darting to Sonos, seeking answers amidst the chaos. That's not what Jax had indicated. They were supposed to be safe. Had something happened between his last message and now?

"He's lying," Taimani muttered, her voice barely audible.

"Commander Uzoma," Ade continued, "is currently overseeing a grand excavation of the mountains to unearth the fabled treasures of gold that will soon be delivered as the spoils of our victory."

Jubilant cheers erupted from the assembled nobles on the screen; they were reveling in the prospect of newfound riches.

The crowd in the village was notably mute. Charlotte understood their unease.

Ade paused, basking in the adulation of those with him in the throne room, before continuing. "On the eve of this glorious conquest, the Emperor and his mightiest sorcerers helped to ensure this triumph of K'Luma. He transcended into the unseen realm and has transformed into a formidable manifestation of a shadow dragon."

"That's not true," Charlotte whispered, annoyed at the lies. Her eyes again searched Sonos' face, memories from the battlefield tent flooding her mind. "It was you... the words from *El*..."

She opened her jacket to check on Rapha.

Before Charlotte could say anything further, Taimani swiftly leaned in, her finger pressed against her lips, silencing any further conversation.

As Ade's words filled the square, a colossal shadow in the shape of a dragon began to materialize on the wall behind the throne. The shadow seemed to crawl forward beyond the throne and through the screen into the village square.

Gasps of astonishment rippled through the crowd, mingling with an undercurrent of fear and disbelief. The sight alone should have been awe-inspiring, but Charlotte's mind raced, searching for a rational explanation. *The smoke dragon that attacked me was a sorcerer,* she thought. Could this be some elaborate illusion as well? She scanned the square for any dark purple robes that marked out the sorcerers, but it was too crowded.

"Through this power, I now stand as the first Dragon Emperor of the mighty K'Luma Empire. I am the voice and living embodiment of the Shadow Dragon. Together, we wield dominion over the veiled realm of shadows in the unseen realm, and over the ever-expanding empire of K'Luma," Ade proclaimed, his voice resolute and commanding.

The nobles in the throne room erupted into thunderous applause once more.

Murmurs rippled through the square, and then the captain from the stage commanded everyone to bow.

It took only a moment before the villagers started dropping to their knees. Nearby, a young boy stood confused, his mother coaxing him to kneel. A guard took the blunt end of his spear and knocked the boy's knees from behind, causing him to cry out in pain as he fell.

Even though they stood at the square's edge, pressed against the bakery wall, Charlotte was quick to kneel.

Sonos and Taimani did the same.

Her heart pounded, but her gaze remained fixed on the screen. She wondered briefly how Sonos felt, being forced to kneel to his brother, but his face was still hidden, and he gave nothing away.

The audio blared as Ade continued. "At this dawn of a new era, my first act is to fortify the order and dominion of the Empire. The practice or belief in any gods other than the Dragon Emperor shall be met with death and enforced without mercy."

Charlotte's stomach dropped. Previously, religion and following any authority but the Emperor's had been illegal, but if it was hidden, no one made a fuss. Something in Ade's tone and fervor indicated that this would be different.

"Furthermore, there are two rebels who must be brought to swift justice as an immediate priority."

A larger-than-life image of Charlotte and Sonos flashed on the screen, their identities unmistakable. All the blood drained from Charlotte's face. In that heart-stopping moment, she and Sonos became the most hunted criminals in the entire Empire.

The wall of the bakery shifted behind them, and Charlotte gasped as arms pulled her into darkness.

Chapter 5

A SMALL FLAME FLICKERED, casting a faint light on the walls of the gloomy front room of the bakery.

Sonos sighed in relief as the light caught on a tuft of familiar blond curls.

Sibi calmly pushed away Taimani's dart, which she was holding against his throat.

Taimani sucked her teeth in annoyance, but her warrior's facade softened, giving way to a flicker of tenderness as she stashed her darts back in the holder on her thigh.

Sonos pulled the young boy into an embrace. Standing up to the Emperor to save this former palace servant is what put him on this path in the first place. He pushed away the thought of the haunting face of the master-servant he had accidentally killed to save Sibi. "Good to see you, Sib," he said softly, allowing some of the tension from the square to recede.

"You too, Sonny." Sibi winked, knowing how much Sonos hated that nickname. "But Miss Gemma says you need to come inside quickly." Sibi motioned for them to follow him into a back room.

Dayo—the young boy who had narrowly escaped death in Portemore—trailed behind them.

Charlotte reached out a hand to tussle the dark hair that kept falling into his eyes. "Good to see you too, Dayo."

He flashed her a big grin.

Sibi led the way into the kitchen—a room bathed in a warm, inviting glow, a stark contrast to the darkness they had just left behind.

Sonos felt a tinge of doubt, his mind plagued with questions of what lay ahead. He may have stopped his father, but what had they truly unleashed in taking the Emperor out of Ade's way?

Rapha jumped out of Charlotte's jacket and scurried over to nuzzle an elderly woman who stood in the middle of the room.

"Miss Gemma!" Sonos exclaimed as his eyes adjusted, unable to contain the overwhelming surge of emotion that welled up within him. He had been feeling more vulnerable than he ever had in his whole life after Ade's declarations, and after having his and Charlotte's images broadcast to the whole Empire, but at least for now they were somewhere safe.

Miss Gemma placed a finger against her lips, indicating quiet from everyone. "Will you do the honors, Raph?"

Rapha scampered around the kitchen, moving from the doorway they had come through to a thick wooden door at the back of the kitchen and then to a window above the sink, his tiny hands pressing each opening with a delicate touch. He hummed a melody that reverberated throughout the room, infusing the room with a sense of sanctity and safety. After he finished, he returned to rest on Miss Gemma's shoulder.

"There, now we can speak freely without being overheard." She smiled, the tension in the room melting away. Miss Gemma pulled Sonos into a heartfelt embrace. She then turned her attention to Charlotte and Taimani, extending her warmth to each of them.

Rapha went to greet Sibi and Dayo. Their giggles echoed through the room, creating a momentary respite from the weight everyone carried.

Sonos smiled, his heart swelling with gratitude as he recalled the initial mistrust that had clouded their first meeting with Miss

Gemma in Portemore. In the end, though, Miss Gemma had saved many lives that night, including the Salan family who had been sentenced to death. She had even orchestrated their escape from Captain Die.

"We don't have much time, I'm afraid," Miss Gemma's voice broke through the air. "Things have been triggered into motion and are moving quickly."

Sonos thought about the unwanted notoriety that he and Charlotte now shared. He never wanted to put her in more danger, and yet here they were. They had successfully evaded his Uncle Die only to be branded as rebels on an Empire-level scale. The truth was that Charlotte wouldn't even be safe in Jamroq.

"Do you know where my brother is?" Taimani wasted no time asking, her desperation practically palpable.

Miss Gemma squeezed the warrior's hand, even as she shook her head. "I only see what's made visible to me—which is far from everything," she answered. "But *El* knows the end from the beginning, and I feel his story is far from over."

Taimani opened her mouth to say something more, but another figure emerged from the shadows, and a hushed silence fell over the room.

Sonos' heart skipped a beat. He was almost afraid to believe his eyes. "Mother?" His voice wavered, as he stood frozen in shock and disbelief.

She was dressed like an ordinary villager in a loose, flowery tunic tucked into dark leather pants and boots. Her hair was pulled back in a single braid. He had never seen her looking so casual and relaxed, but the undertones of her authority in how she moved—back straight, chin squared—were undeniable.

Sonos rushed forward. He enveloped his mother in his arms; the weight of their separation from his imprisonment until now was lifted in that moment.

"It's good to see you, son," she whispered. Her voice, soft and comforting, washed over him like a balm.

"What are you doing here? How?" Sonos asked after lingering in the embrace.

"*El* warned me in a dream that I wasn't safe," she said, her voice carrying a calm resolve. "I just had to wait for the right moment and the right people to help me escape." She turned and looked at Sibi and Dayo who were playing with Rapha in the corner.

Both boys had been forced to grow up well before their time, and it was good to see them laughing and having careless fun—even if for a moment.

"She doesn't sound like what I expected," Charlotte said from behind Sonos.

The comment caught him off guard, and he turned around more sharply than he had meant.

Charlotte blushed. She was leaning close to Taimani and clearly didn't expect to have been heard.

"I mean... your Highness, I hear the curling Kimwaki accent. Not the harsh, clipped sound that comes from the Emperor... uhm, *came* from the Emperor... I..." Her blush grew deeper.

Sonos glanced at his mother. Was she the reason Charlotte was stumbling all over herself and calling him Highness? It sounded so strange coming from her.

The Empress stepped forward and laid a hand on Charlotte's shoulder. "Roots run deep, and I am now free. Be at ease. I feel more like myself than I have in years." She smiled, allowing unabashed joy to spill through every contour of her face. Then she pulled the scarf down from under her chin and revealed the intricate tattoos that adorned the right side of her neck, starting at her jawline.

Sonos' mouth fell open. He thought the Emperor had forced the Sahemy to remove them.

His mother smiled, noticing his reaction. She traced a finger along her neck. "It was only a trick of makeup that the Sahemy used to hide them—they were never erased."

She was more beautiful now in common clothes and in the kitchen of a small bakery than she had ever been in the most elaborate feasts and dresses in the palace.

Muted noise from outside brought Sonos back to the present. "Where exactly are we?" he asked.

"Harmony," Sibi said, stepping forward with a grin. "Dayo and I got to help Miss Gemma save your mom... er, the Empress. Sorry," he mumbled an apology to Sonos' mother.

The Empress reached a hand out to Sibi and ruffled his blond curls. "I think it's time to embrace my true name, brave one. And not the title once forced upon me." A look of liberation danced in her eyes. "You may all call me Ali'tasi."

The name was clearly from Kimwaki and sounded beautiful and fitting for his mother. "I never knew..." He cocked his head toward her. He knew his mother and her brother, his Uncle Diekolo-laoluwa, had been taken young when Kimwaki had been defeated. His father had insisted on only ever being called the Emperor, and his wife the Empress. Sonos had never fully considered his mother's life before the palace.

"Ali'tasi is what my father used to signify the beginning," his mother explained. "And embracing the name once again at this new beginning seems fitting."

His mother's joy was unmistakable even with the Empire being thrown into chaos.

"The seed is found in the harvest," Miss Gemma said with a matching smile. "I believe your brother will also find new meaning for his original name."

Sonos groaned and hung his head in shame, remembering his uncle. "Mother, I'm so sorry," he started. "I tried so hard to get Uncle Die to stop pursuing us. I didn't mean for—"

The full weight of the memory of how Sonos had cut the cloak of his uncle, forcing the Elites to stop pursuit, but also ensuring Die's failure, crashed into Sonos. Failure was never tolerated in K'Luma, and his uncle would have certainly fallen on his sword because of him.

His mother—Ali'tasi, he reminded himself—pulled Sonos close. "Peace, dear son. It was not your fault. And besides, I've been assured that my brother lives." She glanced toward Miss Gemma.

"But—" Sonos started. How could she possibly be sure?

Miss Gemma simply shrugged. "Isaako lives and has purpose yet to fill, starting with finding his true identity."

"Isaako." His mother smiled.

"It means laughter and joy," Taimani whispered. The warrior had been uncharacteristically silent since the Empress entered the room. "Ali'tasi and Isaako... does this mean... Are you? Will you reclaim your honor as Chieftains of Kimwaki?" Taimani's dark eyes brimmed with hope.

"Ah, your desire is both contagious and dangerous, my warrior," his mother said, facing Taimani. "I do not yet know where my road will lead." His mother looked at Rapha, who had perched again on Miss Gemma's shoulder. Then she pulled back her shoulders and spoke with quiet determination. *"A oo mai le taimi, ou te sauni.* When the time comes, I'll be ready," she repeated in the common tongue.

Miss Gemma cleared her throat. "Man plans his steps, but remember that *El* directs the way forward. Be flexible, all of you. And do not always trust what you feel or see with your eyes."

"The unseen realm," Charlotte said under her breath. She edged closer to Sonos, her fruity scent filling his senses.

Sonos cleared his throat. "Surely you don't plan on waiting here until the right time?" he asked his mother. "Harmony is only a day's ride from Riverton, and it feels far too close to Pergamum and Ade."

"Your brother has proven to be... unstable," his mother inclined her head. "I owe a large debt of gratitude to Miss Gemma, Sibi, and Dayo for rescuing me after Baku was murdered."

"Baku was murdered?" Sonos asked, surprise filling his voice, remembering the terrifying, lanky form of the head of the Imperial Guard. It explained why he hadn't seen Baku in Ade's broadcast.

"Ade would not risk divided loyalties, and Baku was there when the Emperor was allegedly transformed," his mother said. She raised a questioning eyebrow at Sonos. "Perhaps *you* can shed some light on what really happened?"

"Well, he was transformed, but he wasn't transformed into some shadow dragon," Sonos confirmed. "I can't quite explain it myself, but *El* put a curse in my mind, and as I spoke the words, the Emperor was turned into a hairy beast. He's confined to roam the Badlands for seven years."

His mother paced the room. "I knew Ade was trying too hard, and something was off with the sorcerers." Her brow was furrowed, but she spoke calmly. "But if *El* started it, there must be a plan behind it."

Sonos glanced towards Sibi. That sounded like something the young boy would say—that *El* had a plan.

"I am confident our people will protect you in Kimwaki," Taimani said, her chest puffing out slightly.

"I have no doubt," his mother responded. "But my path is first to the Mountain Kingdom. I must meet with King Mason and the leadership council. Together, we will determine the timing and the way forward."

"The Mountain Kingdom will be crawling with Commander Uzoma and the army," Sonos argued.

"Sibi, Dayo, and I will be accompanying Ali'tasi. She will be safe," Miss Gemma said.

"But—" Sonos retorted.

"One one cocoa full basket," Charlotte spoke softly. All eyes turned to her, and her face flushed again. "Sorry, it's something Gran used to say," she quickly added. "It means that slowly, but surely, each thing will eventually fill the basket... or in this case, each thing completed will fulfill the wider purpose."

A sudden desire flashed in Sonos' heart. He wanted to meet Charlotte's Gran and the family she cared so deeply about.

"Don't worry." Sibi stepped up next to Sonos' mother and motioned for Dayo to stand on her other side. "I swear on my life to keep your mother safe," Sibi declared and beat a fist over his heart twice.

"Me too," Dayo said, eyes alight as he repeated the motion.

Sonos recognized the gesture used by Kimwaki warriors and caught the corners of Taimani's mouth turning downwards ever so slightly.

"We have disguises, a special boat—" Sibi paused and looked at Sonos. "You'd be proud of how much progress I've made around water."

Sonos remembered the boy's deathly fear during their first escape from Pergamum. Sibi and the others were great, but Sonos still doubted their ability to evade the force of the Empire.

His mother placed a hand on Sibi's shoulder. "One day, you will regale Sonos and other warriors with the details of your bravery, and the story of how you brought me out of Pergamum to Harmony and into the safety of the Mountain Kingdom."

The boys lit up at her praise.

"I can't wait to hear it myself," Charlotte said, kneeling before Dayo. "I'm so glad you found your way."

Rapha chittered from where he sat on Miss Gemma's shoulder. She rubbed his head in acknowledgment. He then scampered over to Charlotte.

"In the meantime," Miss Gemma said looking at Charlotte, "You have some sisters to free and some towers to burn."

"And a brother to save," Taimani said.

"I know it will be tempting to rush in and act, but Taine is not your mission," Miss Gemma said, fixing her eyes on Taimani.

The warrior tensed, and Sonos worried that she might run off again.

"He will be okay despite whatever you see. Keep focused on the path before you," Miss Gemma warned again.

"Open up, in the name of the Empire!" Someone shouted, and banging sounded from the front door of the bakery.

Sonos' heart dropped. His eyes shifted from his mother to Charlotte and quickly over the others in the room. He felt like they were sitting ducks all together in one room. He couldn't lose everyone that he loved.

"And that is our cue." Miss Gemma jumped into action.

Chapter 6

C HARLOTTE'S HEART RACED, A frantic rhythm matching the chaos around her. She clutched the bag that Miss Gemma had thrust into her arms. Everything was happening so fast, like a whirlwind sweeping them away.

The banging on the front door continued.

Sibi knelt in front of Rapha in the corner of the room, Dayo by his side.

Charlotte was glad Dayo had found a true family. She hoped Sibi and his unbreakable spirit would rub off on the young orphan who had found her in Portemore. Sibi had grown up as a palace servant and been beaten within an inch of death, but still, he radiated life and joy. *May we all walk through this fire and come out on the other side with no smell of smoke on us,* Charlotte thought.

Sonos lingered in a last embrace with his mother.

Charlotte squeezed her eyes shut for a moment, pushing back against an empty feeling that filled her chest when she thought of the loss of her mother. If only her sisters hadn't been kidnapped in the first place.

She took a deep breath and found something else to focus on. *Ali'tasi,* Charlotte repeated the true name of the Empress in her mind. She loved that the Empress knew who she was and where she was going. She wished she had that same certainty, and a clear plan.

Taimani paced near the back door of the kitchen, her movements agitated. She checked her weapons and muttered under her breath in her native tongue.

Miss Gemma leaned in, her voice a whisper against Charlotte's ear. "Sonos and Taimani will need your strength and resolve in the days ahead."

"Me?" Charlotte asked, confused. "Since when would a Kimwaki warrior need strength from anyone, let alone someone like me?" Not to mention Sonos—Charlotte had no idea what she could offer him. He was brilliant and brave beyond what she imagined of a crown prince.

"You," Miss Gemma repeated, her voice filled with conviction. "You started on a journey to free your sisters, but as you've already seen, your purpose is to save many more."

Charlotte remembered the weight of responsibility King Mason of the Mountain Kingdom had placed on her shoulders with the daunting task of destroying the chemical weapon meant to defeat the innocent people of Noiz. It was nothing short of a miracle that she and Taimani had been able to disarm the dragon-shaped weapon in mere hours.

The banging at the front door grew louder, a keen reminder of the imminent danger.

Miss Gemma revealed a hidden trapdoor in the floor, then looked at Charlotte. "You'll head out the back with Sonos and Taimani. Jamin will find you and get you out of the village."

Charlotte recalled the man from Portemore who had led their escape there. They practically owed Jamin their life. "How will we find him?"

Rapha scurried up to perch himself on her shoulder, but Miss Gemma ignored her question, focusing on opening the trap door.

"You two better take care of Empress Ali'tasi," Taimani admonished Dayo and Sibi. "It is your sworn duty."

Both boys looked up at the tall warrior with wide eyes and nodded.

"We won't let you down, Mani," Sibi said. "Besides, Miss Gemma told us, '*Those who are with us are greater than the darkness.*'"

Charlotte smiled as she remembered the exact words from the commander of *El*'s army. The words had saved Sonos' life in the Badlands.

The Empress stepped through the trapdoor that Miss Gemma held open, Sibi and Dayo scrambling after her.

Banging continued on the front door of the bakery. "Everyone is required in the square! If anyone is in there, come out now!"

"We will get to the Mountain Kingdom safely; do not worry," Miss Gemma told Sonos. "Fight we must, but the victory is already won."

Unconquerable, Charlotte remembered the last word of the poem Rapha had given her.

"Now, move that cupboard back over this door." Miss Gemma pointed at the item, gave a final wink, and closed the trapdoor.

Sonos, Taimani, and Charlotte were on their own.

"How is Jamin supposed to find us?" Taimani paced the room. "That woman is insufferable."

"Why does she make you so angry?" Charlotte asked as she and Sonos slid the cupboard over to hide the trapdoor.

"She's so arrogant," Taimani spat. "Always thinks she knows more than everyone else."

"Well, she is right." Sonos shrugged.

Charlotte glared at him. He could be so insensitive to other people sometimes.

"Which makes it worse," Taimani muttered.

"Everything she's said has come true so far. She has a gift for sight." Sonos tried explaining further.

"It sounds like the banging at the front door has subsided," Charlotte said, changing the topic.

"My big question is, why is everyone being called back into the square?" Sonos asked. "Surely there can't be any announcements bigger than what my brother already declared."

"Do you think we'd be allowed to keep the hoods of our cloaks up if we go?" Charlotte asked. They each wore the soft yet durable cloaks King Mason had given them in Noiz. She also wore her dark jacket with many pockets from Jamroq underneath the cloak.

Taimani tsked. "We cannot risk going into a crowd of people." She paused and looked at Rapha who sat in his usual spot on Charlotte's shoulder. "I still don't know how Jamin will find us. Perhaps we should wait for the cover of darkness to move."

Rapha shifted and started chittering.

"I think Rapha wants us to go now," Charlotte said, glancing at the monkey.

"But go where?" Taimani insisted.

"I... don't know. But more important than knowing the details, we must listen to the timing. If he wants to move now, let's move." Charlotte slugged the pack's straps over each arm and settled its weight on her back.

Taimani narrowed her eyes at Sonos as if he was the deciding vote.

Charlotte felt annoyed. Not that it was Sonos' fault, but why did he get the final say? It's not like he was royalty inside the palace anymore.

"Let's follow Charlotte's lead," Sonos said, picking up his pack.

Charlotte's anger melted as quickly as it had formed. "Thanks," she said.

Sonos nodded.

Taimani checked the darts strapped to her thigh, then pulled up the hood of her cloak and cracked open the back door. "Give me a minute to check the alley." She scurried out the door.

There was an awkward silence as Sonos and Charlotte waited. She tugged at her pack, about to ask a question, but a loud, piercing shout sounded from outside.

Charlotte and Sonos exchanged a glance.

"Come on," Charlotte grabbed his hand, running out into the back alley.

Taimani was nowhere in sight, but the sound had come from the direction of the square.

"We need to at least see if Mani is in trouble," Charlotte said, edging them along the alley wall. She pulled up the hood of her cloak, and Rapha buried himself inside her jacket.

Sonos kept his fingers intertwined with hers.

This is probably the first time he's been without a bodyguard or Kimwaki warrior to protect him, Charlotte thought. It didn't mean anything more than that. But no matter what she told herself, her heart still skipped a beat.

She tried to keep them in the shadow of the wall as much as possible as they neared the end of the alley.

Another piercing cry laced with pain erupted, and Charlotte's breath caught as she peered out into the square.

Sonos inhaled sharply from where he stood, looking over her head.

A scene of unimaginable cruelty unfolded before their eyes. A man, stripped of all dignity, was bound to a wooden block, his body marred by blood and pain.

The captain of the Imperial Guard with the red stripes loomed behind him, wielding a whip adorned with sharp stones and metal. His voice boomed as he spoke. "Last chance. Declare Emperor Ade your god, or you will be given a swift death."

The man on the block served as a symbol of resistance. He refused to yield, his head shaking in defiance. Blood streamed down his shoulders, a testament to his unwavering spirit.

Rapha squirmed out of her coat and ran towards the platform.

Charlotte gasped, but Sonos pulled her back before she could chase after the monkey.

"Shouldn't we do something? Help him?" Charlotte whispered.

"Rapha bolted. I'm not sure he wanted us to follow," Sonos said gently.

Charlotte took a moment to think. It was true. Rapha hadn't hummed, pointed, or done anything like he usually did when trying to get them to move.

The captain on the stage raised the whip once more.

"No," Sonos whispered.

Charlotte turned her head into Sonos' chest, unable to watch. She had too many memories of people she loved, like her dad and Jax, being hurt in the name of the Empire.

Sonos wrapped his arms around her.

She pressed her hands against her ears, trying to block out the horror.

The man's cries reverberated through the square.

The silence afterward was deafening.

"It's Jamin," Taimani said softly from behind Sonos.

Charlotte looked up, tears spilling out of her eyes. "Jamin? What?" It was hard to process what the warrior was saying.

"It was Jamin who they just... executed." Sorrow filled Taimani's words.

"Every follower of *El* or any other religion other than total and unwavering faith in Emperor Ade will be found and executed," the captain shouted from the platform.

Charlotte turned and caught a glimpse of a small, furry form moving underneath Jamin's now-still form on the block. *Rapha must have stayed with him during his final breaths.* She felt a wave of thankfulness that he hadn't been alone.

"I can't... I don't know what to say," Sonos croaked as he gazed at the platform, his arms hanging limp by his side.

A silence had fallen over the square. No anger, no rebellion, no fight. Perhaps shock.

But fury boiled in Charlotte's blood now, and she wiped the tear tracks from her cheeks. "Ade must be stopped," she whispered. "No one is safe."

"It's only going to get worse from here," Sonos agreed. "Once my brother has a taste for blood and power, and the people's fear, his appetite will become insatiable."

"We need to save *my* brother first," Taimani said, eyes ablaze.

"Mani, but Miss Gem—" Charlotte started. The stakes were higher than ever, and they couldn't afford to make mistakes.

"I know what Miss Gemma said," Taimani hissed. "But clearly, she was wrong about Jamin getting us out of the village. What if she's wrong about Taine, too?"

Charlotte allowed her gaze to linger once more on Jamin's still form as a small group of villagers was allowed to wrap his body and move him from the platform.

Resolve burned within her. She pulled Sonos and Taimani deeper into the alley, away from the square.

"Maybe Jamin will still help us escape the village," she said. "Not how we expected, but let's move while everyone else is still in the square."

Thankfully, Taimani didn't argue further.

The sinking sun painted the sky with shades of gold, a reminder of the passing time. Once they left the village, finding the road that led east towards Riverton and then on to Pergamum would be easy.

"We keep our eyes forward and our path straight," Charlotte said, embracing the fight that flowed through her veins.

They would win, just like they had against Commander Uzoma.

They would stop Ade, free her sisters, find Taine, and get back home before anyone else was lost. Enough was enough.

CHAPTER 7

—·—

"E VERY LAST FOLLOWER OF *El* will be hunted down. May Emperor Ade live forever!" The captain's voice boomed through the amplifier, even as they made their way away from the square.

This is all wrong. Stopping my father was supposed to help, not make things worse. Doubts plagued Sonos' mind as he followed Charlotte away from the square, their footsteps quickening with urgency.

Taimani walked behind him, her eyes darting around for signs of danger.

As they weaved their way through the side streets, Sonos voiced his concerns to Charlotte. "Are you sure we weren't supposed to save Jamin? And what about Rapha? Shouldn't we wait for him?"

Charlotte shot Sonos a fiery glance, breaking her momentum, and Sonos almost crashed into her. "Stop with the questions. This is not the time. Raph will find us."

His inner tumult must have been evident because her tone softened. "I know that it feels like things keep shifting, and it hurts to be far from those we love," she said, shifting her gaze to Taimani, "but we need to focus on what's in front of us, and keep moving forward."

"Keep moving forward," Sonos repeated under his breath, latching onto the surety of the words.

"People are leaving the square now, so we can follow along and exit on the main road to the East. We're heading to Riverton first, then to Pergamum." Charlotte stated the plan more than posed a question. But all the same, Taimani gave a single nod of agreement, her eyes narrowed and focused.

"My brother is my priority," the warrior said flatly.

Miss Gemma's warning to stay focused ran through Sonos' mind, but his thoughts were interrupted as a little ball of fur ran towards them.

Rapha scurried up Charlotte's side and nestled himself under her cloak.

Charlotte's shoulders relaxed, and she adjusted the hood of her cloak to hide her face. Sonos did likewise. Only Taimani kept hers down, likely to extend her peripheral vision as much as possible.

"Good to have you back, Raph," Charlotte whispered, rubbing his head.

Rapha hummed from inside her jacket. The muffled sound was like a cool breeze.

Even Taimani exhaled a slow breath.

Sonos marveled at the power of the "frequency," as Charlotte had described it. She always loved to explain things from a tech perspective, but in this case, it made sense. The unseen realm couldn't be felt or seen, but just like the tech that powered the gazers, it was there and powering their world.

Harmony was not a large village, but Charlotte led them into the slow flow of the crowd.

Imperial guards stood watch, their imposing presence a constant reminder of the lurking danger.

The villagers' faces were downcast and etched with fear.

Sonos remembered that Harmony would have been in the path of Commander Uzoma when he had led his undefeated army through the village en route to the Mountain Kingdom a few weeks earlier. It was quite possible—and more than likely—that the small village had experienced a foretaste of the cruelty the Empire could exact when driven by entitlement.

But like any tight-knit community, connection to one another was paramount, and talking to each other couldn't be helped. Even so, their whispers were filled with apprehension.

"Emperor Ade is terrifying!" one voice murmured.

"Did you see he's now hunting his own brother and some strange girl as rebels? Where is she from?" another asked in hushed tones.

"What happened to the Empress?" someone else questioned.

"Did you see that shadow dragon behind Emperor Ade? Maybe she transformed, too? Or maybe he ate the Empress as a sacrifice!"

Sonos shuddered, hoping his mother remained safe from prying and ignorant eyes.

Amid the tension, Charlotte suddenly yelped, drawing the attention of those nearby.

Taimani closed in behind them and sucked her teeth in annoyance.

"Sorry," Charlotte whispered, her voice filled with urgency, "My ring started vibrating and caught me off guard." She kept her hands deep inside her cloak, fidgeting with unease.

"Char! Char, is that you? Can you hear me?" Jax's voice was far too loud.

Sonos instinctively wrapped his arm around Charlotte, feigning a casual conversation between them to divert any attention.

Charlotte raised her hand close to her mouth to whisper urgently. "Jax, keep it down. You have to be quiet! Give me a minute."

Thankfully, Jax stopped talking.

But Charlotte remained on edge. "I need to find somewhere to take this call. I don't want to lose Jax..."

Sonos' concern over attracting unwanted attention grew, but before he could voice his thoughts, Taimani intervened, pushing him forward.

She led them off the main throughway, into a more deserted alley. Their hurried footsteps echoed between two buildings as they tried to create some distance from prying eyes.

Charlotte lifted one side of her cloak and whispered to Jax as they ran.

"Are you okay?" Jax's voice broke through, still too loud for the alley. "I heard that announcement come through and saw your picture being shown..."

Charlotte shoved her hand back into her cloak, muting the call.

Sonos whipped his head behind, following the sound of a grunt and a heavy thud.

A guard in a black uniform was slumped over, a red dart sticking out of his neck.

Taimani stood over him. She plucked the dart out with a satisfied smile and strapped it back to her thigh. "I hope these things work more than once."

Rapha hummed, and she smiled wider.

But where there was one guard, there would be more. How were they followed? What was making them stand out? Had someone recognized him even with the hooded cloak? Sonos' thoughts spiraled. He realized with horror that he hadn't even counted the number of steps they had walked since leaving the square. He used to do that practically unconsciously, as he made a point of paying attention to details. He patted the journal tucked into a pocket of his cloak. *Head in the game*, he chided himself.

"Over here." Charlotte pulled them towards a secluded stable that appeared to be on the edge of the village.

She slipped through the unlocked door, Sonos close on her heels. The smell of hay and horses filled the air, reminding Sonos of the stables back in the palace, earthy and alive. A horse neighed in the corner.

Taimani ran off to inspect and secure the area.

Charlotte lifted her hand, pushed her hood back, and projected the holographic video into the space in front of her.

Jax exhaled audibly when he caught sight of Charlotte. "You're okay. I thought for a second..." his voice trailed off with emotion.

Sonos was annoyed at Jax's call and the danger it posed, but the care and concern overflowing was clear. Jax was just worried for his best friend. *Yes, they're just good friends. That's what Char said,* Sonos reminded himself.

"H-hey Char and S-Sonos." Lenora's face appeared next to Jax's in the video feed. The princess of the Mountain Kingdom had dark circles under her eyes, but appeared calm, especially given that their city was currently under siege. Her dark hair was tied back, the obsidian pendant hung on her forehead in place of any crown, and her eyes were kind and observant.

"Glad to see you both are okay, too," Charlotte said, relief spilling through her green eyes. "I was worried about the chemicals seeping through, and now Uzoma and his crazy army are looking for the gold."

Lenora rolled her eyes and let out a sharp laugh. "He d-doesn't realize our gold isn't in th-the ground. The g-gold is our people."

Sonos was about to ask more questions, but Lenora whispered something to Jax.

"We have to go soon," Jax said. "We've been up here longer than allowed already. Something about risking the Sahemy detecting Mountain Kingdom frequencies or something." He frowned.

"It's really good to see you, and to know that you guys are okay," Charlotte said.

Sonos leaned against her shoulder and tilted his head into the video. "Yes, my brother has created quite the story around the defeat of Noiz."

Lenora harrumphed in the background. "Fool."

"Yes, we saw the broadcast," Jax said. "Which is why I insisted I needed to try calling you again."

"We're just outside of Harmony," Charlotte said. "We met up with Miss Gemma and—"

Sonos grunted and shook his head. His mother was heading to the Mountain Kingdom, but he didn't trust the technology fully and didn't want to put the Empress in further danger.

Charlotte caught his eye and nodded in understanding. "And some other old friends."

"Harmony?" Jax said, surprised. "How...?"

"Long story," Charlotte said. "But let's just say we found another temporal portal in the Badlands."

Rapha chittered from beneath her jacket.

Taimani rejoined them, taking up a position that allowed her to keep looking outside through a crack in the barn door.

"Hey, Jax. It's good to see you. Have you heard anything about my brother?" Taimani asked, her voice hopeful.

"Not exactly, sorry. We only know that Wylder is in Pergamum, and we assume Taine is being held somewhere in the palace," Jax said. "We also heard rumors that Baku was mysteriously murdered."

"We know," Charlotte said.

Jax's eyes widened. "It's true?"

"Speaking of murder," Charlotte continued, her voice turning solemn. "Jamin was executed today, here in the village."

"What?" Jax gasped.

Hearing the words spoken aloud came as a new affront to Sonos. *What is my brother thinking?*

Lenora leaned in and whispered something again to Jax.

"Sorry, but we gotta go," Jax said. He started running—or rather hop-limping while holding onto Lenora—and the video became bumpy.

"What's happening? Are you okay?" Charlotte said, her body tensing beside Sonos.

"A drone was spotted nearby, and we need to get back under," Jax panted. He pulled the gazer close to his face again. "I wish I could be there with you, Char. I'm supposed to be there when you get to Ava and Lily..." His voice trailed off.

"Jax?" Charlotte leaned into her gazer. She repeated his name a few more times. But the video feed had frozen, and the sound had cut off.

Charlotte muttered under her breath and tried fiddling with some controls, but it was useless.

A rustling came from the hayloft above.

Sonos snapped his head towards the sound.

A dart was already loaded into the blowgun Taimani raised to her mouth.

"Wait," Sonos laid a hand on Taimani's shoulder.

A man stood up with his arms raised above his head.

"We need to know how much he heard," Sonos added more softly.

Taimani didn't lower the blowgun, but she didn't fire either.

"I'm a friend," the man called out. "And I can help."

Chapter 8

C HARLOTTE'S HEART POUNDED WITH an intensity that threatened to consume her as the stranger descended from the hayloft. Every fiber of her being tensed as she considered the perilous situation she had foolishly led them into.

Why didn't I wait until we knew the barn was empty? I just ran in here and started talking, so focused on Jax. She chastised herself for being so naive, for continuing to rush into things repeatedly.

Taimani kept the blowgun loaded but slowly lowered it from her mouth, her eyes not leaving the man in front of them.

Rapha jumped off Charlotte's shoulder, paused briefly near the stranger to scrutinize his face, and then ran up to the hayloft.

"Are there more of you up there?" Charlotte asked. Rapha hadn't seemed bothered, but she reminded herself to keep her guard up.

The man shook his head. "My name is Torrin." He kept his hands visible as he spoke. "Jamin and a few others stayed here and helped protect us when the army marched through." His voice cracked at the mention of Jamin.

Some of the tension in Charlotte's body loosened once she saw that the man cared about Jamin.

"Why weren't you or any others arrested, too?" Taimani asked, her voice laced with caution, her grip on the blowgun unyielding.

Torrin's gaze flickered to the ground, a fleeting moment of vulnerability before he met Taimani's eyes. "The guards started probing around in earnest a few days ago, trying to find a follower of *El*," he explained. "While outright worship or open discussion of any god other than the Emperor has been forbidden for years, the Imperials haven't actively sought us out. But Emperor Ade seems to have a renewed vigor to fight against *El*."

A heavy silence descended upon them until Sonos sighed audibly. His forehead was creased, his lips were tight, and his eyes looked like a turbulent ocean. The guilt in his voice was palpable as he muttered, almost inaudibly, "It's my fault."

Charlotte wanted to refute Sonos' self-accusation, but Torrin resumed with his explanation, so she just grabbed Sonos' hand.

"The guards were in a tizzy. Jamin decided to draw their attention, even though he wasn't from here. He saved us." Torrin paused again, gathering himself.

In Charlotte's own heart, the embers of indignation only ignited further. *Who did Ade think he was to claim himself as the beginning and the end of the people's needs?*

Torrin's gaze shifted to Charlotte and Sonos. "I know who you are," he confessed.

Taimani raised her hand with the blowgun again.

"I saw the broadcast from Emperor Ade and overheard your conversation on that device." He gestured towards the intertwined hands of Charlotte and Sonos, curiosity evident in his eyes.

Taimani sucked her teeth in annoyance.

Torrin quickly raised his hands in a placating gesture. "I mean no harm," he clarified. "My whole family and all the followers of *El* here in Harmony owe Jamin our lives. I'll gladly do what I can to assist. I can't get you as far as Pergamum, but I can get you to Riverton and introduce you to someone who can help from there."

Charlotte was impressed. Despite witnessing the atrocities committed by the guards, Torrin remained resolute and willing to help them.

"We shouldn't stay here and put you at further risk," Sonos said, releasing Charlotte's hand and rubbing the back of his neck. "I don't want... I can't have another death on my head."

Annoyance flashed over Charlotte. There he went again with his royal ignorance and bias without realizing it. It was Torrin's decision to make and his honor to give, yet Sonos instinctively took responsibility for everything.

"*El* connected us," Charlotte said. She was beginning to believe it wasn't happenstance that had led her to run towards this stable earlier. She glanced up to the hayloft, where she heard soft monkey snores. Rapha seemed comfortable here, too. "*El* will keep us safe." She inclined her head towards Torrin. "We'd be grateful for the help. Riverton is a step in the right direction."

Torrin bowed his head respectfully, acknowledging their decisions. "It's an honor." He paused, then looked towards the door. "I'd invite you to my home, but I think it's safer for you out here if the guards come searching tonight."

Taimani seemed to take that as a cue and slipped out the door into the darkness.

"Why would they be searching?" Charlotte asked. "Surely they don't know we're here, or else they would've been on higher alert earlier."

"If they decide to hunt down Jamin's associates," Sonos said, pacing.

Torrin nodded. "But don't fear." He boldly placed a hand on Sonos' shoulder. "We have love, power, and a sound mind. These are stronger than any guards." He turned towards the door. "I'll bring you out something to eat in a bit. We'll leave for Riverton at first light."

Charlotte stretched her weary limbs within the confines of the hayloft, her back pressed against the rough barn wall. The scent of a hearty dinner prepared by Torrin's wife still lingered in the air. Her full belly threatened to lull her into a peaceful slumber, but the intensity of their situation kept her on edge even in this moment of respite. She thought about the lives they were fighting to save, including her sisters'.

Beside her, Sonos fidgeted restlessly, his movements shaking the small platform a little. He had hardly eaten a bite of his meal.

Rapha had gone to join Taimani in keeping watch on the main floor of the stable.

"You know what would help right now?" Charlotte asked.

Sonos turned and raised an eyebrow. "Another temporal portal that would actually put us where we need to be instead of days away from the capital?"

Charlotte frowned, ignoring the impossible request. "Cocoa tea." Her eyes glazed over as she thought about the near-endless cups Gran would offer to make for her and Jax back in Jamroq during the late nights they spent in the cellar trying to restore the flyer-board. Charlotte squeezed her eyes closed, trying to shut out the worry over Jax and the fact that she still didn't know if her family was safe.

Sonos glanced over, his eyes softening as if he appreciated the lighter response. "Chocolate dipped in sunshine, right?"

Charlotte smiled, remembering the first time she had tried to explain that beloved taste of home. "Exactly. It never fails to help me think about, and remember, what's most important. Or rather, *who* is most important."

"Remember..." Sonos muttered as he reached for his cloak, which was bundled nearby. He retrieved the journal and the pencil Rapha had gifted to him. He flipped through pages that were already filled, then started scribbling notes.

Something fell from the notebook, and Charlotte reached over to pick it up. It was an intricately folded origami tree. She held it close to inspect the details.

Sonos looked up and smiled. "That's from my mom. She used to leave them for me as a coded reminder: *A tiny seed becomes a mighty tree.* Only after meeting Miss Gemma and my former tutor, Sah Timur, did I begin to understand the fullness of what she meant with those words."

He turned back to making notes in his journal.

A flicker of familiarity sparked within Charlotte as she watched Sonos, and her mind filled with fragments of memories and moments shared with her family. The older of her two sisters, Ava—who took great pride in coming out of the womb before her twin, Lily—was a genius and had once dreamed of joining the Order of the Sahemy. No matter that the secret society of scientists, technologists, and sorcerers was only open to Imperials—Ava had been convinced that she could prove her worth and eventually help bring technology to the conquered isles. She had certainly proven her worth, earning the top award for math and science. But then she had been kidnapped alongside Lily at the award ceremony by General Uzoma's wife, Elisa.

This journey had become about so much more than just freeing her sisters. The entire system that sought to oppress her people—and conquer more lands—needed to be burned to the ground.

"You still with me?" Sonos' voice broke through her thoughts.

She opened her eyes and found his gaze fixed on her. "Uhm, yeah. I'm here," she mumbled in response. She hoped he hadn't caught her moment of overwhelming sadness.

He frowned and closed his notebook, giving her his full attention. He had definitely caught her mood. Sometimes, it seemed as if he saw everything with those observant eyes.

"I'm sorry," he said. "I've been all over the place today—well, since the Badlands. But you're not in this alone." He reached out and squeezed her hand. "Losing Taine and watching Jamin give his life… it feels awful. And, what's more, I feel like I've caused so much of it, and I can't figure out how to make things right."

Charlotte's heart swelled with understanding and empathy. "I'm not sure it is up to us to make things right." She shifted so that she faced Sonos. "We're part of a bigger plan that we didn't set in motion," she continued. "Remember what King Mason said on the eve of the Emperor's attack on Noiz?"

Sonos tilted his head, his eyes seeking the connection. "He said, we may be the spark, but we cannot carry the weight of the fire," he recalled.

"Yes!" Charlotte exclaimed. Of course, Sonos would remember. "Don't tell me you have some kind of photographic memory, but for audio."

Sonos laughed. "Not exactly. But those words held power." His brow furrowed, and he sat up straighter, opening his journal again.

Rapha scampered back up the ladder to join them in the hayloft.

"It's almost as if some words get etched into my mind. Like they come straight from the unseen realm," Sonos continued.

"Like when you cursed your father?" Charlotte asked. She remembered the force of those words in the battlefield tent.

Sonos nodded. He opened his journal and started writing again. "Something about remembering and recording these words is helpful. Like the future isn't quite as bleak as it seems." His whole body adjusted to focus on writing.

Charlotte smiled and rubbed Rapha's head. There was wisdom and purpose in each gift they had been given for the journey. *Backward look for forward strength.* The phrase popped into her mind.

Rapha hummed a little louder.

A few moments later, Taimani scurried up behind Rapha. "Good, you're awake. We have a problem."

Charlotte's stomach fell.

"Guards just woke up Torrin and his family," Taimani said. "They are over in the main house."

Charlotte's mind came into sharp focus.

"In the middle of the night?" Sonos asked, stashing away his journal. "They must have some kind of intel."

"There are only four guards," Taimani said. "I can easily subdue them."

Charlotte's eyes had adjusted enough to see the blowgun gripped in Taimani's hand.

"No," Charlotte said.

"Why not?" Taimani asked, voice accusatory.

"We don't know that they'll be harmed, but if you come out and fight the guards, there's no going back, and the family would have to go on the run," Charlotte said. "That's not our decision to make for them."

Taimani hmphed but stayed in the loft.

"All the same, maybe we can keep an eye on them and ensure they're not harmed," Charlotte added. She grabbed her cloak and wrapped it around her shoulders.

Taimani stashed their dinner plates and swept the hay with her feet to hide any evidence they had been there.

"Where's Raph?" Charlotte asked, looking around the loft. She hadn't even seen him leave.

"He ran back to the house," Taimani said.

That monkey was as fast as a warrior.

"You could have mentioned that bit," Charlotte said, annoyed. She scrambled down the ladder. *Should we save the family? Sometimes Rapha is clear, and sometimes trying to understand him is like trying to see through mud.* Either way, Charlotte wanted to ensure that Torrin and his family were okay.

Taimani led the way out of the side door of the barn.

Charlotte did her best to mimic Taimani's silent movements, but she and Sonos were like clumsy oafs compared to the honed warrior.

Light flooded through the main house windows, and loud voices barked orders.

"We are simple farmers, nothing more." Torrin's voice quaked at the end, but his words were loud and sure.

A child whimpered in the background.

How brave is this man, risking himself and his family for us... for what he believes? It reminded Charlotte of Gran, and her mind wandered to imagining Gran and her dad hiding with the Freedom Fighters back in Jamroq. Knots formed in her stomach.

"We'll know soon enough. We are searching every home in this village," a gruff voice said with a clipped Pergamum accent.

What are they looking for? Charlotte wondered. *Or who?*

"You two, go search the stable," the same voice ordered. "Ensure there are no unauthorized persons in this home."

Charlotte pressed against the back wall of the house, cocooned between Sonos and Taimani as they squatted low and out of sight.

Taimani edged up slowly to peer through the window.

Charlotte's pulse raced, worried that the warrior would be spotted. "Mani!" she hissed.

"I needed to ensure they're unharmed," Taimani whispered, returning to a crouch.

"Well?" Charlotte asked when it became apparent Taimani wouldn't offer up confirmation.

A crunch on the ground nearby froze Charlotte's blood.

Sonos tensed beside her, and they locked eyes for a brief moment. She saw fear, but something stronger as well—protectiveness.

Taimani eased off the wall, blowgun to her lips, and peered around the corner.

A few moments later, a meow sounded, and Taimani returned to crouch next to Charlotte, shaking her head.

Boots stomped into the main room. "All clear," a deep voice said.

"Notify us immediately if you see anyone out of place," the head guard spoke again. "Or, if you hear of any follower of *El*. It is in everyone's best interest that any rebels be turned in. And those who prove themselves loyal to the K'Luma Empire will be rewarded," the guard added in a tone that sent shivers down Charlotte's back.

Chapter 9

—•—

THE SKY HELD A fiery glow as the hour before dawn unfolded.

Horses brayed inside the stable, clearly expecting their morning meal, but instead, Torrin was hitching the wagon to two powerful horses.

"My family will come to take care of the other animals after we leave; the less they know, the safer they'll be," Torrin explained.

He opened a hidden compartment beneath the driver's seat in the wagon. The small space was like a long box, and Torrin would sit directly above them.

"It'll be a tight squeeze for three people, but as you witnessed last night, the guards are on high alert," Torrin said. He glanced at the sky through the stable doors as if wishing they were already on the road.

Clever, Sonos thought, realizing Torrin was no stranger to clandestine operations within the Empire.

Charlotte shivered beside Sonos, rubbing her arms.

She's still not used to the cool spring air, Sonos thought. He moved closer, catching the fruity scent that seemed permanently embedded in her hair, which was wild and free this morning.

Rapha squirmed and poked his head up through Charlotte's jacket.

"Thanks again for everything you're doing for us," Charlotte said, embracing Torrin. She was always quick to trust and embrace others—while dangerous, it was something that Sonos appreciated, having grown up in the palace where he had been taught to think everything and everyone was a threat.

"We may not choose our battles, but we can always choose our response," Torrin declared, returning Charlotte's embrace. "Fight we must."

"Win we shall," Charlotte finished the battle cry.

Every time the words were spoken, they sank deeper into Sonos' spirit, reminding him that despite the danger ahead, Rapha had promised the victory was already won. *Words have power.* He remembered how his anxiety had subsided the night before as he had written in the journal, recounting the journey.

Taimani urged Charlotte and Sonos to enter the cramped space first, her eyes constantly scanning the surroundings. "It's way too tight in there for me to be useful. I'll stay up here with Torrin," she declared, determination etched on her face.

Torrin appeared ready to protest, but then shrugged. "I suppose having a Kimwaki warrior on the road in these perilous times won't appear completely out of place."

Rapha scrambled up next to Taimani.

"I'll go in first," Sonos offered to take the position furthest from the opening, the most cramped. He wanted to give Charlotte as much comfort as possible in the tight space. As it was, he had to bend his knees slightly as he lay down, his back pressed against the front of the wagon in the makeshift box.

Charlotte squeezed in after him. Surprisingly, she placed her feet by his head instead of settling into the same orientation as Sonos. Was she feeling uncomfortable about being in such close proximity to him? Maybe Sonos had been misreading their recent closeness; maybe Charlotte still had feelings for Jax. Life as a prince had left him wholly unprepared for simple social interactions and relationships.

He squirmed and tried to settle himself down a bit. Their bodies pressed close together. It was uncomfortable, though, knees and elbows pressing in all the wrong places.

"How long will the journey take?" Sonos asked, just before Torrin closed the lid on their enclosure.

"It'll be a full day, I'm afraid," Torrin replied, a hint of remorse in his voice, "but it's the best we can do."

Sonos nodded, suppressing any complaint that threatened to escape his lips. He couldn't afford to dwell on the fact that he had once traveled in luxurious flying K'Luma carriers before his world had come crashing down.

The wagon jolted forward, pausing only for Torrin to close the stable doors before heading to the main road.

Charlotte moaned when the wagon hit a bump that caused Sonos' knee to prod her in the back.

"Sorry," he whispered.

Torrin sang as he drove the horses forward.

Sonos had to admire the man's joy. *We can always choose our response.* He'd have to remember to write that in his journal later.

There were many times that Torrin called out greetings to others on the road, and other instances when they heard the clomping of other animals' hooves, so he and Charlotte remained silent.

Faint rays of light seeped through small cracks in the wooden enclosure, providing a modicum of relief from complete darkness. Yet, discomfort settled within Sonos—the confined space was pressing upon him.

A *CRACK* of thunder broke the silence.

Charlotte gasped, and Sonos felt for her hand.

Outside, the skies opened, and rain seeped readily through the cracks.

Sonos managed to pull the hood of his cloak over his head, thankful for the well-made Mountain Kingdom garment that kept the worst of the wet from soaking through.

"Ho there!" a man called out.

The sound of approaching hoofbeats sent a chill down Sonos' spine.

Torrin pulled to a stop.

Charlotte's entire body tensed, but she still shuffled silently to try and peer through a crack in the wood near her head.

"Can I help you?" Torrin's voice rang out, steady and composed despite the mounting tension.

"We're spot-checking those on the road," a guard answered loudly enough to be heard over the rain.

Two guards were rustling boxes and goods on either side of the wagon.

Sonos prayed inwardly that Taimani wouldn't make a move on the guards from where she sat near Torrin on the driver's bench. He could imagine her hand tapping the blowgun and darts strapped to her thigh.

"Just a routine delivery to Riverton," Torrin said, shifting on the front seat.

Sonos was thankful for the rain and the shroud it offered. Taimani would have her hood drawn, and it would look normal.

One of the guards rifling through the goods crunched on something with his teeth.

"Hey! That's—" Torrin started.

"A small payment for our services," a voice quipped, mouth full.

Torrin sighed but didn't argue further.

Sonos felt a pang of shame. Was this how members of the Imperial Guard had always acted, even under his father's rule? He had spent far too much time cooped up and sheltered within the walls of the palace.

"Move along," one of the guards commanded Torrin. "Keep your eyes open for anything out of place. Should you discover something, notify a guard immediately, and your loyalty to K'Luma will be handsomely rewarded."

Sonos recoiled at the promise that flowed so easily from the guard. It was as if Ade had somehow found a way to exploit both human weaknesses and human desires, further tightening his grip on power.

As the wagon resumed its journey, Sonos felt the weight of responsibility settling upon his shoulders. Yes, he needed to save Taine and help Charlotte rescue her sisters. But there was a bigger need at play here. He was starting to understand Charlotte and Taimani's pure hatred of the Legacy Towers. They stood as a symbol of K'Luma's corrupted strength and power, while holding the best of the conquered lands captive.

They needed to be burned to the ground.

CHAPTER 10

I T HAD BEEN A grueling day for them, cramped as they were in the suffocating confines of the wagon.

Sonos' body throbbed with fatigue.

The sun had set almost an hour ago, by his estimation. The wagon trundled into the city of Riverton, and the clamor of bustling streets infiltrated the wooden compartment, intensifying Sonos' restlessness.

The tantalizing aroma of street food—spiced meat, fried potatoes, and more—wafted into their space. Sonos' stomach growled loudly. He muttered an apology to Charlotte, but she didn't answer, leaving Sonos to wonder what thoughts were running through her mind. Perhaps even more than food, he would give anything for a glass of water. But they had to be close.

Finally, Torrin pulled the wagon to a stop in a quieter part of town, perhaps somewhere off the main road.

"Stay here a moment," Torrin spoke softly near a crack on Sonos' side of the wagon.

A knock resounded on a nearby wooden door. A few moments later, a jovial voice greeted Torrin. "I wasn't expecting you for another day or so! Good to see you, friend."

Their voices lowered, and Sonos couldn't understand what was being said.

Feet scuffled, and the lid to their secret compartment was soon opened.

They were in a dark alley, but light spilled through an open doorway ahead.

At the end of the wagon stood a small, spindly man clutching a box of produce. He motioned for Sonos and Charlotte to follow him once they had unfolded themselves and stood on solid ground.

Taimani glanced at Sonos and Charlotte before darting off toward the end of the alley.

Torrin took a step to follow, but Charlotte stopped him.

"Don't worry, it's her way. She'll be back," Charlotte said, her voice calm and composed.

Torrin's frown deepened.

"She's just working to keep us safe," Charlotte added, arching her back in a stretch and rubbing her neck while holding onto the hood of her cloak.

Sonos stretched his arms and legs. Every joint was sore and stiff. He was thankful for the risk Torrin made on their behalf, but he hoped never to be shoved into a small compartment again.

Noises from the nearby street reminded him of the danger of being out in the open. He checked that his hood was also in place and quickly picked up a box of produce, hoping to alleviate Torrin's annoyance at Taimani's departure.

Rapha scrambled up to perch on Charlotte's shoulder and emitted a low hum, seeming quite content.

Torrin's features relaxed, and he picked up a box of produce, leading the way inside.

Sonos ducked his head slightly to pass through the doorway and found himself in a vast storeroom. The shelves were neatly lined with an abundance of provisions—dry goods, fresh produce, and jars of preserves.

The man from outside was peering at them as if trying to see their shadowed faces.

"Charlotte, Sonos, allow me to introduce you to Shorty," Torrin said.

Sonos grimaced, not yet trusting the stranger, but Charlotte quickly pulled down the hood of her cloak.

"Shorty sounds like a name they'd likely give you back in Jamroq." A smile played on her lips.

Shorty gave a slight bow of his head to both of them. "Don't worry, no one else knows—or will know—you are here," he told them in a soft yet friendly tone. "I help organize our little group in Riverton, similar to how Torrin works in Harmony and Miss Gemma in Portemore... though I hear she's on the move these days."

Sonos made a point of looking at Rapha and trying to see his reaction. He seemed content enough with Shorty, and since his name was already known... he reluctantly pulled down his hood.

To his credit, Shorty didn't stare or give any reaction.

"Baji is holding down Portemore," Torrin said to Shorty. "But come, let us finish unloading the goods."

Shorty gestured towards a corner of the room, pointing out two chairs. "You two make yourselves comfortable back here, and stay out of sight," he instructed Charlotte and Sonos as he and Torrin left the room.

At the earlier mention of Miss Gemma, Sonos' thoughts had immediately turned toward his mother. *Was she safe? Had she made it to the Mountain Kingdom?* An old woman and two young boys hardly seemed enough to protect the rightful ruler of Kimwaki. Sonos frowned. *Is my mother the rightful ruler of Kimwaki?* For his whole life, Sonos had only known the K'Luma Empire as the mainland with the conquered port of Portemore plus the three conquered isles of Kimwaki, Jamroq, and Salan. *But my mother's father was the Chief and ruler of Kimwaki before Father and General Uzoma had him beheaded and his people broken.* The questions gnawed at Sonos.

Caught up in his thoughts, Sonos didn't immediately notice Charlotte's concerned gaze.

"You okay?" Charlotte asked, her voice tinged with worry. "You have this faraway look."

Rapha had scampered off to explore the room and was munching on a piece of fruit in the corner.

"Sorry, just thinking about my mom and... and trying to figure out what K'Luma would look like if the isles were on their own," Sonos confessed.

Charlotte's expression softened. "Well, my dad and Gran could give you an earful about what Jamroq looked like before the Imperials came." It was her turn to look off into the distance in thought. "They still dream of a time..." She trailed off, her eyes meeting Sonos'. "If we manage to stop your brother, who takes over? You? Your mom? Will there be some crazy contest for the throne?"

The question caught Sonos off guard. He hadn't given much thought to the aftermath of their mission—his focus was solely on saving Taine, helping Charlotte, and ending his brother's tyranny. "I don't..." He faltered, searching his heart. What would stopping his brother actually mean for him? Thankfully, his uncle hadn't fallen on his sword because of Sonos, but he still had nightmares about the servant he had accidentally killed when saving Sibi. And what if *El* were to make Sonos curse his brother and banish him from the throne, like what happened with their father?

"I don't want anything to do with the throne," he finally declared. He knew that much.

Charlotte raised an eyebrow and looked like she was about to ask another question, but Rapha emitted a loud, assertive hum as if in agreement with Sonos' sentiment.

Charlotte cast a glance at Rapha, then turned back to Sonos. "I think it would be important to figure that out before we confront Ade, wouldn't it?"

"The right choice will be made clear at the right time," Torrin interjected, rejoining the group with a box in his arms.

Sonos hadn't realized they had been talking loudly enough to be overheard. But Torrin's face held only peaceful confidence.

Nodding in agreement, Charlotte said, "Yes, you're right. Until then, we focus on the next right choice, one step at a time. It's something Gran would say."

A sudden yelp from Charlotte interrupted the conversation. She held up her hand, a blush creeping up her neck. "Sorry," she apologized. "I'm still getting used to the new tech."

At that moment, Taimani burst through the door, her cheeks flushed, and her expression filled with urgency. "Char, did you catch it? I didn't see it, but everyone's talking about Ade's new broadcast."

Shorty followed Taimani in and laid down a box. "Torrin, I'll catch you up while we stable the animals. Let's give them some privacy."

Charlotte activated the gazer, and Jax's face materialized before them. His voice was heavy with concern. "Char, you're okay?" he asked.

Charlotte slid the gazer off her finger and set it on one of the nearby boxes. Jax's video feed hovered directly above the gazer. There were so many similarities to the Sahemy-developed gazers worn like bracelets, but hopefully, the frequencies developed by the engineers from Noiz had no such similarities to those used by K'Luma.

"Oh! Hi, Mani! Hi, Sonos," Jax's eyes darted around the room. "And Raph! Good to see you all."

"We w-were worried when... we saw the broadcast," Lenora said, leaning over Jax's shoulder. Her eyes settled on Taimani.

"Do you have a copy of it?" Taimani asked, a vein pulsing in her neck.

What kind of rumors had she heard on the streets? Sonos wondered. He had never seen her so upset.

Rapha climbed onto the warrior's shoulder, but Taimani lifted the monkey and pushed him into Sonos' arms. Sonos spluttered in surprise, but Rapha caught himself and swung onto Sonos' shoulder. Sonos was getting more and more worried about Taimani.

"You can get... get access to a copy of th-the broadcast," Lenora said, looking at Charlotte. She then explained the controls and how to access the K'Luma feed through an undetectable back door.

Taimani paced behind them, muttering in her native tongue.

Sonos didn't hear everything, but he picked up enough to know she'd never seen technology move so slowly. She then switched to reciting how she would save Taine, no matter what.

Sonos bit his tongue, thinking it unwise to remind Taimani of Miss Gemma's caution about not going after Taine. The weight of her love for her brother and the urgency of the situation hung heavy in the air. Sonos felt a surge of empathy for her.

"This is amazing," Charlotte said, finding the video of the broadcast and using her hand to slide it across to form a second hologram next to the one from Jax's feed. "And I can play it at the same time as having you guys up?"

"Yep." Lenora nodded.

The video started playing, and the room fell into a stunned silence.

Ade stood in the foreground, but a bruised and battered Taine was tied to a chair behind him, surrounded by Elite guards. The sight was harrowing, and Sonos balled his hand into a fist.

"No!" Taimani fell to her knees, hand over her mouth.

The sight of Taine hit the room like a blow. They were running out of time.

Ade's words cut through the silence, dripping with self-assuredness. "Citizens and servants of the eternal K'Luma Empire," Ade started the address. Dark circles ringed his brother's eyes, and he seemed to have aged even over the last few days. "I regret to say that my rebel brother and his newfound compatriot, Charlotte King, have not yet turned themselves in as demanded. Every city and village have seen that I am true to my word—rooting out all dissent and those who put their faith in invisible gods when the living power of the greatest Empire stands right before their eyes."

The shadow dragon moved on the wall behind his brother: the blasted Sahemy and their tricks.

Ade paused as if waiting for adoration to pour in. Maybe it was from the throne room, or... Where were they broadcasting from? Something about that round room and curtained windows was familiar.

"A Legacy Tower!" Sonos said suddenly.

"What?" Charlotte asked, briefly glancing his way before looking back at the video.

"They're broadcasting from the Kimwaki Tower," Sonos said, realizing where Ade was.

Taimani stood. Tears streaked down her cheeks, flowing from her charcoal-lined eyes. But her hands were balled into fists as she walked closer to the video feed as if trying to jump right into the room.

"Perhaps my brother and his girlfriend need a little more motivation to come forward," Ade said, his voice full of malice. He turned and looked back toward Taine's bound form. Taine was shirtless, and the tattoos that ran from his earlobe down to his right shoulder and over his chest were stained dark in places.

At least he's alive, Sonos tried to tell himself, but his breath came in short bursts. *He'll be okay. We'll be there in a few days.*

Ade nodded to the most senior Elite. *Wait, is that Fetu? Ade's personal bodyguard?* Fetu was Kimwakian, the same as all of the royal bodyguards. What was Ade doing?

Fetu's eyes were hard, and his movements calculated, but he stepped up to Taine all the same.

Sonos held his breath. He had a sinking feeling.

Fetu raised his double-edged sword. It activated, glowing blue with the tech infused into it by the Sahemy.

"No, no, no..." Charlotte whispered, watching in horror.

Ade wouldn't be so rash as to kill Taine. This was to send a message. To give them motivation, his brother had said.

Fetu's sword swung toward Taine's hand, and Taine cried out.

Jamin's guttural shout echoed in Sonos' memory, amplifying the moment in his head.

Fetu stepped back in line, his mouth drawn tight.

Blood flowed from Taine's hand, but he was alive.

A stub lay on the ground next to Taine.

"His thumb," Sonos whispered with disgust. An awful memory flooded Sonos' mind of the two thumbs and a tongue he had been served on a breakfast platter one morning during his lockdown. They had belonged to his former tutor, Sah Timur. Baku had discovered the man's betrayal and had wanted to send a message.

Bile rose in Sonos' throat. How could his brother be so cruel? Cutting off a warrior's thumb? Having Fetu, who was practically a brother to Taine, be the one to mete out the punishment? *That's the point—to demand absolute loyalty and prove his power*, Sonos thought.

"Every day that you refuse to turn yourself in, Sonos, you will cause more pain and suffering." Ade looked directly into the camera as he spoke. Then, the video went dark.

His words turned Sonos' blood into ice.

"I'm so sorry, Mani," Charlotte said, standing beside Taimani.

"*O le a ou fasiotia Ade. Saeese o ia. Fai atu ia te ia e aioi atu mo le alofa mutimutivale,*" Taimani screamed out.

Sonos didn't bother to translate her threats to kill Ade and rip him apart for Charlotte. Taimani's anger and intent were clear enough.

"Mani, we're going to save him," Jax said through the video.

"When?" Taimani spat. "What if Ade decides his head goes tomorrow? I cannot wait."

"My brother won't kill him," Sonos said softly. Guilt racked his heart. And the stakes had just been raised to a very dangerous level. "He has value."

Taimani's eyes sought to burn holes in everyone and everything.

"I'm still trying to find a way to get to you guys—to at least meet you in Pergamum," Jax said.

Lenora cleared her throat.

"I can't say much, but King Mason keeps talking about waiting for the right time." Jax sighed. "I'm trying, though."

"It's okay, I know. We'll find our way to Pergamum, too." Charlotte said. "Walk good."

"Walk good." Jax echoed, and the video cut off.

The room was consumed by a heavy silence once again. The tension was almost palpable.

Rapha shifted his weight on Sonos' shoulder and started to chitter.

"Rapha, we do not need a lecture right now," Taimani glared. "We need to save my brother." Her grief had morphed into a fierce resolve, her dark eyes ablaze with unwavering determination.

Rapha crossed his arms, staring back at Taimani.

Sonos couldn't deny the urgency of Taimani's plea. The image of Taine's thumb severed from his hand replayed in his mind.

"You really think anything is more important than saving Taine? He's in the most imminent danger!" Taimani clenched her jaw, unrelenting. "And if you refuse to help, I'll do it myself."

Her words hung heavy in the air, leaving a lingering uncertainty.

"Mani, we all want to help," Charlotte said.

Taimani shifted her gaze to Charlotte. "You will? Then we've agreed to save my brother first?" The warrior paced around the room.

"I..." Charlotte glanced at Rapha. "Timing and getting the right order of things are important. I learned that when I tried to insist on saving my sisters before the Mountain Kingdom."

"Your sisters are safe with their people inside a tower," Taimani argued. "Taine is being actively tortured by a madman. He doesn't have the luxury of time." She pulled up the hood of her cloak. "And I will not argue further." She moved towards the door.

She had only taken a step when Torrin and Shorty rushed in, their faces etched with urgency.

"New curfew in effect," Shorty said, out of breath. "Nobody is allowed to move for any reason, under threat of arrest."

CHAPTER 11

WHERE IS EVERYBODY? CHARLOTTE thought as she looked around at the empty space. It was bright and airy, with no person and nothing in sight. Then she looked down... and screamed.

Below her was a mass of trees and buildings. The Ti're river stretched as far as she could see.

Did I turn into a bird? She wondered. She stretched her limbs and saw two arms and legs, just as normal.

"Where are we?" Sonos asked from beside her.

Charlotte yelped. He hadn't been there a moment ago.

They were both floating in midair.

"I... I don't... know," Charlotte stuttered, still trying to get her bearings. "Raph? Where are you? Is this some kind of crazy portal?" *But if so, where are the others?*

Sonos flailed his arms and legs, but his eyes were focused, not fearful.

"What are you doing? Trying to fall?" Charlotte asked, her panic levels rising.

"Trying to figure out if this is some kind of invisible K'Luma carrier or something," he answered. "I don't understand how we're just hovering and unable to go anywhere."

Charlotte's mind raced, trying to make sense of their situation. She recalled the flying hover-pods used exclusively by only the most important nobles and Elites from Pergamum. She had dreamed of flying in one, until her sisters had been forcefully taken in the carrier used by Elisa Wumi, wife of General Uzoma.

Charlotte pushed the thought from her mind. Her breath caught every time she tried to look below. It felt as though they would fall at any moment.

"Rapha?" she tried again.

No answer. Nothing moved apart from her and Sonos. This had to be a dream.

"Where do you think we are?" Charlotte asked, her voice trembling. She tried desperately to make sense of the bizarre landscape below. If it was a dream, it seemed too real to be a mere illusion.

"Riverton," Sonos answered, his voice filled with confusion and amazement. "There's the main road leading to the west, and you can make out Harmony in the distance."

Charlotte squinted and was finally able to understand the scene below them.

Just then, a powerful gust of wind pummeled Charlotte, causing her to lose her sense of balance. The world blurred below, and her heart raced in fear.

As she struggled for air, she frantically reached out to try and find Sonos. His strong arm quickly grabbed her around the waist and pulled her close to his side.

Almost as abruptly as the wind had come, it stopped. Now, they hovered over a sprawling, heavily fortified city.

Charlotte sucked air into her lungs, her eyes wide with disbelief.

"Pergamum," Sonos whispered. His jaw clenched, but his arm remained wrapped protectively around her.

The palace appeared like the inner layer of an onion, surrounded by massive walls that protected the entire city. The palace stood above all other structures—connected buildings and open courtyards sprawling within the walls. The Ti're river bordered one side, and tall, tiered towers stood proudly to the north.

"The Legacy Towers!" Charlotte exclaimed, her voice filled with wonder and realization. This was the closest she'd come to her sisters. But they were trapped in a dream-like realm, suspended, with reality just out of reach.

Now, if I could just get down there, Charlotte wished, her mind racing with possibilities and filled with uncertainty.

The sky darkened, and a sound like thunder rumbled louder and louder until Charlotte's whole body trembled.

Sonos pulled her closer.

"Do not presume you know the way," a deep, thunderous voice boomed, resonating throughout the sky. "Trust me, as I have trusted you."

Another gust of wind pushed against Charlotte, and the world went dark.

Charlotte shot up with a start, gasping for air, her heart pounding in her chest. Sweat coated her forehead as she frantically tried to make sense of her surroundings.

Beside her, Sonos was in a similar state, his breathing labored, eyes wide with confusion and awe.

They were each on a straw mat in Shorty's storage room, and soft light trickled under the door from the alley. Charlotte's mind slowly began to separate the dream from reality.

Rapha lay curled up and snoring next to Charlotte. *Figures*, Charlotte thought. The entire world could crumble, and Rapha would still snore.

"Did you...?" Sonos started, then stopped, rubbing a hand through his cropped hair.

"Just have a crazy dream?" Charlotte finished his sentence, her voice trembling with the remnants of the intense experience. She nodded, confusion, awe, and determination swirling in her mind.

Sonos exhaled loudly. "That was intense."

"It happened to me once before—on the way to Salan." Charlotte paused, her thoughts still caught between the dream and the waking world. "But this is the first time I've had a dream *with* someone."

She thought the corners of Sonos' mouth lifted—but the room was dimly lit; maybe it was her imagination.

"It's the second time *El* has come in a dream and asked me to trust him," she said, remembering the red-masted ship in the storm. The dream had foretold her of the ship she and Jax would find to take them to the mainland of K'Luma.

"*Trust me, as I have trusted you,*" Sonos repeated the last words of the dream.

"Wait. You heard the same thing as me?" The realization that they were in the same dream continued to amaze Charlotte. "Trust me, as I have trusted you," she repeated the phrase. "I guess he has trusted us with pretty big things... like stopping the army and the Emperor," Charlotte thought aloud. She couldn't shake the feeling of being part of something much larger than saving her sisters, and even rescuing Taine. What kind of power could bring two people together in the same dream?

"Mmhmm," Sonos agreed. But his brow furrowed, and his gaze shifted to Charlotte's other side. "Where's Taimani?"

Charlotte turned, her eyes widening in realization. Taimani was nowhere in sight. Panic crept into her voice as she reached to touch Taimani's vacant mat and said, "The straw is cool as if Mani hasn't been here all night."

Charlotte stood and walked towards the door. There were no windows in the storage room, only the door leading to the alley and another to Shorty's storefront. He ran a small grocery, as he had explained the night before. Torrin had taken the extra room in the living quarters above the store, while the others had been given space in the storeroom.

Charlotte unlatched the door to the alley and opened it just enough to stick her head through. The sky was pale; dawn would be coming soon.

Sonos walked up behind her and stuck his head out above hers.

"Nowhere in sight," Charlotte muttered. She squirmed out from beneath Sonos' head and shoulders and stepped back into the dimly lit room.

She found a candle while Sonos closed and latched the door.

Rapha finally stirred and came to sit on the high table where Charlotte lit the candle and placed it in a jar. She took a seat on the sole barstool near the table.

Sonos picked up a small piece of paper that rested on Taimani's mat, along with her blowgun and darts, and brought them over into the candlelight.

"I can't stand by and do nothing to help my brother," Sonos read from the paper. "I'm turning myself in. There's no quicker way to get to the palace. I'll find a way to break my brother free from there. Best of luck to you both." Sonos flipped the page to the other side, but there was nothing more.

"Taimani knew we were specifically told not to go after Taine," Charlotte said, her voice filled with both frustration and concern.

Sonos hung his head. "It's my fault. I knew she was upset. I should have talked to her more directly. I shouldn't have hesitated in the cave. If we had jumped the first time, Wylder would never have had a chance to capture Taine."

Charlotte scowled, her anger surfacing. "Stop trying to take responsibility for choices that are not yours," she said firmly. She grabbed Taimani's note from Sonos' hand and burned it over the flame of the candle. She was determined to protect her friend's plan from being discovered—even if it was foolish.

"I understand why Mani ran, but it does not excuse her selfish decision." Charlotte's eyes burned with an anger that seemed to flow from somewhere other than her own heart.

Sonos looked up, surprised. "Selfish?"

"Yes, selfish," Charlotte repeated. "Don't you think we all want to see Taine safe? Don't you think Ava and Lily will be in even more danger once Ade realizes they're linked to me? He may have already figured that out."

Charlotte started pacing.

"Taimani knew we were specifically told not to go after Taine. Yet she decided to put us all at risk by alerting the Imperials to us being in Riverton," Charlotte said. "So yes, it was incredibly selfish of her to run off."

She glanced at Rapha, but he didn't try to interrupt her. In fact, he seemed to be nodding.

"And you heard the voice in our dream," Charlotte stopped and looked Sonos in the eye. "*El* is trusting us. This journey didn't start with us, and I think it would be dangerous for any of us to do our own thing now. Even if it *feels* noble."

Rapha hummed a few notes after Charlotte's last words.

"That sounds familiar," Sonos muttered, his brow furrowed in thought. He knelt by his sleeping mat and dug through his cloak until he found his journal. He flipped through the pages. "Here it is," he put his finger on a particular page and read. "Man plans, but *El* directs the way forward. Be flexible. Don't always trust what you feel." He looked up. "Miss Gemma said that back in the bakery."

"Don't always trust what you feel," Charlotte repeated. She looked at Rapha. "We must do better. We have bigger responsibilities now and can't afford to let each other down. I can't let my sisters down. And Taine. And *El*. I can't let *El* down." She allowed the weight of that to sink deep inside her core.

A soft knock sounded on the door from the grocery side. Torrin popped his head in. "Oh good, you're both awake. We have a problem."

He walked into the storage room, followed by Shorty. Their faces showed unmasked concern.

Charlotte's heart skipped a beat as she braced for more bad news.

Shorty scanned the room, his eyes lingering on Taimani's empty mat. A deep frown was etched on his face. He explained, "I received an alert from one of my contacts in the Guard. A rogue Kimwaki warrior turned herself in and demanded transport to Pergamum. She claims to know the rebels' whereabouts. And since you are both the most notorious rebels in the Empire, I assume that means you."

Charlotte crossed her arms. This is precisely why she got so angry. Did Taimani not realize that her actions and choices affected more than just herself? Now Shorty and everyone in Riverton would be under even more suspicion.

"Surely she won't give up our location," Sonos said, his voice holding a glimmer of hope. "Maybe she'll even try to throw them off track."

Torrin sighed, his tone filled with resignation.

"Does it matter what she says?" Shorty asked. "She was here and claims to have intel on you both. They're going to lock down the whole city looking for you, even if she doesn't name us or lead them to the store."

A mechanical rumble sounded from the sky, adding tension to the room.

"And those must be the K'Luma carriers coming now," Shorty said. "I'm going to have to find a better hiding place for you both, but your movement out of here will be delayed. I'm sorry." He scurried out of the room.

"Hang tight here, and we'll work something out," Torrin assured them. "Shorty has a lot of contacts in Riverton. In the meantime, I think the best thing I can do for you is make breakfast. I feel it may be your last warm meal for a while. Do you like cocoa tea?"

Charlotte's eyes widened in surprise. "You know about cocoa tea?" It felt selfish to get excited about something when the whole place was under threat.

"I'll take that as a yes," Torrin replied with a slight smile. "I'll allow you two some space to talk and freshen up, and I'll get to work in the kitchen." He stepped out through the door.

Reality sank back in.

Another *vroom* sounded overhead, making the walls vibrate slightly.

An idea started forming in Charlotte's head.

"Remember that dream?" she asked, slowly putting the pieces together.

Sonos raised a questioning eyebrow.

"I have an idea," she said.

"No... surely you're not thinking..." Sonos' voice trailed off.

It was exactly what she was thinking.

Chapter 12

"**T**HIS IS A TERRIBLE idea," Sonos muttered through gritted teeth as he trailed behind Charlotte through the streets towards the river.

Thankfully, people were allowed to move around the city between sunrise and sunset, but Sonos knew his brother would not relent in his pursuit.

To his shock and chagrin, when Charlotte had described both the dream and her plan to Torrin and Shorty over breakfast, they had agreed.

"*El* speaks in many ways," Torrin had said, and his voice had carried an unsettling certainty.

"Miss Gemma once told me, '*First be sure, then be really sure, then be quick.*'" Shorty had added.

After hastily gulping down the tantalizing cocoa tea that had surpassed Charlotte's description, they embarked on the reckless plan with Rapha, leaving Torrin and Shorty behind.

The sun lazily ascended the sky, casting an ominous glow on the awakening city. Storefronts creaked open, and vendors cautiously moved through the streets, an air of gritty tension in the atmosphere.

Abruptly, Charlotte came to a halt, causing Sonos to crash into her, their collision echoing the chaos of their situation.

Rapha chittered from where he sat on Charlotte's shoulder.

She grunted and pulled Sonos to huddle beside her against the brick wall. "Aren't you supposed to be Mister Observant? Now would be a good time to pay attention," she hissed.

Charlotte's face was hidden underneath the hood of the cloak, but he could imagine her frown and the blaze of her green eyes.

"I was just..." Sonos muttered an attempted apology.

As they stood there, hoods up, a disgruntled fisherman carrying a basket of fish on his back stormed past them. "Imperials trying to stop me from docking. Where was I supposed to go? Float away in the sea?" His voice faded as he walked away.

The Imperial grip on the city was tightening with each passing moment.

"Shorty said the K'Luma carriers would be landing in and taking off from a field just north of those buildings, near the river." She squinted towards the squat buildings.

Sonos nodded, his mind trying to maintain focus amidst the whirlwind of doubts. The dream had shown them hovering in the air, but what if they had overlooked a crucial detail? What if their assumptions were flawed?

"Are you sure about this?" Sonos risked asking again. "It wasn't specifically a K'Luma carrier in the dream. What if it was something else?"

A steely resolve solidified in Charlotte's eyes; her patience had worn thin. "If you want to run back and try your luck hiding out with Torrin and Shorty, leave." Charlotte let the words hang for a moment. "But if you're staying, do not question me at every turn—especially when the decision to move forward has already been made."

Sonos opened his mouth to apologize, but Charlotte had already walked off. She turned down a narrow street leading north, flanked by two one-story structures resembling windowless warehouses with oversized front doors.

Summoning every ounce of willpower, Sonos silenced his doubts, focusing on taking the next right step and moving forward.

Charlotte held up a clenched fist, signaling for Sonos to stop. She pressed herself against the wall, pointing around the corner.

Before them lay an expansive open field devoid of structures save for two imposing K'Luma carriers.

A surge of disbelief washed over Sonos, threatening to drown him in the realization of their audacity. Stealing a carrier in broad daylight was sheer madness. Yet, there they stood, ready to do just that.

During the hurried planning, Sonos had to explain how the carriers couldn't fly very far at night, their solar-powered hover platforms rendering them powerless in darkness. The Sahemy hadn't yet found a better way to store the energy required.

He allowed his mind to wander for a moment. *With her ingenuity, Charlotte could figure out a solution to the storage problem.* He marveled at her technological prowess, recalling the first time he witnessed her effortlessly manipulating an Imperial gazer in that dim alley in Portemore.

Charlotte's hushed voice snapped him back to the present. "There are more guards than I anticipated," she whispered, frustration spilling out through her words. "There are two carriers, and I count four Elites milling about."

Sonos frowned. "Each carrier can hold at least a dozen people. They must be waiting for more information from Mani before deciding on their course of action. The other guards are likely inside those buildings we passed or hunting for us in the streets." He instinctively glanced over his shoulder.

A flicker of worry crossed Charlotte's face, showing through the shadows cast by her hood. "I only have two red darts to knock them unconscious. I could use the blue darts to cause blindness, but I don't think I'm good enough with this blowgun to load it and hit four targets before one of them takes me out." Charlotte tapped her foot and sighed heavily.

Against the odds, he and Charlotte may have to face two dozen Elites by themselves. Even the four currently in sight seemed insurmountable. He desperately needed one of his warriors.

Something caused him to wince internally. Charlotte would bite his head off if she heard him say that Taine or Taimani was "his" warrior. And she would be right. He had to fight the assumptions of ownership taught to him from birth.

Rapha chittered from Charlotte's shoulder.

"What, Raph? You have an idea?" Charlotte asked, her voice held a blend of desperation and anticipation.

Sonos strained to decipher Rapha's chitters as well. He was so engrossed in his deliberations that he didn't hear the footsteps behind them until it was too late.

"You there. What are you two doing here?" a deep voice asked with the familiar Pergamum clip.

Sonos turned to face the looming threat, his heart pounding.

Two Elites, their double-edged swords glinting ominously, confronted them with an air of unyielding authority.

Caught off guard, Sonos struggled to find his voice. "I... we..." he stammered.

A flurry of movement scurried past him, and in the next instant, the guards had two red darts sticking from their necks. Their eyes went wide for the briefest of moments; then they crumpled to the ground.

A triumphant Rapha stood atop them and pulled out the two darts, handing them back to Charlotte.

"Nice one, Raph! You think you could do it again with four darts?" Charlotte asked.

Rapha chittered, and Sonos wasn't sure, but it didn't sound like Rapha was agreeing to anything.

"I'm glad to see that whatever chemical powers the darts have don't seem to run out," Sonos said, acutely aware of the uncertainty that still hung over their heads. They hadn't been able to test whether both darts would work beforehand, and Taimani had already used a red dart back in Harmony.

Charlotte glanced around the alley. "If these two were on patrol, it's safe to assume there are more lurking nearby. We need to move," she said resolutely. "You and Rapha create a diversion while I disable one of the carriers. Then we'll meet in the second one and make our escape."

She stepped forward but halted abruptly, her body tense, as a deep rumbling resonated from above.

Sonos' blood turned to ice as another K'Luma carrier descended from the sky, landing gracefully in the field before them.

He peered around the corner, and his heart sank further as he recognized the last person he expected to see exiting the third carrier—Wylder himself. The merchant's floppy hat was absent, but his dark, tech-infused trench coat was something Sonos would recognize anywhere.

"What do we do now?" Charlotte's voice barely registered in Sonos' mind as she whispered, her gaze fixed on Wylder, too.

Wylder and the Elites accompanying him dispersed towards a nearby building closer to the river. That must be where they were holding Taimani. Sonos clenched his jaw, both anger and guilt coursing through him. Everything he touched seemed to crumble beneath his fingertips.

"Six guards now," Charlotte said, counting the Elites near the carriers.

"Plus, whoever is patrolling the town," Sonos added.

Charlotte turned and frowned at him. "Point made. But let's move now before any more carriers decide to land."

"As you said, Rapha and I distract, you disable, and we meet up at the third carrier." Sonos put as much encouragement into his voice as possible.

"The carrier Wylder arrived in," Charlotte confirmed. She thrust three darts—one of each color—into his hand, then tucked the remaining darts and the blowgun into her pocket. Her hood shifted slightly, and her eyes locked onto his. She grabbed him in a quick, urgent embrace and then whispered, "Go."

Sonos drew a deep breath, steeling himself for the imminent storm. *Eyes forward*, he told himself.

Rapha scurried ahead, rushing towards the carriers, then cutting towards a nearby building.

Sonos stepped out and shouted after Rapha, allowing his voice to carry. "Hey! Get back here!" He flailed his arms, his voice loud as he tried to pull all the attention to himself.

Out of the corner of his eye, he saw Charlotte making a beeline to the closest carrier.

"Stop!" an Elite called out; his authoritative voice cut through the air. "What are you doing here?"

Sonos breathed a sigh of relief when he confirmed that the guard was focused on him rather than Charlotte. He turned toward the building, maintaining the facade. "Trying to retrieve my frisky pet," he replied.

Rapha was now throwing stones at both Sonos and the guards.

A stone whacked Sonos on the shoulder. "Ow!" Sonos let out an authentic yelp.

He heard another Elite curse under his breath.

How much time does Char need? Sonos wondered. She hadn't been able to say for sure, because she'd never even seen the inside of a carrier. Sonos worked to quell his rising anxiety. *It's okay; she'll figure it out. Technology is her thing, and* El *is with us.*

"Get that confounded monkey!" another guard shouted.

Sonos risked a quick glance. He counted four Elites. That meant Charlotte would still have to deal with two of them on her own if she didn't keep out of sight. She had the exact number of darts needed. There was no room for error.

Rapha screeched from the rooftop above.

"What kind of rabid pet do you keep?" an Elite asked from next to Sonos.

Sonos jumped. He hadn't realized someone had come so close. "It's a white capuchin monkey." He tried to mask his voice and impersonate Charlotte's accent, but it came out distorted.

"Pull down your hood," the guard ordered. Three others circled where they stood.

Okay, that means only two are left unaccounted for.

"What?" Sonos spluttered.

"You heard—"

The Elite was interrupted by a stone that hit him directly on the forehead. He gasped and dropped to his knees.

The other guards pulled their swords from their backs, and the blue glow of the tech infusion hummed.

I hope Charlotte is faring better than me, Sonos thought. He still didn't dare glance at the carriers. His palms were sweating again. He didn't have enough darts and felt woefully unprepared.

The Elite who had been struck by the rock stood again, still dazed. He walked toward Sonos.

I need to do something. Sonos was panicking. He assumed a fighting pose, putting one foot behind him and raising his fists. All it would take is one touch from the sword, and he'd fall unconscious, but at least he wouldn't go down without a fight. *Maybe I'll even meet Taimani, and we could try to save Taine together.* His mind dared to hope. But he couldn't leave Charlotte. Not like how they'd left Taine to the enemy...

The Elites circled in.

The closest one reached a hand towards Sonos' hood. Sonos ducked and tried to land an uppercut on the Elite. He prayed the training from the past year would kick in. He dodged the Elite's hand, but his fist barely grazed the guard's chin.

One of the guards let out a chuckle. "At least the ruffian has some spirit. Should make it a little more fun."

Their words reminded Sonos of how Ade had always teased him on the practice fields. *"Give it up, little brother. Might as well go stick your nose back in a book."* But during his year-long lockdown, Sonos had become stronger... better than this.

He didn't need to defeat four Elites. He just needed to keep them distracted long enough for Charlotte to do her part. He could do this. He slyly pulled out one of the darts and held it securely in his closed fist.

Sonos locked onto the one guard who didn't have his weapon raised. He lunged. *I might as well go all in.*

He wrapped his arms around the Elite, tossing them both to the ground.

His body landed on top of the guard's, and he tried to use this to his advantage, but Elites trained for years. They were the best of the Imperial Guard—the ones who had proved themselves worthy to rise through the ranks.

In half a heartbeat, the guard kicked Sonos' legs away and flipped him onto his back, but Sonos managed to stab the dart into the guard's neck and then pull it back quickly. He gave it a quick glance before he closed his fingers back around it; it was the blue dart that caused temporary blindness.

Perfect, he thought.

The guard jumped off Sonos and cried out, "I can't see!"

Sonos glanced at the other Elites. Two were trying to help their comrade. But one had his gaze locked on Sonos.

"It's Sonos!" the guard shouted in realization.

Sonos' hood had dropped in the tussle. His cover was blown.

The guard who called his name made a movement with his hands to turn on his gazer. The entire mass of Elites would soon descend.

But Sonos was faster. He sat up, aimed a green dart at the guard, and threw with all his might. It hit the guard in the thigh and, thankfully, seemed to stick. *A small miracle*, Sonos thought. The green dart would cause hallucinations. Hopefully, it would be enough, Sonos prayed as he pulled up his hood again.

Sure enough, the Elite with the green dart sticking from his thigh turned his glowing sword toward the other Elites.

"What are you doing?" one called out, shifting to a defensive position.

Sonos took the opportunity to move into a crouch. He pulled out the remaining two darts, his fingers closing around them like a lifeline.

He was going to give Charlotte every moment he could.

With a surge of determination, he launched the first dart at the nearest Elite, his aim true. But the guard proved too swift, skillfully dodging the projectile.

Confused, the Elite pointed the glowing sword towards Sonos.

Two others engaged with the hallucinating guard and the other who was blind. Sonos hoped that meant it only left one guard for Charlotte to handle. But Sonos had to focus all his attention on the last Elite who circled Sonos, his gaze unmoving.

Desperation coursed through Sonos' veins. With a final burst of resolve, he threw the last remaining dart, his vision fixed on the guard closing in on him.

But the dart sailed right past its intended target, again.

Sonos backed up, about to run, but an agile ball of fur ran past, picking up the red dart from the ground and running toward the Elite focused on Sonos.

Bravely, Rapha jabbed the Elite, but another guard grabbed the monkey before he could jump away.

Panic again rose inside of Sonos.

"Got you, little varmint," the guard spat, then turned his gaze to Sonos.

Rapha chittered, discreetly pointing to the carriers, then hummed with determination.

No, Sonos thought. *I'm not going to leave you here. I can't...*

But Rapha's humming intensified. It confused the guard, but Sonos knew what Rapha was trying to communicate. He needed to run.

He lingered a moment longer to be sure. To see if Rapha had one more dart or another plan. But Rapha was unmoving. He didn't fight the Elite.

Guilt flooded Sonos' brain, but he turned and sprinted towards Wylder's carrier, towards Charlotte.

CHAPTER 13

"WHERE'S RAPHA?" CHARLOTTE ASKED, breathless. She tried to inhale deep gulps of air after her sprint to Wylder's carrier. She had just disabled the other two.

Sonos had hastily climbed in moments after her, but Rapha wasn't with him.

"I... he..." Sonos stammered.

Charlotte got distracted as she caught sight of an Elite running towards them. The urgency of their situation fueled her short temper, overshadowing any sympathy she might have mustered on a normal day. Why wasn't Sonos answering? She needed to get them out of there but didn't want to leave Rapha behind.

"Where is he?" Charlotte snapped, but then focused on the holographic dashboard being emitted by her gazer-ring. Her eyes locked onto the dashboard's swirling data. Her mind raced, searching for a way to log into the K'Luma carrier's controls to take charge and secure their escape.

"He's not coming," Sonos choked out, his voice heavy with guilt. "He gave himself up for me so I wouldn't get captured."

Charlotte's heart wrenched at his words. She was mad, but it sounded exactly like something Rapha would do. She needed to do her part, too.

She took a deep breath, her eyes never leaving the dashboard. She couldn't afford to lose focus, to let her emotions overwhelm her. She needed to find that back door that the Sahemy always seemed to leave open in their tech...

"I'm in," she gasped. She found a way to lock the carrier just as the Elite reached them.

He pounded on the door with fierce determination. The urgency pushed her further, and she activated a shield mirroring the deadly power of the Elite's swords.

"Uhm, Char... Not to rush you, but I think the reinforcements are coming," Sonos said, his voice trembling slightly.

Charlotte's grip tightened on the carrier's controls, her knuckles turning white as the banging reverberated in her ears.

She needed to get this carrier off the ground. Disabling the other two carriers had been more straightforward. The Sahemy were rudimentary in their understanding of energy, and she had severed the power source.

But to fly... that was another matter entirely. She looked back and forth between the holograph on her gazer-ring and the actual levers on the carrier.

She had retrofitted a flyer-board back in Jamroq and fixed a Sahemy motor on a ship from Salan. But how to make this work?

Find the right thread, and you'll untie the knot, Gran's words echoed in her mind. Her eyes darted back and forth, scanning through the Noiz data projecting out from the gazer-ring and at the Sahemy tech of the carrier, searching for the key to pilot the carrier.

"Okay, I think I got it," she declared. Her heart raced; her palms were slick with sweat.

"Mmhmm," Sonos murmured, his voice strained.

Charlotte risked a quick glance away from her task. "Oh my!" she gasped.

Dozens of Elites surrounded their carrier, their menacing presence almost suffocating. They radiated a murderous intent, and their eyes glared at Charlotte and Sonos.

Summoning her resolve, Charlotte flipped the blue switch and swiftly pressed two other buttons, her fingers moving purposefully. The carrier roared to life, a surge of power coursing through its metallic frame. An involuntary smile spread across Charlotte's face. She knew their lives were hanging on a razor-thin margin, but the technology was astonishing.

"Char..." Sonos' anxiety was palpable.

"Getting there," Charlotte said.

The clanging of metal against metal rang in Charlotte's ears. The Elites relentlessly attacked the electric shield, their swords emitting a haunting blue glow. They clearly were not used to attacking their own tech.

Gritting her teeth, Charlotte determined not to falter.

"Not much longer." Her voice was steady—more steady than her racing heart.

With a surge of adrenaline, she shifted her focus to the holographic steering wheel, the image emitting from her gazer-ring. It acted as a real-time tutorial for the carrier. She reached out, her hand trembling as she grasped the physical level on the dashboard.

The carrier shot upward, defying gravity's grip, propelling them into the vast expanse of the sky.

The sheer force of their ascent stole the breath from Charlotte's lungs, leaving her gasping for air.

Beside her, Sonos inhaled sharply, his eyes wide.

"Woo!" Charlotte exclaimed when she finally caught her breath.

She guided the carrier using a delicate balance of physical levers and holographic controls, her heart pounding in her chest. This was everything she dreamed of and more.

The cloudless sky gave unhindered views of the Empire for hundreds of miles. *This is what flying feels like...* Nothing but wonder filled Charlotte's mind.

"That was... uhm... Good job," Sonos said weakly.

Charlotte looked over; his face was a few shades paler than normal, and his eyes were wide. "Sorry, this is my first time. I guess that takeoff was a little quick," she said, still unable to keep the silly grin off her face.

Sonos nodded, his gaze turned to her rather than the sky. He must be used to the view, having flown many times before. Or maybe he was just horrified at her lack of flying skills.

Charlotte turned her attention back to the controls. "I think this should get us going forward."

The carrier jolted forward in the direction of the capital. She tried to ease back the physical lever as she steered with her other hand. The carrier steadied at a more controlled pace.

After a few moments, Sonos turned his head. "It normally takes pilots months of training before they can operate a carrier on their own." His voice was full of admiration.

Charlotte's heart skipped a beat, and she watched him out of the corner of her eye, suddenly afraid to catch his gaze fully. The way he said that...

"I mean it," Sonos continued, his voice softening. "You've never flown *anything* before, had no access to tech on Jamroq, no training—" His words cut off. He must have caught her sudden scowl.

"Oh... I'm doing it again, aren't I?" He shifted uncomfortably.

Charlotte huffed. The ignorance that just flowed from his statements had the immediate effect of boiling her blood. Her homeland was not a mere conquered isle, an insignificant backwater place existing only because of the Empire's rule. "I have flown before... well, a flyer-board," Charlotte felt the need to explain.

"We make do with what we have. We're not ignorant slaves to the Empire."

She gazed out at the sweeping landscapes that sprawled below as far as the eye could see. How often had Sonos flown these skies with the Emperor—seeing the breadth of the land they ruled? A mix of admiration and frustration welled within her, the stark contrast of their perspectives casting a shadow over her thoughts.

"But with this tech, and bird's-eye views like these, no wonder you think you're destined to rule over everyone," Charlotte said. The realization of their very different upbringings threatened to drive a wedge between them, a divide she wasn't sure she could bridge.

"Char, I'm sorry," he said, his voice gentle—not defensive. "After we get your sisters, and Taine and Mani... and Raph, I want you to show me Jamroq if you're willing. I want to see your home as you do." His blue-grey eyes shone, and the sky paled in contrast.

Charlotte managed a silent nod in response. She deliberately turned her attention back to the scenes below them. Now was the time for focus, not for butterflies in her stomach.

Fields of green blurred below them as they followed the Ti're River north towards Pergamum. The Badlands and the Mountain Kingdom were nowhere in sight, but Charlotte knew they lay somewhere to the west. *Jax, I hope you find a way to the palace. We're going to need you*, Charlotte thought. Their small group continued to dwindle, with the responsibility now resting on her and Sonos.

"Remember the poem that Rapha gave you in the portal?" Sonos asked. He dug through his cloak and pulled out his journal.

The lack of Rapha's presence weighed heavily on Charlotte's heart. But she remembered the poem. She had read the words over and over.

Sonos read from his journal, "*Hear the mighty thunder of Noiz, See the numbers who stand in Truth, Feel the tremble as* El *arises, You have touched one who is unconquerable.*"

"Unconquerable," Charlotte repeated. It was a promise from *El*.

"Some things are bigger than what we can see," Sonos said, his eyes drifting toward the window. "And I'm beginning to learn that our job is to fight, to do the next right thing. And in the end—"

"We win," Charlotte finished.

"Win we shall," Sonos echoed the phrase that had carried them throughout the journey.

The waters of the Ti're raced beneath them. Flying was everything Charlotte had imagined it would be. They were taking what would have been a two-day journey upriver with motorboats and turning it into a trip of roughly an hour or so; at least, that was Sonos' estimate. Given the speed at which they were traveling, Charlotte believed it.

A new holograph popped up from the physical dashboard. It was in the shape of a circle, and blinking red dots appeared at the top of the circle.

Charlotte cocked her head, curious.

"We've got company," Sonos said gravely.

"But I disabled the other carriers..." Charlotte said, her words trailing off as she counted the dots. There were six.

"Those aren't coming from Riverton," Sonos said. "They're coming from the north, from Pergamum."

Charlotte's heart dropped. Of course, Ade would send other carriers to intercept them.

"I'm not sure this shield will stave off an attack from six other carriers." Charlotte tried looking for information in her gazer to see what it could hold off. The plan had been to land their carrier at a rarely used base located just outside the palace. Why did she think they'd go undetected long enough to get there?

"*El* didn't bring us so far just to kill us," Charlotte muttered. She clung to the words she had repeated to Sonos in the Badlands. There had to be a way out.

"How far away from the capital do you think we are?" Charlotte asked. She was having a hard time judging their travel time while flying the carrier.

Sonos snapped his head up from where he'd been staring at the holographic image showing the other carriers. "Huh?" he asked. His fingers were white from clutching his knees.

Despite the alarm that now beeped incessantly inside their carrier, and all the buttons and levers that called out to Charlotte, she shifted her body to face Sonos and gave him her full attention. She knew the signs of a panic attack all too well. She gripped his forearm with a fierceness she hoped wasn't over the top. "Hey. We're going to get through this. You hear me?"

Sonos looked up and held her gaze, but she could see the fear warring with hope in his eyes.

"What were we just rehearsing about being unconquerable?" she asked. "We're not going to die. We're not going to get captured. But I need you with me, okay?" This vulnerable side of Sonos made her nervous—especially as they were about to jump into a battle. But she knew they had to do this together.

He swallowed and nodded, determination returning to his eyes.

"I know Rapha isn't here, but we're not alone, and we *will* win this thing," Charlotte said. Her grip tightened, conveying a silent plea.

"Win." It was only one word that Sonos repeated back to her, but it was enough. It was the most important one.

She returned her focus to the speeding world in front of them. The other carriers were not yet in sight, but the blinking red dots were getting closer on the circular hologram.

"We have about twenty minutes of flying left to reach Perga-mum and about..." Sonos squinted at the hologram, "ten minutes until the other carriers reach us."

"You're sure?" Charlotte asked. Her pulse was racing again. She had hoped to get closer to the palace before having to ditch the carrier.

"I know carrier speeds well enough, and I know the route. I'm sure," Sonos said. Confidence seeped back into his words, and for that, Charlotte was grateful.

"We can't fight them in the air, and landing at the palace with them right behind us would be pointless. We have to land some-where around here before they see us, and try to make it on foot." Charlotte spoke their options aloud. But the plan was flimsy at best.

"There may be another way," Sonos said. His eyes darted to the back of the carrier. "But you have to trust me."

Charlotte didn't trust the way her heart flipped—this was not the time for it. But she had no better ideas and loved the spark in Sonos' words. It was much better than the scared and defeated version of Sonos that kept sneaking out ever since Taine's capture.

"Tell me," Charlotte answered.

"We don't have much time," Sonos hurriedly explained. He flipped a switch on the physical dashboard and entered a code on a panel that emerged.

"Auto-pilot engaged," a mechanical voice said.

"How—" Charlotte started.

"It's the one thing I learned when we flew in the carriers. For emergencies." Sonos stood, his confidence fully restored. "Now, follow me." He led Charlotte from the cabin to the holding bay where passengers usually sat.

He dug around in a pile of items Charlotte could not identify and found two packs, one of which he strapped to Charlotte's back.

"Ready to *really* fly?" Sonos asked, eyebrows raised.

Charlotte wasn't sure if the spike in her pulse was from fear, excitement, or a little bit of both.

Chapter 14

—   •   —

"HEY, WAIT UP, YOU crazy reptile!" Diekololaoluwa called after the dragon lizard weaving ahead of him in the dim cavern.

Only small cracks or holes in the red stone of the Badlands terrain above allowed in slivers of light.

Maybe Die imagined that he had heard the dragon speak. *"It is time. Follow me,"* it had said in a raspy voice.

Failure to capture Sonos—his nephew—and the humiliation of having his cloak cut, but not his body, had earned him a death mandate.

Only the death of Captain Die—the captive turned head of the Elites. The identity and name given to me by the Emperor, Die thought to himself. He had chosen to end one life, the one that had been forced upon him by the Emperor and, in doing so, had activated the life his sister, the Empress, had always told him existed. Die had been only eight years old when Kimwaki was defeated, and he and his sister, the children of the Chieftain, were taken to Pergamum as spoils of war.

Die spit dust from his mouth. Almost two decades of training in the Imperial forces had honed Die's senses and taught him to trust his instincts, and something about this reptile felt important.

The dragon lizard puffed out its chest up ahead, and a flare of color caught a ray of light. The creature looked back as if waiting for him to catch up.

"It's not exactly easy for someone my size to keep up with a lizard in this place," Die muttered as he hunched his shoulders further to adjust to the narrowing tunnel.

The lizard flicked its tongue in response and scuttled forward.

"Cheeky little guy, aren't you?"

Die hurried along as the lizard's tail slipped from sight.

Soon, he was crawling. When the tunnel narrowed further, Die hesitated, stopping with his hands and knees on the hard stone floor. He'd have to drop to his belly to keep following the lizard. What if he got stuck? What if the lizard was a trick of the Sahemy sorcerers and was leading him to his death? Perhaps he should turn back and take his chances with his squadron—his former squadron.

The dragon lizard reappeared and darted back to Die, stopping near one of his hands. It puffed out its chest once more.

"Trying to say something?" Die asked, cocking his head. "I thought you could speak."

The lizard slid under his hand and pulled it slightly forward.

Die caught the meaning—and perhaps the urgency. He sighed and adjusted to belly-crawling forward. He kept his arms in front of him so they wouldn't get stuck at his sides. Who knew where this lizard hole would lead?

The tunnel grew darker and narrower as Die crawled along. Thankfully, there was always just enough space to keep moving forward. He started to wonder how long he'd have to keep going. Thirst burned his throat. How long had it been since he'd seen light? An hour? Time was strange, and there was nothing but darkness, the sounds of his own breathing, and the lizard's soft movements to mark any sign of life.

Every inch forward was a battle of will and survival, but he was determined to keep moving.

His hands brushed against something solid in front of him. *Finally, something*, Die thought. But was it a dead end?

Loud scratching filled the tiny space, and the dragon lizard huffed out a breath.

Finally, a trickle of sunlight snuck through a slit the dragon had cut through the wall.

Die reached out to lend his fingers to the frenzy.

The light grew brighter, almost blinding, as the lizard and Die scratched.

When the hole got big enough, the lizard scuttled through.

Die used both hands to force away the loose stone. He only hoped that whatever wall he was prying a hole through didn't collapse completely. Dust limited his sight, but it sounded like a cavernous room ahead. That was encouraging.

Soon enough, the hole was wide enough for him to reach his arms through, and he squeezed his head and shoulders forward and pulled himself the rest of the way through.

As soon as he was out of the dark, narrow tunnel, Die took a few deep breaths, relishing the fresh air.

The circular room he was in was spacious, but not massive. It was cozy. Stone shelves lined the walls and were filled to overflowing with stacked books. A deep green patterned rug covered the hard floor, making the place feel more homey.

Die stood and walked the circumference of the room. There didn't seem to be a door or a way out, apart from the hole they had created. Similar to other places in the underground of the Badlands, holes in the red and orange stone allowed light to come through the ceiling and a few spots in the wall. Perhaps they were near the surface, or possibly inside one of the myriad hills that made up the Badlands.

After scanning the room for potential dangers and trying to orient himself, he finally stopped and stood in the center of the rug. "What is this place?" he asked aloud to no one in particular.

"It is a beginning," a scratchy voice responded.

Die scanned the room again, surprised to hear someone answer. But the room was empty, apart from all the books... and the lizard. The dragon lizard!

"You *can* talk," Die walked toward the creature perched on a nearby shelf atop some books.

"My name is Nissi." The words slithered around its pointed tongue.

Die shook his head. There was something different about this room. It was almost as if the air crackled with energy.

"Your name is Isaako," Nissi said.

"No. My name is Diekololaoluwa." Die crossed his arms. *Does this lizard think I'm someone else?* Die worried for a moment.

"Your name is Isaako." Nissi puffed out his chest, displaying an array of colors.

The air again seemed to spark with energy. Why did that name seem so familiar... like something from a distant past?

"Your name is—"

"Isaako," Die finished this time. The memories came rushing back to him in a flood, and he dropped to his knees. He saw his father and mother standing in a vast, open field. Ali'tasi—that was his sister's true name—chased him, laughing and calling his name.

"My name is Isaako," Die whispered. "It means joy."

The Emperor had done everything possible to rename him, reshape him, and train him to tirelessly protect the Empire. But he finally remembered the truth.

"Your name is Isaako, formed by *El*, known before the beginning of time." The room seemed to pulse with energy. Nissi made his way over to perch on the rug nearby.

Isaako sat back on his heels and wiped at a tear that had made its way down his face. He was found. After all these years, he remembered. He was not conquered. He was not lost.

A flash of light caught his attention. One of the books emitted a glow he was sure wasn't there before. He got up, walked to the low shelf, and pulled off a leather-bound journal. The light faded, and Isaako turned it over in his hands. It felt both ancient and new at the same time.

Nissi flicked his tongue from where he now sat on the shelf.

Isaako turned to the first page.

This is the record and names of Davin's mightiest warriors.

The first was Jashobeam the Hacmonite, the leader of the Three. He once used his spear to kill 800 enemy warriors in a single battle.

Next in rank among the Three was Eleazar, son of Dodai, a descendant of Ahoah. Once, Eleazer and Davin stood together against the enemy when the entire army had fled. He killed the enemy until his hand was too tired to lift his sword, and El gave a great victory that day.

Next was Shammah, son of Agee from Harar. One time, the enemy gathered in a farmer's field, and the army attacked. But the enemy was strong, and the army fled. Only Shammah held his ground in the middle of the field and beat back the enemy.

"I don't understand." Isaako glanced up at Nissi. "What am I reading? What does this have to do with me?"

"These are records of the heroes of *El*," Nissi answered in his scratchy voice. "You have been called out. This is your destiny."

"But these are warriors. I have no army, no commander." Isaako shook his head, confused. Doubt crept back into his mind with the thought that Nissi had the wrong guy.

"Read again," Nissi said. "Each warrior stood, even when he stood alone. You have been chosen to fight for *El*."

Isaako knew precious little of any religion. He remembered whispers and hints from his sister over the years.

There is more than what you can see with your eyes, little brother. Her voice rang in his ear: *E leai se mea fa'afuase'I, na'o le fa'amoemoe.* "There is no coincidence, only purpose," he repeated the words aloud in the common tongue.

Nissi hissed in what seemed to be agreement.

"Do you accept?" Nissi asked.

"Accept the call to fight for *El*?" Isaako asked the question more to himself than to Nissi. His sister and nephew had already sided with *El*. But even more than the family connection, *El* had power. Neither the Emperor nor his sorcerers had ever been able to speak through an animal or create an ancient room in the middle of the Badlands.

Isaako had already made the choice to live, not die. This was his chance not just to survive but to live with purpose. "Yes, I accept." He bowed his head toward Nissi. He wasn't sure of the protocol.

"Come closer," Nissi said.

Isaako stepped toward where the lizard was perched.

"Closer," Nissi said again until Isaako was at eye level and mere inches away. Then, the lizard puffed out its chest and blew.

Isaako's first instinct was to recoil, but Nissi's breath covered him in a refreshing, peaceful mist. Smells of jasmine and mint filled his nostrils. He closed his eyes and inhaled, allowing peace and hope to settle over his mind and heart.

The sound of soft scratching pulled Isaako from his reverie.

Nissi had formed a small window, more of a slit, on the wall behind the shelf.

Isaako leaned closer to look outside.

A hairy creature about the size of a man was prancing around in a gully between two high, red and orange stone walls. It had cloth wrapped around its legs and something almost cloak-like flapping against its back.

Something is oddly familiar about this thing, Isaako thought to himself.

The creature paused its erratic movements and knelt beside the stream, dropping its head into the water. Isaako guessed it was the same mysterious stream that had led the Elites to Sonos and Charlotte. There wasn't supposed to be any water or life that survived in the Badlands.

When the creature lifted its head, Isaako gasped.

He recognized the clasp on the cloak, and those eyes. It was the Emperor.

"How? What?" The questions slipped out of Isaako as he turned towards Nissi.

"The Emperor has been cursed." The *s* sounds were always drawn out when Nissi spoke. "*El* has humbled him, so all will eventually know who is God."

"I thought the Emperor was still back at the palace, waiting until the eve of battle to come to the Mountain Kingdom," Isaako said, trying to put the pieces together.

Nissi stuck out its tongue before speaking, almost as if tasting the air. "Time works differently here."

"In the Badlands?"

"We're in a temporal portal... that happens to be in the Badlands."

Isaako looked back out through the slit in the wall. The Emperor splashed water all over himself in a moment of mad glee.

"It's been a week since you spoke to Sonos in the cavern," Nissi said.

A week? Isaako should be glad it wasn't years, but still... what had happened with the battle? With Sonos? With his sister, now that the Emperor was cursed?

"The Mountain Kingdom is safe, even though Uzoma foolishly searches for gold that he thinks is precious stone," Nissi hissed.

Isaako's mind went into focused battle mode. Who knew what chaos was happening in the Empire with the Emperor roaming the Badlands like a beast? Isaako had been called for a reason.

"What are my commands?" he asked Nissi.

"You will be sent on a rescue mission," Nissi said, jumping off the ledge and scuttling to the other side of the room. "But first, you must know who you are and who you are fighting for. That is your first battle."

Nissi puffed out his chest and blew on the wall. The stone changed to a cloud of red dust. Screams and sounds of angry shouting spilled through from the other side.

Isaako dropped into a warrior's lunge, ready to run into the fray. He no longer had his sword, but he had never been bested in hand-to-hand combat in over ten years. He looked to Nissi for instructions.

"Go. Watch closely, listen carefully, and you will know the way."

"But—" Isaako wanted to know *who* he was supposed to rescue.

"Go!" Nissi hissed with an urgency that left no room for argument.

Isaako narrowed his eyes toward the cloud of dust and jumped through.

CHAPTER 15

"DO IT," CHARLOTTE COMMANDED, her green eyes blazing, and her errant curls whipping wildly in the fierce wind coming in through the open door of the K'Luma carrier.

Sonos swallowed his nerves and pushed her into the sky.

He tried to ignore her screams as he adjusted his parachute and the slim flyer-board that was strapped to his chest. He stole one last glance around the carrier and then plunged out of the hatch after her.

Air rushed into his lungs, and wind filled his ears as he plummeted towards the ground. Frantically scanning the sky for Charlotte, he finally caught sight of her arms and legs spread wide just as he had instructed. He counted the seconds, praying that her parachute would deploy on time.

Eight... nine... ten. Relief surged through him as Charlotte's parachute popped open.

After angling himself closer to her, with a racing heart, he pulled the cord on his pack and was jerked almost to a stop as the parachute filled with air.

The immediate silence that followed as he hung suspended in the air was always his favorite part. He pulled at the toggles to get closer to Charlotte.

"This is... amazing!" Charlotte exclaimed. Her excitement was infectious even in the face of danger. Her vibrant grin spread from ear to ear as she continually shifted to look around her.

Sonos scanned the horizon. The carrier they had been in quickly disappeared to the north, staying on course just as the autopilot was programmed to do. The other carriers were mercifully still out of sight. *This may just work*, Sonos thought.

"You're a natural... yet again," Sonos said with genuine admiration.

Charlotte turned to catch his gaze, wild curls framing her face.

He was momentarily speechless. Here was a girl who had been forced to flee her homeland, and who'd had everything stripped away. Elites were tracking them. She was separated from her best friend and family. Their life was in constant danger, but Charlotte managed to embrace joy in the moment, and her determination and leadership were undeniable.

"Am I doing something wrong?" she asked, worry crinkling her eyes.

He realized he had been staring. "No, no," Sonos reassured her, quickly finding his words. He shifted focus and glanced at the ground. They still had a few minutes. "I just wanted to thank you."

Her eyebrows scrunched in confusion. "It's *you* who taught me to fly." She closed her eyes and threw out her arms. When she looked at him again, he continued.

"My whole world has been turned upside down—our whole world," he quickly added. "I know I've had a few bad moments, and I just wanted to thank you for being strong and taking the lead to keep us moving forward." There, he had said it. And he believed it. Charlotte's words in the carrier had cleared a fog. They would win... even if it meant the fight of their lives.

"Forward ever, backward never," Charlotte said, a hint of vulnerability in her expression. "That one is from my dad. Now, how do we land these things?"

Charlotte never held a grudge, and she always focused on the next right step, as she'd say. He made a mental note to add her dad's words to his journal later that night.

But she was right—they needed to land safely. He scanned the ground below them and pointed to a small clearing near the river. He showed her how to adjust the toggles to direct her parachute. Landing took practice, and he tried to explain how to hit the ground with soft knees.

"You sound like Jax," Charlotte said, a wistfulness in her voice.

Jax had gone radio silent since their last communication. But Sonos would have to worry about that another time.

They neared the clearing, and he allowed her to land first. She touched the ground and started running as he'd instructed, but she was too close to the river.

"Char!" Sonos shouted. He hit the ground as quickly as he could and released the chute. He sprang after Charlotte. She had left the chute connected to her pack, and now it threatened to fill again in the wind.

"Sonos!" she called out, eyes wide.

Sonos managed to grab hold of a piece of the parachute and threw his body over the billowing material, ignoring the press of the flyer-board against his chest as he hit the ground. "Cut the lines!"

Charlotte was perilously close to the rushing river.

The tension in the chute finally released. Sonos found himself entangled in a mass of cloth but fought his way free.

Charlotte was lying face down in the mud near the bank.

He ran over to her, calling her name.

She propped herself up onto her elbows. Her face was covered in mud, but she was alive. They were both alive.

"I guess I need to work on my landing." She shook her head and gave a nervous chuckle.

Sonos exhaled as she stood and brushed some of the mud and dirt from her clothes.

"Thankfully, I think the board is okay." She shrugged out of the parachute pack and turned the board over in her hands.

Before overthinking it, he dropped his pack and board onto the ground and pulled her into a tight embrace. "You're okay. We're both okay." He took a couple of deep breaths, grounding himself in her presence, then let go and stepped back before it got awkward.

Charlotte's face flushed a bit, and she looked away. But it only took a moment for a smile to return. "Who knew I'd get to fly a K'Luma carrier and jump from one on the same day!" She was unfazed by the danger and the embrace.

"And survived to tell the tale." Sonos smiled in return. He pulled a cloth from a pocket in his cloak and dipped it in the river. He walked over to Charlotte, who was still inspecting the board, and gently lifted her chin to turn her face toward him.

Her eyes went big; he couldn't ignore the racing of his own heart either. He held up the damp cloth. "Just trying to help get some of the mud off."

"Oh!" Her face flushed as he wiped away the grime.

For one scary moment, he had thought she would be swept away. But here she was; they were both safe.

He glanced at the sky. Not safe, exactly. "We need to gather the chutes and hide them," he said. "So far, I haven't seen the other carriers, nor an Empire ship on the river, but they'll have search parties out soon enough."

She nodded, pulling her curls back into a loose bun.

They bundled up the chutes and shoved them under some brush at the edge of the tree line. They then covered them with twigs and leaves. Hopefully, it would be enough.

"Now we get to fly a little closer to the ground?" Charlotte asked as she picked up one of the flyer-boards. Sonos was thankful to have found a few in storage on the carrier.

"Just make sure you can disable any tracking mechanism before we turn them on," Sonos said.

Charlotte already had her gazer-ring activated and was projecting a virtual dashboard. She found her way into the flyer-board controls of both the boards.

Sonos scanned the area as she worked. They had shifted out of sight of the river and had the covering of trees overhead. Their landing still seemed unnoticed, but he was anxious to get moving.

"Okay, all tracking disabled," Charlotte declared.

Both boards were activated and humming, a blue-white glow emanating from their undersides.

"These work just like the older model you said you retrofitted back in Jamroq," Sonos explained. "They're just a lot more sensitive."

Charlotte had already slid her feet into the slots and was standing balanced on the board.

"I set my gazer to keep us going north. I didn't see any major towns on the map between here and the city, and we can maintain a course between the road and the river," Charlotte said.

"We may have to walk when we get closer," Sonos said, hopping onto his board. He hadn't ridden or used any tech during his year of lockdown, so he was a little rusty. Thankfully, the boards had a self-balancing mechanism, so he didn't fall on his behind. "All things being equal, I estimate we'll reach the city gates in about four hours." He glanced at the sky. "Hopefully, just after midday."

"No time to waste," Charlotte said, leaning forward to propel the board ahead. It wasn't long before she was deftly maneuvering in and out through trees.

Sonos followed close behind. He did his best to watch their surroundings, including above and behind, for any signs of others, but he missed having Taine and Taimani nearby. It felt like a swarm of Elites would pop out at any moment and surround them.

Halfway through the journey, they paused to rest and eat some ration bars they had gotten from Shorty.

Charlotte tried to reach Jax again through the gazer but was only prompted to leave a message.

"Jax, I hope you're safe," she said into the ring. "There's been a change of plans, but we're on our way. Hope you can meet us there. Walk good." She ended the call.

"Still no response?" Sonos asked.

Charlotte shook her head. "He'll be all right. He's always been a fighter."

"He's a good friend," Sonos said, hopeful she wouldn't defend Jax as anything more.

"The best." Charlotte agreed.

Sonos tried to keep his face neutral, but inwardly, he allowed the spark of hope for the future to grow just a bit more.

If Charlotte noticed anything, she didn't show it. She stood and turned her flyer-board back on. "Ready?"

"To break into the palace and stop my brother?" Sonos kept his response casual.

"And rescue my sisters and Taine and Taimani," Charlotte added.

"No time to waste, then," Sonos said, hopping onto his board.

Although carriers flew overhead and rumbled in the sky at one point, the rest of the ride was uneventful until the city walls came into view.

The forest thinned, and Charlotte and Sonos took to walking. Sonos helped Charlotte strap the board to her back before putting on his own and then adjusting his cloak over the board. Hoods once again covered their faces.

He looked up at the sky, but no cloud was in sight. A storm or a little chaos might actually do them some good.

They stepped out of the woods and onto the dirt track leading to the market gate. Sonos was glad his memory and his maps training were strong.

"It's so much bigger than I could have ever imagined," Charlotte whispered as glimpses of the top of the wall became visible through the trees. "Portemore was huge compared to even our biggest city in Jamroq... but this..."

Sonos didn't point out that this was only the outer wall. The wall that insulated the Inner City, where the nobles lived, and where the palace sat, was even more grandiose.

"The last time I used this gate was for our escape out of the city," Sonos said. "Taine, Mani, Sibi, and I were all supposed to be fishermen."

Charlotte chortled. "You? Mani? Fishermen?"

"It's actually where we first met Wylder, and he tried to kidnap me," Sonos frowned.

At the thought of Wylder, images of the merchant standing over Taine in that cave in the Badlands came rushing back. But there was no time to linger on the past. As they turned a corner of the dirt track, Sonos stopped short, pulling Charlotte closer to his side.

Angry groups of people clustered outside the city gate, which was decidedly closed.

A glance at the top of the walls showed Sonos that the capital was on high alert. Archers were in active positions, and every guard tower was manned.

A wagon rumbled up from behind, and Sonos pulled Charlotte to step out of the way.

"Ho!" the driver called out to a nearby group. "What's going on?"

"Pergamum is locked tight," a man answered. "No one allowed in, no one allowed out."

Chapter 16

"**I**. Hate. Gates," Charlotte muttered through clenched teeth.

"This is not good," Sonos agreed, his voice low and tense beside her.

"Do you think we made the wrong choice? Should we have stayed in the carrier and tried to land closer to the palace?" Charlotte deliberately kept her hands pressed against her thighs, ignoring the impulse to check the gazer on her finger. Jax always knew how to squelch her self-doubts.

Sonos turned, but she couldn't see his face behind the shadow under his hood.

A loud voice boomed from atop the city wall, startling them both. "City gates are closed indefinitely!" A guard in a black uniform with crimson stripes declared, his words echoing from the amplifier in his hand.

Beside him, two life-size holographs flashed to life.

Charlotte gasped, a sense of dread creeping up her spine. One holograph was a life-size image of her, and the other was of Sonos.

"Be reminded that capturing these two rebels is of utmost importance," the guard bellowed. "Anyone who has information on these criminals will be richly rewarded. And anyone who is found to have aided them will be swiftly punished."

Charlotte wanted to turn and flee into the forest, dive into the river, or melt into the ground. The hood of her cloak was still safely hiding her face, but all the whispers and disgruntled mumbles seemed to have become immediately malicious. She took a step back, huddling closer to Sonos.

"It's okay. No one can know yet," he whispered for her ears alone.

The last word hung suspended. They were going to get caught. All this time, all those escapes, and this is where it would end.

"No," Charlotte spoke the word aloud, stopping her thoughts from spiraling further.

Sonos looked from side to side, likely trying to figure out what she was seeing.

Charlotte straightened her shoulders, determined not to let fear control her actions. "I refuse to cower in fear."

Sonos shifted uncomfortably, continuing to scan the crowd.

"I'm not trying to be reckless. But Ade..." she paused and lowered her voice. "He is not the one in control. *El* must have some way in." She cleared her throat. "I hope."

Their holographic images disappeared as Charlotte spoke, replaced by a massive, square holographic screen.

Charlotte's ring vibrated. "Now he calls back?" she muttered. She wanted to run back into the woods but didn't want to draw attention, so she dismissed the notification and hoped Jax would leave a detailed message.

Ade's smug face appeared on the screen, his dark hair slicked back, exuding arrogance and entitlement.

Charlotte was grateful for Sonos' small act of defiance that had led him to shear his hair during his lockdown. It made him seem even more distant from the nobles and his brother—even if he still carried the mindset of a prince sometimes.

"Citizens and servants of the great K'Luma Empire." Ade's voice boomed over the crowd.

Everyone's eyes were turned upward.

"I made a promise and am true to my word," Ade continued. As he spoke, a large, menacing dragon shadow slithered in a figure-eight pattern on the wall behind his throne. It looked eerily alive.

A knot grew in Charlotte's stomach. Ade was no longer broadcasting from a tower, but she wasn't sure if that was a good thing or not.

The camera panned across the room to show Taine strapped to a chair and surrounded by Elites. His face was bruised, and his hand was bandaged from where they had cut off his thumb the day before. He was shirtless, and his extensive warrior tattoos were obscured by dark red in places. But despite the bruising, every muscle in the warrior's body seemed taut and straining against the ropes that encircled him.

"My brother still has not turned himself in. I promised consequences; thus, his failed bodyguard will lose something more. It seems that an appendage was no great matter, but I have heard that long hair is of great honor in Kimwaki."

"No," Sonos gasped.

A guard near Taine stepped forward with a gleaming piece of metal in hand. At first, Charlotte thought it was a knife, but no. As the guard raised it towards Taine, she realized it was a razor.

"At least it's not Fetu this time," Sonos muttered.

Charlotte remembered Sonos explaining that Fetu was Ade's personal bodyguard and also from Kimwaki—which made the punishment all the more personal.

To Taine's credit, he did not shout or thrash about as his head was shaved. Only the closest observer would see the twitch of his muscles. But as the locks of his long hair fell to the ground, it seemed like a fire roared to life in his dark-coal eyes.

A woman in the crowd covered her mouth in horror, and a few others showed visible restraint to their emotions, but the looming guards with watchful eyes prevented any real action from erupting.

Sonos' frame was as taut as a fishing line beside her.

Anger and frustration arose in a dangerous combination inside of Charlotte. Who did Ade think he was? They needed to get to Taine and Taimani. And may *El* keep Ava and Lily's relationship to her hidden.

Finally, the guard finished shaving Taine's head, and the camera turned back to focus on Ade.

"No one else needs to get hurt." Ade was again talking on the video. "Let the rebels turn themselves in. My brother and his little girlfriend are not worth it." Ade's bitterness was bleeding through, but he caught himself. "Blessed is the great K'Luma Empire, and we will all share in the spoils of the Year of the Dragon." Cheers erupted on the video feed, but the crowd outside the walls of the city gate was notably quiet.

Charlotte knew that things would only get worse.

The video from the throne room turned off, and the life-size images of Charlotte and Sonos were again on display.

Mumbles and murmurs rose from the crowd.

"I traveled two days to get here," one woman said. "Where are we supposed to stay?"

"They expect us to pitch tents here?" another added.

One of the farmers led a donkey pulling a cart away from the city gate. He walked past Sonos and Charlotte, grumbling. "Politics and useless royalty. Why can't the spoiled prince save us all the trouble and go back to the palace?"

Charlotte grabbed Sonos' hand and pulled him further away from the crowd, closer to the edge of the forest. They leaned against a tall pine tree whose bottom branches had been trimmed. They were just out of sight of the wall and those around it.

"What other ways are there into the city besides the gates?" Charlotte asked.

"None," Sonos answered flatly, frustration filling his words. "It's built as an impenetrable city. My father used to say that even blind and lame men could hold the city because it was built so well."

Charlotte rolled her eyes, even though her face was still hidden. Arrogance was so blinding. "Nothing is impenetrable. What about the Ti're? Or does the wall extend down to the river as well?"

"Well, there's a section of the palace that leads to the baths that connect to the river," Sonos began. He held up a hand to stop Charlotte from jumping in. "But that section is heavily guarded by Elites all the time."

Charlotte sighed in frustration.

"My father was paranoid. He also doubled the size of the Inner City wall to make it even more secure than the Outer City wall you see here." Sonos waved his hand toward the massive wall they had just come from.

Charlotte had a hard time imagining that there was something even bigger that they'd have to pass through on the inside, if they could even get into the city. *One step at a time*, she reminded herself.

"I remember when Ava was studying city design—back when she dreamed about joining the Sahemy." Charlotte struggled to remember the details. "I think there was something about how fresh water was secured... a water shaft or something."

"There's a fresh spring underground, and the Sahemy designed a way to secure access to the water in case the inner city was ever under attack. That way, we'd always have a fresh supply of water." Sonos paused and turned his hooded face towards Charlotte. "They made the knowledge public to show off just how *impenetrable* and impossible it would be to conquer us... them... uhm, my father." Sonos stuttered over his last words and turned away.

Charlotte remembered how Jax had responded when Sonos had first revealed himself to be the crown prince of K'Luma in the forest outside of Portemore. Jax had been so angry and skeptical about whose side Sonos was on. Even though she had only known Sonos while he'd been on the run, and he had stood up to his father, and he had never done anything to deliberately hurt their group, the fact remained that he had been born and raised his entire life as a royal... the son of the conquering and ruthless Emperor. Was there any chance he was having second thoughts about turning his back on his brother, especially now that they were back at the palace?

She shook her head. *No, now is not the time for second-guessing*. She'd keep her eyes open, but it was better to trust Sonos and be wrong than to allow mistrust to take root inside of her mind. *El* was her ultimate protector, anyway.

The sound of angry voices erupted from near the wall.

Charlotte stepped around the tall pine tree to get a better view.

The flash of glowing blue swords caught her attention first. The guards were weaving through the crowd and looking... looking for them. Her heart raced as she recalled the night over three years ago when her sisters were taken in Kinstun. She remembered the chaos and the wanton harshness of the guards and Elites with the glowing swords as they quelled every fight and attempt to save her sisters. She had been entirely useless. She grabbed onto the trunk of the tree behind her as the image of her parents in a heap, paralyzed by the electric shock of the swords, blanketed her mind.

An arm wrapped around her shoulder, and Charlotte yelped as she was reminded of the guard who had held her to stop her from reaching her parents. *"No one fights the empire and wins,"* he had warned.

"Char, it's me. It's okay." Sonos' voice brought her back to reality—not that reality was much better. Guards were still swarming through the crowd nearby.

Charlotte's breaths came in short spurts. The horror of that night with her sisters was on sickening replay in her mind.

Sonos pushed his hood back just enough to show her his face, and then he reached inside Charlotte's hood and cradled her face in both hands. "Look at me," he said.

Charlotte forced herself to meet his gaze.

"Take a deep breath. I need you with me. Right here. Right now." Sonos spoke calmly but forcefully.

Slowly, Charlotte's breathing stabilized as she kept her eyes fixed on Sonos, listening to his voice.

When she finally settled, she was thankful that she hadn't passed out like before, when Captain Die had humiliated her dad, Jax, and Gran on Feast Day in front of the whole village, in an effort to find her. She had no sooner been dragged to the stage, when all she could think of was the night her sisters were taken, and she had blacked out.

"How did you know?" Charlotte asked, returning her focus to Sonos.

He dropped his hands, but stayed close to her side. "I've had anxiety attacks before. I almost had one up in the K'Luma carrier before you pulled me back. My tutor, Sah Timur, was the one who taught me how to control them."

"Well, thank you," Charlotte said. "The Elites in the crowd with those swords... I just kept thinking about when Ava and Lily were taken. How helpless..." She didn't finish the sentence. Instead, she straightened her shoulders. "But that's not who I am now."

Sonos nodded. "It's true. Now, you're one of the most wanted rebels in the Empire."

Charlotte cringed. "Don't remind me."

Sonos grinned but then turned serious. "We need to get out of here, though. They may not expect us at the gate so soon, but my brother will grow increasingly desperate to find us."

"Take me to the water shaft," Charlotte said.

"It's not accessible like that." Sonos shook his head.

"Gates are not looking like an option, nor is the Ti're River. We don't have a carrier or another way to fly over the gates, but crawling up through a small, unexpected space may be just the way."

Sonos frowned but relented and walked towards the river.

"I've only been here once when Sah Timur showed me what it looked like. I had asked a hundred questions before he relented," Sonos explained. "He got in trouble for it with the Sahemy. As you know, they love to guard the details of their secrets."

Charlotte could hear the flowing river and felt the cold wind that seemed determined to keep spring warmth at bay. She pulled her cloak tighter around her. She remembered the call to her gazer earlier and checked for the message using the sleeve of her cloak for cover. There was nothing. *Strange*, Charlotte thought, double-checking the calls.

The sun was starting to slip down in the sky, quicker than she wished.

Sonos kept looking around, backtracking at times, and muttering to himself. "I remember it was exactly 1,596 steps from the city gate."

Charlotte again admired his genius level of attention to detail and incredible memory.

After digging through the logs on the gazer-ring, Charlotte realized the buzzing had come from a notification of a broadcast. *But it's not supposed to be connected to the Empire*, Charlotte thought, biting her lower lip with worry. Perhaps it was only the same connection that Lenora had shown her to access broadcasts.

"There was a stump... near a cluster of hickory trees, which you can identify by the shaggy bark and long leaves..." Sonos continued. "Yes! Here it is." He stood triumphantly near a large stump.

Forgetting the mystery of the broadcast coming through on her gazer, Charlotte walked over to join Sonos. She leaned over and ran a finger over a small symbol of the Sahemy that had been stamped, or rather burned, onto a corner of the stump. It was a snake in the shape of a circle with a flame in the center. Lily had once drawn the symbol for Ava as a gift, and the picture had been pinned above Ava's bed ever since.

Shouts rang out from the crowd near the gate. They were still distant, but something was brewing.

"Not to rush you, but I'm not seeing any entrance." Charlotte paced around where Sonos knelt by the stump.

Sonos ran his hand over the old bark. "Found it," he said after some searching. "There are four buttons, and you just have to enter the code..."

His sentence trailed off, and then a loud click sounded.

Charlotte glanced around. The shouts seemed to grow closer.

Sonos kicked away some brush on the forest floor and grabbed hold of a long handle. He grunted as he lifted open the door of a small hatch.

Cold breeze and the smell of earth and stone wafted up through the opening. The thought of the unknown still gave Charlotte jitters, but there was only one way to go. And they couldn't linger out in the open.

Then, Charlotte paused on the first step of the ladder that led down the hatch. "What's the code?" she asked.

The sounds of movement in the forest grew louder.

"What?" Sonos asked, confused.

"What's the code you used to open the hatch? I may need it." If the Sahemy treated physical security the same way they did technological security, it was likely that she could, or would have to, use that code again in another place and time.

Sonos frowned and glanced over his shoulder. "Can we talk about this later?"

Charlotte didn't move. She couldn't explain the urgency she felt to know that detail, but she didn't want to ignore the feeling.

"East, West, South, North. No matter how they're arranged, in any shape, you'll always find four, and then you press them in that order." The instructions flew out of Sonos as he rushed to climb into the hatch after her.

She committed the sequence to memory, hoping that the pieces of Sahemy knowledge would start fitting together.

The hatch closed with a metallic thud, and Charlotte cringed, imagining the echo in the forest.

"Keep moving forward," she whispered into the darkness—one step at a time.

CHAPTER 17

As Sonos climbed down the ladder after Charlotte, he wondered if Timur had shown him these secrets knowing that he might one day find himself in rebellion against his family—or rather, against the crown.

He stepped onto the cold stone floor.

Charlotte turned on her gazer, and it cast an eerie glow that illuminated the small tunnel.

Sonos reached for a torch and flint hidden behind the ladder, and the stone tunnel soon danced with flames and shadows.

As the shadows flickered, he swallowed a wave of nausea that surged at the memory of the shadows attacking him in the Badlands.

"Finally, a message!" Charlotte exclaimed, her voice echoing through the tunnel, breaking the silence that had settled in. She projected a video of Jax from her ring.

"Char! I just got your messages. I hope you're okay. Flying a carrier? I can't even imagine." Jax turned his head sharply in the video. "Okay, we only have a few seconds. Uzoma is desperate to find gold, so we must stay in the sanctum. Tell Sonos his mother arrived safely."

Sonos let out a sigh of relief. Miss Gemma and the boys had found a way. But things were escalating in the Mountain Kingdom.

"I'm still working out a plan to get to you, don't worry. Soon come," Jax said, and the video went abruptly dark.

Charlotte's worried frown deepened. "I don't trust Uzoma and the lengths he will go to to please the Emperor."

Sonos didn't have a response. He wouldn't underestimate Uzoma either, but he didn't want to add to Charlotte's worries.

Charlotte pulled at the strap that held the flyer-board to her back. "Do you think we can use these to speed up?"

Sonos considered it briefly but shook his head. "We shouldn't need to. From what I remember, the reservoir isn't too far. And the tunnel will narrow even more," Sonos said. He held up the torch and led the way through the cool and damp tunnel.

It wasn't long before he had to bend his shoulders as they walked. But it was only 487 steps, and the tunnel opened into a vast cavern with a deep, clear pool.

"Oh! It's even bigger than I imagined." Charlotte's eyes were wide as she gazed around. Her voice echoed in the vast space.

Sonos pointed to a metal hatch towards the left. "That's a small dam connected to a filtration system that pulls from the river if the reserves ever get low. But the underground spring that created this place has never run dry."

"Ava's books were never this detailed," Charlotte said, her voice still full of awe. "She would love to see a place like this."

Sonos again admired the bond that these sisters shared. The importance of saving Ava and Lily became clearer with each passing day.

He pointed to their right where the ledge stopped and there was a small opening in the wall a few feet above the water. The opening was even smaller than he remembered. "And that is the water shaft. Where they can pull up buckets of water direct to the palace."

"Oh," Charlotte let out a disappointed sigh. But she edged past Sonos and bravely walked out onto the narrow ledge that led towards the shaft.

"From what I understand, after the containers enter the hatch, it's an almost vertical climb to the point where it enters another tunnel that leads to the palace kitchens," Sonos explained. He looked again at the tiny opening. This was a bad idea. He should have done more to talk Charlotte out of it before coming here.

Charlotte dropped to her knees beside the hatch. "It's going to be tight," she muttered. She glanced back at Sonos. "Do you think it gets even smaller up the shaft? And how long is the climb?"

"It has to stay wide enough for the containers, so it can't get much smaller. I remember seeing the containers once... I think they were less than two feet across." Sonos tried to picture the containers he had only glimpsed years ago. "And the shaft is probably about..." he racked his brain. "Sixty feet? Or maybe closer to seventy."

"Okay, that's less than one of our royal palm trees back home," Charlotte said.

She was unfazed, even though Sonos was already trying to figure out an alternate plan. "Char, I don't think..."

But she was already shrugging off her cloak and unstrapping her flyer-board. "I need to lose all the bulk I can." She abruptly glanced up at Sonos. "But—"

He shook his head slowly. She had reached the same conclusion he had when he had seen the size of the shaft. "There's no way I'll be able to squeeze into that opening, much less climb the shaft."

Charlotte frowned.

As much as it pained him to split up, maybe this was the best way forward—at least for Charlotte. "You need to find your sisters," he said, his voice steady despite the fear churning within him. "Plus, we stand a better chance of at least one of us making it, if we're not together."

"I'm not so sure about that." Charlotte scrunched up her brow.

"I'll find another way in," Sonos assured her. "But at least one of us will be on the inside immediately. Plus, this shaft leads to the kitchens, and Seena Sweethand is a friend. She can help." The more he spoke, the more sure he was.

Charlotte hesitated, then jumped up and pulled him into a tight hug. "Thank you." She placed both hands on his shoulders and waited for him to meet her gaze. "Find your way in. We need you... I need you," she said, her voice filled with emotion. "Fight we must."

"Win we shall." Sonos put on a brave smile. Braver than he felt on the inside.

Charlotte knelt back down at the end of the ledge and reached out into the shaft's opening to try and find a grip on the wall. She swung her legs, her toes finding just enough footing, and pulled herself inside. Her shoulders brushed either side.

Sonos remembered how she complained about her sisters getting all the height, but being petite was working in her favor now.

"It's pretty slick in here," Charlotte's voice was muffled. "But I'm finding little divots in the wall. Just like—"

Suddenly, her feet came into view and splashed down in the water as she yelped. She used her upper body to catch herself before falling entirely into the water.

"Char!" Sonos ran over to her.

"Okay, I misjudged a hold up there." Her voice was still muffled because her upper body remained in the shaft. "And oh, is that water cold!"

"Maybe we can both find another way," Sonos said. *What if Char slips when she is higher up? And what if someone tries sending down a container while she's climbing?* A hundred worries filled his mind.

Charlotte ignored him and pulled herself fully back up into the shaft. "It's okay. I'm going to treat this like climbing a tree back home." She grunted, and water trickled down the hatch from her soaking wet pants and boots. "I just need to take my time. And keep moving..."

After a few more minutes, her voice came back from further away. "I'm making it! I'll see you on the inside! Find your way in."

Begrudgingly, Sonos stood there, helpless.

He tried to peer into the hole with his torch, but it was useless. He could barely see where the shaft turned vertical, which was pitch black. But the water had stopped dripping down, and there were no further sounds or scuffles.

Sonos knew he couldn't linger. He needed to move and find another way into Pergamum. But he had never felt so alone. Even in his isolation and lockdown, Taine had been there. On their escape, he had two warriors with him and Sibi's eternal optimism. Then, there was Rapha, Charlotte, and Taimani. Now... it was just him: no tech, no gazer, no Rapha, nothing. The shadows cast by his torch seemed to grow even more ominous.

Those who are with you are greater than the darkness. The unbidden words broke through his thoughts. He first heard them from the commander of *El*'s army in the Badlands. They had saved him once before, and he thought about the reality of what they meant. He wasn't alone.

Just as his breathing settled, a *CLANG* of metal sounded from down the tunnel. His heart skipped a beat.

Someone had opened the hatch, which was his only way out.

Chapter 18

CHARLOTTE HEAVED HERSELF OVER the top edge of the water shaft, overcome by relief. Every muscle in her body pulsed from exertion and strain—but she had made it.

She slumped against the stone wall of a tunnel, her wet legs and feet spread out in front of her. The tunnel was small but felt like a wide expanse after that water shaft. Her breath quickened as she recalled the harrowing climb upwards. There had been moments when the stone had pressed against her on all sides, and she was sure it was closing in and getting smaller. She squeezed her eyes shut, trying to shake off the panic. She was safe—out of the shaft.

Had Sonos made it safely out of the cavern? Was he finding a way into the palace even now? What if he's been caught? Her thoughts spiraled as the cold seeped into her bones.

A shiver wracked her body. She needed to keep moving and hopefully find some warmth. Fast.

First, she checked her gazer. It might be the last time she could put it on for a while. No new messages. And her location showed her in the heart of Pergamum. She was here. She inhaled sharply—memories assailed her of her mom, dad, and Gran huddling in the cellar of her family home, plotting and planning how to get here and rescue the twins. Those faded into memories of her and Jax after her mom and his parents had disappeared at sea and her dad had given up.

No, he hadn't given up entirely. He just didn't want to lose anything more to the Empire, Charlotte thought. "Soon come, Dad," she whispered to the air.

She adjusted her gazer. The dim light cast eerie shadows on the rough walls. She had to focus. And find her sisters. That was all that mattered.

Charlotte forced herself to get up onto her hands and knees as a draft cut through her wet clothes. The tunnel was cramped, and her movements restricted as she pushed forward.

Her palms and knees were bruising from the never-ending crawl, but she ignored the pain. There was only one option: to keep moving forward.

Finally, the sounds of muffled voices wafted through the tunnel.

Charlotte immediately turned off the gazer, plunging the entire area into darkness. But she kept crawling forward, ensuring her movements were silent. One accidental sound could give her away.

The voices grew louder, and a sliver of light peeked through a crack in the ceiling ahead.

"Did you pull that bread from the oven, Maya?" a woman's voice echoed through the tunnel.

The kitchens! Charlotte suppressed a sigh of relief. She remembered what Sonos had said about where the tunnel would lead.

And if she wasn't mistaken, the woman sounded like she had a Salan accent. The lilt reminded Charlotte of Gran... and her mom.

She crept closer to the light, her eyes fixed on the ceiling with desperate hope.

Slam! Her chin smashed into something solid, sending a shooting pain through her jaw. A muffled yelp escaped through her clenched teeth. She clamped both hands over her mouth, willing her pounding heart to slow. She silently cursed the oversized bucket that must be used for transporting the water. Gingerly feeling around in the darkness, her hands brushed against a large pile of rope.

"Maya! Did you hear something in that pantry?" The Salan woman called out with an edge of irritation. "It better not be another rat in there. Go check!"

Charlotte's throat constricted with anxiety. Soft light suddenly spilled in through a small opening in the ceiling of the tunnel—it looked like a grated hatch.

"Yes, Miss Seena," a young voice called out as feet pattered above Charlotte's head.

Seena! Sonos had said that Seena Sweethand was a friend. Was this her chance?

Boxes shuffled overhead. Maya wouldn't be in the pantry long.

Charlotte made her decision. She shifted the bucket aside as quietly as she could, then pressed her hands upward against the hatch. And... nothing. It didn't budge at all, sealed tight. She crouched and shoved her shoulder against the wood with her full weight. Still nothing. It was locked from above. She stifled a curse, frustration welling within her.

Summoning every last ounce of courage, Charlotte called out tentatively. "Hello?" Her voice shook with equal parts fear and hope. She held her breath, praying she hadn't just doomed herself.

Maya yelped, and her footsteps ran from the pantry. "Seena! Seena!" the girl called out.

"Hush, girl. Can't you see we have a guest?" Seena's strong Salan accent carried through the hatch, but her tone was impossible to read.

A guest? Charlotte's stomach knotted impossibly tighter. Was that good or bad? She could barely think straight.

"Mrs. Elisa Wumi, what can we do for you?" Seena continued.

Elisa. At that name, Charlotte's blood ran cold. The wife of the commander who was attacking the Mountain Kingdom right at that moment. And the woman who had overseen her sisters' kidnapping.

This is it. She knows I'm here. She will catch me and put me with Taine as more bait to catch Sonos. We're all going to die. Charlotte's thoughts spiraled.

"With the palace on lockdown, we are making extra checks." Elisa's cold voice filled the kitchen.

If there were any rats about, even they remained silent and frozen in place.

Heels clicked as Elisa's voice moved about the kitchen. Charlotte could picture a tight bun and harsh features—the woman's face was etched into her memory.

"My husband has always said that unchecked rebels breed more rebels... and no one wins in a rebellion." The implicit threat hung in her words.

Charlotte's whole body tensed, poised for flight, though there was nowhere to run.

The sharp clicks of Elisa's footsteps came ever closer until they entered the pantry and stopped just above Charlotte's head. She didn't dare move a muscle, barely breathing. The silence seemed to last an eternity.

Finally, Elisa spoke again. "You must ensure strict rations for all the staff during this lockdown." Her tone brooked no argument. "Even though I expect this foolish girl and Sonos to be caught quickly, we must always be prepared."

"Yes, Ma'am, of course," came Seena's quick reply.

"And it goes without saying if you see or hear anything suspicious..."

Please let Maya be silent, Charlotte prayed.

"You will be the first to know, Ma'am," Seena responded. Was that resentment Charlotte detected in her voice? She couldn't be sure.

Elisa grunted a response, and her footfalls eventually faded away.

Charlotte sagged against the wall, exhaling shakily. That had been too close. She should never have called attention to herself earlier. What if Maya had said something? Stupid mistake. She berated herself, emotions swirling.

"Maya, be a good girl and put that bread on the table," Seena instructed. "You two, fetch jam from the cellar. And you, boy, bring in more wood for the fire."

Multiple footsteps hurried to obey Seena's commands.

Charlotte pressed her eye to the crack, straining to see any details in the pantry above her.

"Now, Maya, what upset you in the pantry?" Seena asked, and footsteps once again moved above Charlotte's head.

"The rats... or something... someone called out," the girl responded, clearly flustered.

"Your head is spinning with everything happening," Seena said kindly. Her footsteps circled the pantry.

Then suddenly, Charlotte found herself staring directly into Seena's eyes through the crack as the woman peered down at her hiding spot.

Charlotte gasped involuntarily.

But Seena placed a finger over her lips, commanding silence.

"Rats don't suddenly speak," Seena scolded Maya lightly. "There's nothing here but flour, lard, and all the usual provisions. We have a meal to finish."

Charlotte sank down again, equal parts confused and relieved. Seena knew she was there now. Could she be trusted to help? For the moment, it seemed Charlotte had no choice but to wait. She pulled her knees to her chest, trying to capture warmth as she shivered uncontrollably in her still-wet clothes.

The rhythmic sounds of the kitchen eventually faded into background noise as exhaustion crept over Charlotte. She slipped into a fitful sleep, plagued by nightmares of being discovered by Elisa.

Charlotte was jolted awake by a loud scraping noise. Had Elisa come for her after all? Her heart seized in her chest once more. But there was no angry shouting nor the heavy treads of guards.

The hatch above her head swung open with a creak, and a petite face surrounded by bouncing blonde ringlets smiled down at Charlotte. "I thought it might be you or Sonos," Seena whispered warmly. "Charlotte, I presume?"

Charlotte hesitated, but what use would there be in lying? She released a shaky breath and nodded.

Seena helped pull her up into the panty, then ushered her into the kitchen.

Everything seemed comfortingly familiar after Charlotte had been listening to the kitchen activity for so long.

"You... look familiar," Charlotte half-said, half-asked, looking at Seena's face.

Seena chuckled, her eyes twinkling. "I've heard you met my son, Sibi."

Recognition dawned on Charlotte, and she nodded enthusiastically. "Oh, yes! I only spent the briefest time with him, but Sonos and all the others speak so highly of him," Charlotte said. "He's the spitting image of you."

Seena's smile widened with pride as she guided Charlotte to a tucked-away corner near the fire. The warmth seeped into Charlotte's bones as she sank into a chair and began to devour the hot meal Seena provided. In between bites of spiced meat and mashed potatoes, Charlotte asked anxiously, "Are you sure it's safe for me to be here? Shouldn't I hide better?" Seena's run-in with Elisa still weighed heavily on Charlotte's mind.

Seena's reassurance was steady. "Don't worry. I have young guards posted at the doors, and they know when I need my privacy. We're safe."

Charlotte wanted to believe her, but she couldn't shake her concerns completely.

"How did you know it was me in the water shaft?" she asked, trying to keep any edge from her voice.

Seena chuckled. "Somone coming up through a secret passage in the middle of a siege? It wasn't hard to piece together. Besides, Sibi sent word to tell me he's okay and to expect you and Sonos."

Charlotte's eyes widened in surprise. "He did?"

Seena's smile turned fond. "Yes, he did. He's quite resourceful, my son." She dropped her voice. "The Empress couldn't ask for a better attendant." She winked, then resumed moving about the kitchen. She pulled a kettle of water from the fire. Listening to Seena hum as she worked, it was hard for Charlotte to imagine that the city was under siege.

Seena took Charlotte's empty plate and offered her a cup of herbal tea.

"Thanks." Charlotte inhaled the scents of mint and other herbs she couldn't quite place.

Seena took a seat across from Charlotte. "Where is Sonos?" she asked.

Charlotte pulled her mouth into a frown. "I... he..." While she knew they had made the right choice, she was worried for him. "He couldn't fit inside the water shaft," she explained. "I was barely able to fit myself. He promised to find another way in, but..." She couldn't finish the thought.

Seena's demeanor shifted, and she reached across the small table, squeezing Charlotte's hand gently. "Those who are with us are greater than the darkness. He'll be okay."

Those who are with you are greater than the darkness... Charlotte remembered Sibi quoting the Commander of El's army. The piece fell into place.

"You're a follower of *El?*" Charlotte asked. It made sense, given what she knew of Sibi. When she stopped to consider, perhaps what made her feel so comfortable with Seena, aside from the Salan familiarity, was the frequency Rapha had taught her to recognize. It operated like an internal tuning fork—not audible, but connected to the unseen realm, and Charlotte was learning to recognize it.

Seena nodded, but then leaned back in her chair and took a long sip of her own tea. "I admit these last few days have been hard on us as followers of *El.*" She paused. "It reminds me of the ferocity from when the Emperor, Sonos' father, first rose to power."

Charlotte's interest was piqued. Her parents often talked about what Jamroq and Salan were like before becoming part of the Conquered Isles, but they rarely discussed the invasion itself. "Tell me more."

Seena leaned back in her chair, her eyes distant. "The Emperor's fear and lust for power knew no bounds. Those who posed even the slightest threat to his rule were ruthlessly silenced. The followers of *El* were especially targeted, as they represented a force of resistance against his tyranny."

Charlotte's mind whirled, connecting the dots between the history Seena described and the current state of the Empire. "My Gran fled Salan with my mom before the Emperor conquered their home. They went to Jamroq, where my mom married and had me and my sisters."

Seena's gaze softened, a tender smile gracing her lips. "Your Gran's courage is commendable. That also explains the mix I see in you. You have the Jamroq edge to your words, but I thought something was softening it. And your look is a special blend."

There was no animosity in Seena's voice at the word *blend*. While Charlotte and her family were well-loved back in her village of Mina, standing out and not looking exactly like anyone else had been... uncomfortable at times. But Seena made it feel special. *There's no one else in the world like you, Char. You bring out the best of both your father and me*, her mother used to say.

As Charlotte's thoughts began to drift to her family and the painful memories of losing her mother, she abruptly shifted her focus back to the task at hand. "I need to find my sisters. They were taken three years ago and brought to the Legacy Towers. Can you help me get there?"

Seena's expression turned grave, and Charlotte's heart sank. "That may be a problem," Seena admitted, her voice filled with regret. "I'm afraid I don't have good news about the towers and those who lived there."

Charlotte's chest constricted sharply. "*Lived*—as in past tense?"

Seena nodded. She reached again for Charlotte's hand, but Charlotte barely felt it. Her head spun as panic clawed up her throat.

"The Legacy Towers are empty," Seena said.

CHAPTER 19

SONOS' FOOTSTEPS POUNDED AGAINST the stone floor as he sprinted through the dim tunnel. His breath came in ragged gasps, and sweat dripped down his back where Charlotte's cloak and the two flyer-boards were strapped to him.

"Get back here!" A deep, commanding voice echoed off the narrow walls.

Sonos ran faster, focusing solely on getting Charlotte as much time as possible.

He had barreled past the Sah, racing toward the entrance with the ladder. Relying on the element of surprise, he made it. Barely.

"You're not going to make it far!" Desperation filled the shout now.

Sonos didn't care. He knew he'd be caught sooner or later, but Charlotte had to reach Seena.

The dark tunnel blurred—Sonos' momentum was reckless. A stumble sent him crashing against the stone wall. In that split second, his touch triggered a hidden mechanism, the wall spinning him into blackness.

The hidden door clicked shut as Sonos regained his footing. He cursed, fumbling in vain for a torch in the dark. Where was he?

Footsteps and a muffled voice sounded through the wall. There was no time to waste. He had to buy Charlotte every last second, then face his brother.

Hand sliding along the cold stone, Sonos felt his way forward. What he wouldn't give for a gazer or some tech. The passage was tight, the ceiling barely inches above his head. The darkness overwhelmed and disoriented him. Still, he forged ahead, counting each hurried step.

He had just reached his 1,761st stride when he ran smack into a large form. Sonos stumbled backward as a dim orb flickered on, illuminating the tunnel. A formidable Sah stood before him draped in a deep purple robe—a sorcerer, Sonos deduced, different from Timur who once wore a blue robe symbolizing the sciences.

"I don't know how you managed to get into this passageway, Highness, but your escape ends here." The soft, high-pitched voice belied the Sah's imposing form.

Sonos wasn't prepared to yield, however. Swiftly, he turned to flee back the way he came.

"I wouldn't recommend being apprehended by the others. They will not be offering a helping hand," the Sah called out.

Sonos paused. Was it the calmness in the *Sah*'s voice that gave him pause? No. *He knows who I am... he called me Highness*, he thought. And the title hadn't been spoken with contempt.

"That's right. I'm your better choice," the Sah said, coming closer.

Sonos turned back around. His gaze shifted to the light coming from the glowing orb hovering near the Sah's head.

The Sah grinned, following Sonos' gaze, a gesture that made his thick beard, muscled neck, and round face seem much less intimidating. "It's a little thing I'm working on." He tapped the gazer on his wrist, and the sphere floated forward to hover in front of Sonos, growing slightly brighter.

A distant shout echoed down the tunnel, and Sonos' heart skipped a beat.

The burly Sah tsked. "I'm forgetting myself. Come... before we both get caught. And please, call me Sal." He turned and started walking.

Sonos hesitated. He felt stuck between two hard choices. He didn't trust Sal, and worried about how the Sah knew who he was immediately. But at least the direction they were headed in took him further away from Charlotte and gave her a better chance to make it. He ran to catch up.

Sal's gazer blinked on his wrist, and he tapped a few buttons. The Sah's posture stiffened at words only he could hear. "Nothing to report in S-22. All clear."

Why is he helping me and lying on my behalf? Sonos wondered.

"Sal," Sonos whispered, "where are we going?"

Halting abruptly, Sal turned to face Sonos, his expression grim. "There are those who would seize you and hand you over to Emperor Ade, or even Wylder."

"But not you?" Sonos asked, suspicion gnawing at him. Why was Sal exempt from this loyalty to his brother's regime?

"No. At least, that decision to turn you over will not be mine." Sal fell silent as muffled footsteps passed nearby. "Now, come. We're close."

What game was Sonos stepping into? The Order of the Sahemy was so shrouded in secrecy that even Sonos wasn't sure of its structure aside from the three disciplines of sorcery, science, and tech. They lived to serve the Empire and build its strength.

Charlotte's sparking, green eyes flashed in Sonos' mind. *She would have glared at me for saying something like that*, Sonos thought. *Mindlessly saying that a people existed only to serve the Empire. Well, at least I'm catching myself now.* Being wrong but aware, and trying to change, was progress from being unconsciously wrong.

Sal paused at a seemingly random spot in the stone wall. He tapped a pattern into his gazer, and a doorway opened. He led Sonos into a small, circular chamber. A lamp hung from the ceiling. Sonos couldn't figure out how it was powered, unless there was a long line running up to a sun collector above ground. Or maybe it was a better version of Sal's orb.

Even though his chest was pounding, he thought about how much Charlotte would adore the place and new tech.

"Wait here," Sal instructed, crossing to a door on the far side of the room.

Sonos paced the small chamber as he contemplated the tangled web of events that brought him to this secret room. And to whom—or what—lay beyond the door Sal had disappeared through.

Chapter 20

"WHAT DO YOU MEAN the Legacy Towers are empty?" Charlotte asked in disbelief. The fire burned steadily in the hearth, but she no longer felt its warmth, and a chill ran through her bones.

"Emperor Ade had them emptied after he returned from Noiz. It seems Baku had discovered a security breach underground." Seena frowned slightly, eyebrows furrowing. "Details were a little sketchy by the time they reached me. But the prisoners have been moved."

Charlotte tried to take deep, calming breaths, willing her heart to slow its frantic pace. How was she going to find her sisters now?

"I remember Sonos talking about escaping through a tunnel," Charlotte thought aloud. "I guess they found it. But... do you have any idea where the prisoners could be?" She looked up, trying to control the desperation that must be flowing through her eyes.

Seena let out a heavy sigh, her shoulders slumping. "I wish I could be of more help. I can only guess that the Sahemy are involved with hiding them somewhere."

"I need to find them, no matter what it takes," Charlotte said.

"If I had to guess, I doubt they kept everyone together," Seena said. "There were hundreds of prisoners between all four towers."

"Jamroq, Kimwaki, Salan, and Portemore." Charlotte counted off the Conquered Isles, plus the port city from the mainland. "Where could they possibly hide so many?"

"There's no prison that could take on hundreds of extra prisoners. Especially not with the influx of arrests they've made of followers of *El*."

Charlotte's face fell. "We saw… a friend of ours executed in Harmony. Right after Ade's first announcement." She quickly wiped her eyes, willing herself to stay strong.

Seena grasped Charlotte's clammy palm and gave it a gentle, reassuring squeeze. "Public executions and beatings happened here in Pergamum, too. It seems every village and city square teemed with examples of this new edict."

A heavy silence hung in the air.

"But for what it's worth, I heard that not a single person recanted their faith or claimed Ade as their god, even at the end." Pride shone behind the tears in Seena's eyes.

A horrible thought struck Charlotte. She remembered how defiantly Gran had stood up for her when Captain Die—Isaako—had come to arrest her and Jax. "Do you know the names of those who died?" she whispered, almost too scared to ask.

Seena slowly shook her head. "We're still trying to gather all that intelligence. Did you have family or friends you're worried about back home?"

Charlotte gave a slight nod. "Back in Jamroq. My dad, Josiah King, and Gran, Donna Soa."

At the names, Seena's eyebrow arched in interest. "Josiah King, you say?"

"Does it sound familiar? You think something bad happened?" Charlotte's heart began to race all over again.

"Not exactly, no," Seena said, shifting in her seat. "But, as you may know, surnames on the isles often relate to one's occupation or identity." She paused, gathering her thoughts before continuing. "For instance, my family has worked in kitchens and inns for generations, and we were known for our cooking skills long before that—hence the name Sweethand. Your grandmother likely was gifted at sewing and weaving—Soa."

"Yes, Gran is amazing with sewing—my mom, too... she was... before..." Charlotte couldn't finish the sentence, unable to speak of her mother's death. Instead, she pulled her jacket a little tighter around her, even if it was still damp. "But my dad is a teacher—hardly a king."

"But before that?"

"I..." Charlotte's voice trailed off as uncertainty filled her. The truth was that her father had never talked about his family or childhood. Had they been killed when Jamroq was invaded all those years ago, like the Empress and Isaako's parents had been killed? The thought made her stomach twist painfully.

"I promise to see what I can find about your father and grandmother. But for now, I encourage you to keep focused on what's right in front of you. Find and free your sisters. That's what you came for, right?"

"Yes. Ava and Lily." Charlotte stared into the glowing embers of the dying fire. A coldness held her stomach in knots. "But I honestly don't even know where to start. I've never set foot in Pergamum or the palace before now. I know nothing of this place." Speaking the words aloud felt like a crushing admission of failure.

Seena cleared her throat, causing Charlotte to lift her eyes. "You know there's a difference between truth and fact?"

Charlotte blinked in confusion. "Huh?"

"It is a fact you've never visited the palace before today." Seena held up one finger. "It is also factual that you currently have no idea where your sisters are being kept." Up went a second finger. "And I think it's safe to say you lack resources, and you also have

Emperor Ade himself as your adversary." Seena held up a third and fourth finger, waving her hand to indicate that she could go on listing discouraging facts.

"I get the picture." Charlotte sighed.

"But—" Seena waited until Charlotte looked up and held her gaze before continuing. "All those facts don't add up to the deeper truth here. The truth is that the battle is already won."

"Win we shall," Charlotte muttered the familiar words that seemed so distant from reality.

"Beyond the words, let the reality sink into your spirit," Seena said, placing a hand over her heart.

"Miss Seena?" A hesitant, young voice called out from behind where Charlotte sat.

Charlotte quickly turned her face to the glowing hearth, sinking down in her chair, every muscle tense. She wished desperately for the anonymity of her hooded cloak rather than just her thin jacket. While she trusted Seena—having little other choice—Charlotte remained wary of endangering anyone else in this unfamiliar place.

Seena stood swiftly and guided the boy towards the other side of the kitchen, where they spoke in hushed voices.

No, Charlotte resolved as she sat there. *I will not stay and endanger anyone.* El *help me and guide me.* She pulled on her now-warm boots.

Seena returned to Charlotte alone.

"I need to leave," Charlotte said before Seena could speak.

Seena nodded. "You do. They've already started a thorough search of the palace." She hastily wrapped a loaf of bread and some dried meat in a cloth.

"Head north toward the outer wall. There's a stable where all the royal family's animals are kept, and you can trust the boy who looks after the sheep." Seena kept her voice low as she urged

Charlotte toward the side door. "In the northern hills just beyond the city, there is rumored to be a complex network of caves and caverns, enough to conceal even an army, some say."

Charlotte felt a spark of renewed hope. "That sounds promising, if I wanted to hide a large group of prisoners."

"It's also been whispered that that is where the Sahemy have set up workshops and other spaces, all high-security areas, for their projects—their experiments. It's heavily guarded, both by Imperial guards and by technology." Seena handed over the sack of supplies to Charlotte. "I have no way to help you get there."

"It sounds like just the spot where Ade would send the prisoners," Charlotte said darkly.

Seena leaned in close, gently grasping Charlotte's shoulders and staring intently into her eyes. "Listen closely, pay attention, and look carefully. *El* will guide you, but he rarely shouts the way forward."

Seena handed Charlotte a long piece of dark cloth. "It's not a cloak, but this should help you conceal your face at least."

Charlotte quickly wrapped the fabric around her head and lower face. "Thank you for everything, Seena."

Seena's eyes glinted. "It's my pleasure. You're family." She pulled Charlotte in for a brief but fierce embrace.

Charlotte hesitated and wondered if Seena meant that literally, or if it was just a reference to the family-like community in which followers of *El* operated. "Thank you for everything." She said again. She hoped that Seena and Maya would be safe.

"Be brave and courageous, young one. One step at a time is all it takes." Seena cracked open the side door just wide enough for Charlotte to slip through.

The cool night air hit Charlotte's face immediately, reminding her that she was far from the island warmth of home. Overhead, the blanket of unfamiliar stars gave no obvious clues as to which way to turn.

She slid a hand inside her jacket, carefully switching on her gazer ring to its dimmest setting. She quickly oriented herself northward in the pale greenish light and turned the tech back off.

She followed the side of the outer kitchen wall, trying her best to keep to the shadows. The scents of a well-tended garden filled her nose. Jasmine and mint helped to calm her nerves. But they also reminded her of Jax and his well-loved herb box. *Where is he now? Could he be on his way?* She twisted the gazer ring around her finger anxiously.

A million worries and questions spun through Charlotte's mind as she picked her way through the moonlit garden. But they scattered like leaves in the wind when shouts and stomping boots sounded somewhere nearby.

She whirled toward the noise, senses on high alert, poised to fight or flee into the night.

Chapter 21

I F Sonos had to choose one word to describe the man who stood in the elaborate office, it would be scraggly. A deep purple robe with golden cuffs marked him as the head of the sorcerers, but he was a small, pale fellow with thinning hair that seemed determined to stick up and out in every direction.

In addition to the golden cuffs, he wore a tight crimson collar around his neck. This marked him as head of the entire Sahemy—all three orders. Sonos was in disbelief that this man led the sorcerers, much less the whole Sahemy.

The room was dim, the only light coming from a few candles on the massive desk and Sal's orb. The candles cast ominous shadows across the stone walls. Sonos felt a creeping unease as the shadows seemed to writhe and dance of their own volition.

"Please, Highness, have a seat." The head Sah motioned Sonos to an empty chair.

Sonos was still unused to people using his title without snarkiness. After the year of lockdown and then being on the run, it felt odd—a part of a life he had left far behind.

He eased into the well-worn seat, wary of snubbing the Sah's kindness. He had to adjust the flyer-boards on his back. These new models were so light that it was easy to forget they were strapped under his cloak.

Sal remained standing near the door, his size fitting the form of a bodyguard.

"I take it you know who I am?" the scraggly man asked while looking down his nose at Sonos, sitting behind a desk that was easily double the size it needed to be. His arrogance seemed to suit his role—even if his appearance still threw Sonos off.

"You're the head of the Sahemy," Sonos ventured. The man seemed more concerned with titles than names.

The man sniffed, and the corners of his mouth turned upwards. "Yes, I am. You may call me Grand Magus."

A knot formed in Sonos' stomach. Men who took on their titles as their identity were some of the most dangerous sort—as his father, the Emperor, had proven.

"We've been tracking you and the rebel girl since Riverton," Grand Magus said, his eyes narrowing.

Sonos tensed, wondering if Charlotte had been captured.

"Don't worry; we haven't bothered to apprehend your little girlfriend." Grand Magus leaned back in his chair. "If she gets those nuisance prisoners out of these caves, all the better. They're a waste of space, to begin with—and your brother is throwing his problems at us?" He snorted in disgust.

Anger arose inside of Sonos. He thought of Taimani, who had been a prisoner in the Kimwaki Tower, and of Charlotte's sisters. The people taken to live in the towers were the best and brightest from their territories. "I wouldn't say they're a waste of space." Sonos worked to keep his tone controlled.

"What?" Grand Magus snapped. He waved his hand dismissively and shook his head. "My point is that we won't stop Charlotte. Now, if one of the novices or one of those loyal to the Crown catches her, I can't speak for them... but those true to the Order will not interfere."

Sonos' head spun with the information he was receiving. There were different factions within the Sahemy, and Grand Magus was anything but loyal to Sonos' brother. Did this mean he wasn't going to turn Sonos over to Ade?

Grand Magus pulled a burning candle to the middle of the desk and softly blew into the flames. Mysteriously, a massive puff of smoke formed a rectangular shape that hung between Grand Magus and Sonos. Soon, details formed in the smoke, and Sonos recognized it as a map of Pergamum. Two sparks flickered unnaturally—one in the heart of the palace, near the kitchens, and one north of the city in the hills. The second dot must be him. The first dot...

"How?" Sonos whispered. But as soon as he asked the question, he realized the answer wasn't necessary. He'd seen sorcerers operate before, and he knew his uncle had used items from him and Char to track them previously.

Grand Magus swiped away the smoke with his hands. "Given that you are in my office and under my command, I think I will ask the questions."

Under his command? Sonos gulped. Things were quickly looking worse and worse. This man only wanted power.

Grand Magus leaned forward, candlelight glinting in his pale eyes. "I would like to know how you hid from us for so long. How did you get from Noiz to Riverton?" Grand Magus pushed the candle to the side and focused on Sonos.

Is he trying to mind-control me? Sonos wondered. He felt in control of his thoughts, but something was strange about how Grand Magus was looking at him.

"Why did you only become visible to me in Riverton yesterday as you were leaving, Sonos? Where were you for the past week?" All pretense of calling him Highness was now gone.

Sonos' heart pounded as Grand Magus stared at him expectantly. He racked his mind to piece together the details... They stepped through the portal into Harmony, but Grand Magus only saw him in Riverton. Why? He and Charlotte had a shared dream. Taimani ran off. Jamin was executed. What would have made the difference? Rapha had been caught. He inhaled sharply at the revelation. Yesterday, Rapha had been caught and separated from them in Riverton. It had been Rapha who had protected them.

Grand Magus frowned. "Who was with you? What power did they use? Tell me."

Sonos was not about to give up Rapha. He wasn't sure if the Elites had captured the monkey, but he wasn't about to reveal anything to put Rapha in more danger. He pressed his mind to construct a believable story, something to appease Grand Magus.

"Have it your way," Grand Magus said in a low, ominous voice. "Don't say I didn't try to ask nicely." He splayed his fingers out on the desk and again blew on the candle flame. Shadows seemed to crawl out of his skin and slink towards Sonos.

Horrified, Sonos tried to get up from the chair and away from those creepy shadows. But Sal's hands pushed down on his shoulders, holding him tightly in place in the chair.

"Tell me what I want to know," Grand Magus hissed as the shadows slithered ever closer.

Sonos' breath came in panicked gasps; blood was pounding in his ears. He barely heard the Grand Magus' words. The shadows were moving like those that had come alive in the Badlands.

Words have power. Sonos remembered how he defeated the shadows before. He spoke the words again. "Those who are with me are greater than the darkness."

"What was that?" Grand Magus' head snapped up, and he stared at Sonos.

The shadows that were practically touching Sonos seemed to waver.

"Those who are with me are greater than the darkness," Sonos repeated, this time a little louder.

An idea came to Sonos, and he reached into his cloak to grab the journal, finding the poem Rapha had given Charlotte in the portal.

"Your fight is futile; you come against eternity with time." Sonos read the words aloud.

"What are you reading? Fool!" Grand Magus shouted.

"Your roar is harmless, You come against truth with lies." Somehow, Sonos knew these were exactly the words for this moment. *"Your mammoth shows of power are no more than wisps; you come against El with humanness."*

"Stop it! Stop speaking." Grand Magus stood as the shadows dissolved into tendrils of smoke.

Sonos skipped ahead. *"But hear this—Hear it loud, Ringing clear, The shout of a king is among us!"*

"Take that book!" Grand Magus commanded.

When Sal released the pressure on his shoulder, Sonos slipped out of the chair and ran towards the door. He recited the last part of the poem from memory while dodging Sal. Even though it made logical sense to focus on escape, he felt the deep need to speak—to shout, rather, the words from Rapha. *"Hear the mighty thunder of Noiz, See the numbers who stand in Truth, Feel the tremble as El arises, You have touched one who is unconquerable!"*

Grand Magus' face contorted in anger, disgust, and, if Sonos wasn't mistaken, fear.

Sonos turned and tried to open the door to flee, but there were no handles, and it was closed tight. He desperately pushed against the door, realizing the peril of angering a sorcerer in a locked lair.

Sal's heavy footsteps were behind him, and Sonos felt the prick of a needle in his neck.

The world went dark.

Chapter 22

CHARLOTTE TUCKED HERSELF INTO a ball in the shadows of a small crevice in the palace wall. Her pulse throbbed as she strained to listen for any sounds in the dark gardens.

Heavy footfalls grew louder. Two guards rounded the corner.

"Check the back door to the kitchen," one barked.

Charlotte flattened herself against the cold stone. Had she been spotted? How could they know?

The guards stormed past her hiding spot toward the kitchen. She whispered a prayer for Seena's safety.

With the guards distracted, Charlotte crept along the wall's edge. She kept low, eyeing the tidy rows of tomato plants and squash vines. Their shapes and scents reminded her of home, of lazy summer days in Gran's garden. Charlotte blinked back tears, swallowing her longing. She had to focus on finding her sisters.

The pungent scent of animals grew stronger as Charlotte approached a large barn silhouetted in the moonlight. At first, Charlotte thought the smell was coming from fertilizer for the gardens, but then the soft sounds of animals grew a little louder. A sheep bleated, followed by echoing bleats.

She kept low to the ground as the garden ended at a fenced-in pen filled with fluffy, round sheep.

A lanky figure appeared in the doorway of the barn door. "Ho, sheep. Come in," a boy called out to the animals.

Charlotte held her ground, observing and hoping to see something that might confirm that this was the caretaker Seena had told her to find.

Two guards approached the barn from the outer wall. The bleating of sheep grew louder, the sheep jumpy now that their movement inside the barn had been disrupted.

Charlotte dropped to the dirt and lay flat on her belly.

"I told you the barn is clear!" The boy crossed his arms. "It was just searched an hour ago, and you're upsetting the animals."

The two guards paid him no mind and continued their walk around the barn's perimeter.

The boy stood unmoving, muttering after the guards until they finished their patrol and walked further down the wall.

As the boy called the sheep in once more, Charlotte took a deep breath and decided to make her move. It was now or never. She just hoped that Seena was right, and the boy wouldn't call out to the guards as soon as he saw her.

Charlotte steeled her nerves and slipped through the fence rails into the animal enclosure. Mud squelched under her boots.

"Hey!" The boy called out. His watchful eyes must have caught the moment she entered the pen.

Charlotte slowed, her arms raised in surrender. "Seena sent me."

The boy's expression was hidden because the light from the barn was behind him, casting shadows on his face. But he motioned for her to follow him inside.

She breathed a sigh of relief and followed the flow of the sheep. She kept the scarf wrapped around the bottom half of her face, still unsure whether she could fully trust this stranger.

Inside, the scent of animals enveloped Charlotte. She wrinkled her nose at the sour tang of manure and hay. The animals shuffled in their pens, bleating and snorting.

"Go up to the loft and wait for me there," the boy said softly. "It's safer, in case any more of those confounded guards burst in." He held a small oil lamp, and the flames danced across his young, ruddy face. He couldn't be more than thirteen—his voice hadn't yet broken into a young man's baritone.

Charlotte nodded, and he turned to finish putting the sheep away for the night.

She made her way up a rickety ladder.

A short time later, the boy climbed the ladder and plopped down opposite her in the hayloft.

"Who are you?" he asked. His eyes were direct but kind.

"It's better if you don't know," Charlotte said, still hesitant to remove her face covering.

"Look. You said Seena sent you, right? Well, I trust her. I won't hurt you—unless you plan on hurting my sheep." He raised an eyebrow at his last statement.

"No, I won't hurt your sheep," Charlotte assured him.

"Great. Well, I'm Davin. And you are?"

Charlotte sighed. He'd probably figure it out soon enough when she told him where she wanted to go. She slowly pulled the scarf off her head.

Davin squinted more closely until a flash of recognition sparked. "Oh!" he exclaimed. But instead of anger or fear, his face split into a grin. "Sending one of Ade's most wanted rebels to the barns? Seena doesn't mess around."

Despite herself, Charlotte smiled back. This skinny boy seemed utterly unintimidated by the danger. His boldness was refreshing.

Davin continued to stare at her and pursed his boyish lips.

"What?" she asked slightly defensively.

"They made you look fiercer in that hologram," he said, face serious.

When Charlotte's eyebrows shot up, Davin quickly held up his palms. "Sorry. I didn't mean any offense. Usually, it's just me and the sheep, so I tend to speak whatever comes to mind. But seriously, Ade is making you out to be this scary criminal mastermind. But you look kind of... normal."

Charlotte shook her head. He wasn't wrong. "I always told Rapha that he picked the wrong girl. My twin sisters, on the other hand... they're the real geniuses."

"Well, nobody ever thinks much of me." Davin shrugged. "But I'm quite fierce."

Charlotte worked to keep a straight face. She was in a dire situation with the whole force of the Empire looking for her, but here she was with a young shepherd who thought the world of himself.

"It's true," Davin continued. "Once, a mountain lion came from the hills and started trying to pick off some of my sheep."

Charlotte didn't bother pointing out that the sheep were the Emperor's—not his. She had to respect the boy for taking his job so seriously.

"I said a quick prayer to *El* and ran straight toward the lion. You see, it picked off one of the mothers who had recently given birth to some lambs. They needed their mother..." Davin hesitated, turning serious for a moment. Charlotte recognized that ache in his eyes and thought he was speaking of more than just the lamb's mother.

"Anyways," he continued. "I ran toward the lion who had the ewe in its mouth. I hooked my staff around the lion's neck—I didn't want it running off with the mom. A large stone lay on the ground, and without hesitation I grabbed it, jumped on the back of the lion, and smashed in its head."

Charlotte recoiled slightly at the violent turn in the story.

"I know *El* put the stone there, just for me." Davin smiled, unfazed. "And He may have also helped to ensure the lion didn't snap my head off. Either way, the lion ran off with a bloody head, and the ewe was saved with barely a scratch."

"Impressive," Charlotte said. And it was impressive. As crazy as it sounded, she believed his story. A sudden worry gripped her for the young boy. "Aren't you worried about being caught? I mean, talking so freely about *El*?"

Davin shrugged. "Not really. I guess if one of the guards heard me singing on the hills…" He cocked his head in thought for a moment. "But mostly, my life is just me and the sheep. And they don't seem to mind hearing about *El*." He chuckled to himself.

Charlotte couldn't suppress a yawn that suddenly overtook her. Granted, she had dozed off a bit in the tunnel above the water shaft, but the safety of the hayloft and the long day that had started in Riverton overtook her.

"Come," Davin motioned toward a spot at the back of the loft. "There's a little spot here where you can rest." He helped her crawl into a narrow space between two hay bales. "I'll keep the guards distracted during their searches—it's not too hard once you know their routine. You can help me take the sheep to graze in the morning, which'll get you outside the palace. *El* will help us."

Davin's confidence rested on Charlotte's heart. She couldn't even muster the words to ask how he knew she wanted to get out of the palace. She snuggled deeper into the hay, using the scarf as a makeshift pillow.

It felt like her eyes had barely closed when Davin shook her awake.

"Get up. Come quickly. We need to move."

Chapter 23

Sonos awoke with a start, his head exploding in agony. He groaned. Nausea overwhelmed his senses.

"Help! He's waking up." A young voice cried out, followed by a scuffle of panicked footsteps.

Sonos forced his eyes to crack open, but even the candlelight caused a fresh wave of pain to crash over him as his eyes tried to adjust.

He didn't recognize the small windowless room.

Worse, he was strapped to what looked like a narrow table.

Where am I? He strained to remember where he was last, but his mind was foggy, thoughts muddled.

Be brave and very courageous. Do not be discouraged. The words found a way through the fuzz and instantly brought clarity to his mind.

Sal burst into the room, followed by a young robed Sah.

Do not be discouraged. The words repeated in Sonos' mind. He tried to fight against the restraints on his wrists and ankles, but his muscles were sluggish. His body was completely out of his control.

Sal muttered, saying something about it not being time yet. Then he stabbed something into Sonos' arm, and blackness overtook him once more.

Chapter 24

CHARLOTTE OPENED HER EYES with a start, disoriented. She must have slept longer than she thought—her brain was a fuzzy mess.

Sunlight streamed into the barn through cracks in the walls. The sheep bleated loudly nearby.

"I let you sleep as long as I could," Davin said, crouched beside her. "It seemed like you needed it."

A black cat jumped from a nearby hay bale, and Charlotte sat up quickly, fully awake.

Davin chuckled, looking in the direction the cat had gone. "Don't worry, Ross helps keep the rats away."

Charlotte stretched and untied her bun, trying to shake loose pieces of hay out of her hair.

"You sleep like a rock," Davin chuckled. "The guards came through a few times, but you never stirred. The sheep woke up hungry and loud, and no movement from you. I banged around while feeding them, and still nothing."

"I get the point. I was tired," Charlotte muttered, putting her hair into two braids. Davin may be only a few years younger, but his social skills were clearly developed with the sheep.

"You need to wash up quickly." Davin stood and stepped onto the rickety ladder. "The guards are due for their next check soon. And it'll look mighty suspicious if me and the sheep are still here."

Charlotte followed him down to the floor of the barn.

The sheep bleated even louder at the sight of Davin.

Davin pointed her to a small washroom beneath the hayloft. It was not much bigger than a closet. Once inside, Charlotte took a moment to check the gazer on her finger. No new messages. She worried about Jax and Sonos, frustrated that she couldn't communicate with either of them or check in in real-time. She left a quick message for Jax, updating him on what happened and telling him to call her back.

A few minutes later, she stepped out of the room, and Davin handed her a slice of buttered bread and a bottle of water. "From Miss Seena."

Charlotte scrunched her eyebrows, showing Davin the cloth sack Seena had already packed for her the night before. "She already gave me enough rations for days."

Davin laughed. "Food is her love language. What can I say? We'll eat that for lunch or something."

Boots scuffled near the entrance to the barn. Davin turned immediately serious and pointed to the little room where Charlotte had washed up; she nearly dove behind the door.

The barn door slid open, and voices came through the thin wall of the washroom where Charlotte crouched. She didn't dare move a muscle.

"Who were you talking to?" a gruff voice asked.

"You know me," Davin said casually. "I like talking to the sheep... and myself."

The guard grunted. "It sounded like two voices."

"Sometimes I have conversations with myself," Davin quipped. "And change up de accents tuh mek it interesting." He attempted a higher-pitched, very poor Jamroq lilt with the second line.

"Why haven't you taken the sheep out to graze yet?" Another voice asked.

Feet shuffled around the barn, and one drew near the washroom where Charlotte was hiding.

"Maybe because I keep getting interrupted by endless searches," Davin snapped. "But Jimmy is supposed to be helping today—he's in training—but he's running a little late. We'll be leaving soon."

Jimmy? Charlotte wondered. She didn't like the thought of another person being pulled into this ruse. Already, Davin and Miss Seena were directly helping her escape.

A guard thrust open the door to the washroom.

Charlotte stood behind the door. Thankfully, it was ill-made and opened inwards, and her petite frame fit snugly behind it. But if the guard so much as stuck his head in...

"C'mon! Do you want me to get moving or what?" Davin called out. "And you just looked here less than twenty minutes ago."

"Just doing our job," the guard said, closing the door without another glance.

Charlotte let out a silent breath, her pulse still thumping in her ears.

It wasn't until she heard the barn door close and Davin poked his head into the washroom that she started breathing normally again.

"We need to get out of here," he said softly but urgently. He handed her a long, brown, woven cloak and a large floppy hat. "Put these on."

"Who's Jimmy?" Charlotte asked.

"Huh? Oh, he's a young stable hand who normally handles the cows, but he sometimes trains with me on the sheep," Davin answered, putting on a hat and cloak that matched the ones he had handed Charlotte. "I told them he was coming so they're not suspicious when they see two people going to the fields."

"But won't they get even more suspicious when they see Jimmy with the cows?" Charlotte pressed.

"I promise I'm not as young or naive as you must think I look," Davin said with a frown. "When the kitchen boy dropped off breakfast, I told him to tell Jimmy to lay low for the day. And before you ask, I'll double back when bringing in the sheep to make it look like two of us coming back."

Charlotte's cheeks grew warm as she realized how much she'd underestimated him. "Sorry, I just... I appreciate all you're doing. I want to ensure you don't get in trouble because of me."

"You'd be surprised at how much people *don't* pay attention to farmhands and shepherds. If the guards weren't on such high alert, they wouldn't give me a second glance." Davin took up a staff and handed another one to Charlotte. "Keep your head down, and let me do the talking."

Davin moved to the far side of the barn and slid open a large door. The sheep huddled around him as he spoke. "Good morning, lovelies. Good to see you, too. Ready for some open air?" He chattered almost non-stop, and on their part, the sheep baaed and meh-ed in return.

Charlotte stayed in the rear to ensure no sheep stayed behind, but there was almost nothing for her to do. The sheep loved their shepherd.

Sunlight mixed with a cool breeze as Charlotte followed the herd through the barn door, through a small, fenced passageway, and finally to the outer city wall. The wall was enormous—even bigger than it looked from the outside. As Charlotte passed under the first raised iron gate and through the stone tunnel, she shuddered at the sheer power of Pergamum. She thought about how Sonos had described the protection closer to the palace. No wonder they believed their city so strong that even the lame and blind could protect it. *And yet...*

Davin and his sheep continued talking to each other the whole way. The cacophony of sound turned out to be a protection of sorts. Davin just smiled and waved from where he led in the front, and Charlotte kept her eyes down.

She made sure to keep close to the herd so she wouldn't be picked or singled out by the guards. She thought she heard a few chuckles—she must have looked awkward fumbling around with the staff—but she felt oddly safe.

Once they passed through the second iron gate and were safely outside the city walls, Charlotte took a deep breath of fresh air.

Davin walked a well-worn dirt track through some fields. As they crested the first hill and Pergamum faded into the distance, Charlotte paused, drinking in the stunning view. Rolling green hills and fields spread out before her. It was beautiful.

She thought of Lily, her artistic sister, and wished there was a way to capture the image to show her later. But she couldn't risk turning on her gazer... not yet.

As if in response to her decision, a drone flew by overhead. She stopped herself from looking up at it directly, but saw it out of the corner of her eye as it descended over nearby hilltops. The Sahemy must be testing it out—it didn't sound like the drone that had chased them near the Badlands, or any other that Charlotte had seen thus far.

She saw a little lamb drifting behind the herd and stopped to pick it up. It squirmed, and a few of the nearby sheep started baaing at her, so she set it back on the ground. It ran back into the herd, and Charlotte continued down the hillside.

By the time she reached the crest of the second hill, Charlotte was breathing heavily. Thankfully, Davin stopped halfway down and reclined against a small, budding tree. He patted the ground next to him, and Charlotte took a seat.

"Sometimes, I go a lot further, but I figured you'd want to stay close enough to find the Sahemy caves," he said.

"How did you know?" Charlotte asked.

"It's not hard to piece together once you have eyes to see," Davin answered. "I saw a bunch of prisoners from the Legacy Towers being led from one cave to another the other day."

Charlotte's eyes perked up.

"And if you're one of the rebel leaders, I figured the only reason you'd be coming to the palace—aside from confronting stinking Ade—would be to set people free, right?" Davin turned his brown eyes toward her with a knowing look.

"You're quick," Charlotte said, more and more impressed with the young man. "And not wrong." She hesitated but decided to share more, given the risks Davin had already taken for her. "I want to help the prisoners, but most importantly, my sisters are in that bunch. They were kidnapped three years ago by the Emperor." A question nagged at her. "But how do you know the prisoners you saw were from the Legacy Towers?"

"The long, brown robes and roped belts," Davin answered. "Eerily similar to the garb I wear as a shepherd." He frowned, then shrugged.

Charlotte was about to ask more questions, but Davin had a far-off look on his face.

"I know how it feels to lose family," he said finally, still staring into the distance. "My mother died in childbirth, so I didn't know her. For a long time, it was just me and my dad; he had shepherded these flocks since he was a boy. Last year, Baku—" Davin spat on the ground after saying the name. "He thought he had uncovered a plot against the Emperor, and he blamed my dad. They took him and killed him. Hanged him, and insisted that his body be left out for a week as a warning to others."

"I'm so sorry," Charlotte whispered, horrified.

Davin turned back to her with a fierceness in his eyes. "My dad didn't do anything wrong. He was strong in his faith, but wise enough not to blab about it in the open. He simply stood up for what was right, and protected those who couldn't fight for themselves. And that was a threat against the Emperor?"

He crossed his arm over his knees and turned back to watch the sheep. "So when I have *any* chance of helping, and doing my part to fight for *El*'s way, I'll do it."

Charlotte laid a hand on his arm. She didn't know what else to say, so she repeated the promise that had defined the journey. "Fight we must..."

Davin turned and grinned despite the sadness in his eyes. "And win we shall." He cleared his throat and looked to the hills to their right. "Now, about getting into the Sahemy's underground lair... Most of the entrances are hidden, guarded, or both. But just over the next few hills, there's a lake the Sahemy built. I've used it to water the sheep before, and I'm thinking we can go together. They should have an access point near the water."

The suggestion made sense to Charlotte—at least, it sounded better than running up and down hills looking for entrances at random. "Let's go," she said, standing up, and filled with new determination.

She stopped when the gazer-ring vibrated on her finger. Her heart skipped a beat, hoping it was Jax. She dropped back under the covering of the tree, and Davin huddled close, lifting the sleeve of his cloak to provide more cover.

Her stomach dropped when Ade's face filled the screen for a new broadcast.

Chapter 25

A SHARP, ACRID SMELL caused Sonos to suck in a deep breath.

His eyes popped open. He was still in the windowless room and his wrists and ankles were still hopelessly strapped to a table.

"Grand Magus is on his way," Sal said as he secured the lid of a vial and placed it on a nearby table.

Sonos' tutor, Sah Timur, had once taught him a science class that included segments on smelling salts and other remedies. Sal must have used something like that to wake him up.

Sal waved the glowing orb that always hovered nearby over to a small table. He tapped the gazer on his wrist, and soon, the orb projected a holographic screen. "We can't have you missing the show, though." He winked and went back to tapping his gazer.

Sonos pulled at the leather straps that bound his wrists while Sal was occupied with the tech. He found that he could turn his wrists ever so slightly, but there was no pulling his hands through. His ankles had the same amount of room.

Ade's face filled the center of the projected screen. The dark circles under his brother's sharp, blue eyes were even more pronounced than before.

Sonos glanced at the orb. He had the panicked thought that this was some kind of video call, like when Charlotte and Jax spoke to each other. Or maybe Ade planned on broadcasting Sonos' capture from this dungeon, cave, or wherever he was. He pulled more frantically at his restraints.

Sal glanced up. "Worried, Highness?" A crooked smile distorted his face.

"Citizens and servants of K'Luma," Ade started. The shifting shadows behind the throne where Ade sat formed into the now familiar shape of a dragon. It kept up the deceit about the Emperor's transformation. "I am informed that my wayward brother has not yet had the courage to turn himself in."

Sonos was confused. Did that mean…? He frowned toward Sal, but the big man's back was facing him. Were Grand Magus and the Sahemy not working with Ade? His mind raced. Sal had said Sonos shouldn't get caught by the other Sahs near the water shaft—perhaps he was implying that the faction Grand Magus led was on its own.

"However, we have another accomplice in custody." His brother sounded too pleased.

Sonos snapped his attention back to the screen.

The camera panned from Ade, and over to Taine strapped to a chair surrounded by other Elites, his right hand covered in a white bandage. It took a moment for Sonos to recognize the warrior with his bald head. But the coal eyes of his friend flamed with an unmistakable fire.

Bile rose in Sonos' throat. Taine had lost a thumb—an inconvenience for most, but devastating for a warrior. He was then shamed by the shaving of his head, removing the honor of a Kimwaki warrior. Guilt and fear flooded Sonos' thoughts. What more might Ade do this time?

But then Sonos focused on the empty chair beside Taine. He had a sinking feeling…

His suspicions were confirmed a moment later when a tall female warrior with two long braids was dragged thrashing onto the screen. When Taimani's eyes locked onto her brother, the thrashing stopped, and she looked around the room as if finally realizing where she was.

Oh, Mani. What did you get yourself into? Sonos thought, feeling more helpless than ever with two friends now captured. But he also felt a thread of anger at Taimani. She could be with Charlotte now instead of being used as a hostage in the throne room. Why did she have to run away?

An Elite strapped Taimani to the chair next to her brother.

Sonos caught the flicker of her fingers beyond her defensive fighting. She was communicating with her brother. Sonos picked up on the movement only because he knew them so well.

Taimani settled on the chair and looked directly at the camera.

Clever girl, using the trick Charlotte taught you to find the camera, Sonos thought.

"Fight we must!" Taimani yelled with all her might.

A shiver ran down Sonos' spine.

The whole throne room was silent. Everyone sat frozen.

Even Sal's jaw dropped open.

They surely weren't expecting Taimani to come out of the gates with that response.

The anger, frustration, and fear swirling in Sonos' mind receded with Taimani's shout. The power of the unseen realm came into sharp focus. "Win we shall," he whispered back.

There was a scuffle as the shock of Taimani's shout wore off, and the nearby guards shoved something in Taimani's mouth.

The camera turned back to focus on Ade's red face. "More hurt, more pain, is all that awaits any and every rebel follower of *El.*" Ade spit out the last word. "Unless Sonos turns himself in by sunrise tomorrow, two more deaths will hang on his head." His eyes glinted as a more sinister look twisted the corners of his mouth and eyes in all the wrong ways.

The screen went blank.

The momentary burst of courage Sonos got from Taimani's shout melted into horror as he realized that Ade would kill Taine and Taimani if he didn't find a way to escape and turn himself in.

Grand Magus stepped out of a shadowy corner of the room. Or was it a hidden door?

"I must say, your brother seems quite determined to find you." The wizened man's hair looked just as unkempt as before. His voice filled the air with a coat of slime.

"Let me go," Sonos commanded, trying to use the royal tone his brother had mastered.

Grand Magus stepped towards the table, turning Sonos' journal over in his hands. He thumbed through the pages. "You write in a code I've never seen before."

Sonos frowned but tried to keep any confusion from showing on his face. He didn't write in code. He used the common tongue.

Grand Magus flipped through the pages and held the open book before Sonos' face. "What does it say?"

Sonos was genuinely confused. The writing and journal entry was clear as day to his eyes.

"I see." Grand Magus' eyes narrowed. "You choose to hide *El*'s secrets rather than save your friends."

What? Sonos' mind raced. "No." He needed to get out there and reach his brother. Taine's capture was one thing—but his death, alongside Taimani's? Sonos might not survive that blow.

Grand Magus grunted and threw the journal onto Sonos' chest.

Sonos struggled to sit up. "If I write things in the common tongue, you'll let me go?" He had to try to for his friends.

Grand Magus gestured to Sal to unbind Sonos' wrists.

With a shaky hand, Sonos scribbled one of the lines.

"Waste of time," Grand Magus muttered.

Sonos looked up horrified. Why did the words appear as coded to Grand Magus? They were clear as day to him. He picked up the pencil, trying again. "Wait."

Grand Magus turned to Sal, ignoring Sonos. "Make him copy every last word into the common tongue. Only then will he be allowed to speak." He then said to Sonos, nose held high as he spoke, "You had your chance. Now, I want every last word. And you had better write quickly. The warriors' lives depend on it."

Chapter 26

"I HAVE TO GET to my sisters." Charlotte tapped off the gazer-ring, jumping up from under the tree with renewed determination and urgency.

"I take it those two warriors from Kimwaki are friends?" Davin asked, grabbing his staff and joining her.

"They are," Charlotte answered. "And if Ade gets wind of the fact that my sisters are with the prisoners, they'll be next."

"Let's pick up the pace then," Davin said. "We still have a good hour's walk to the lake."

The sun hung high in the sky by the time Charlotte panted her way up the fourth hill—which was now starting to feel like a mountain. The sheep meandered in their happy gait, following Davin. They passed Charlotte with ease.

Charlotte risked sending another quick message to Jax, hiding under the sleeve of her cloak. She told him where she was heading, and that she hoped he and Lenora were okay. There had been nothing from him, and she felt more than a little anxious.

She poured all her energy into putting one foot in front of the other, doing her best to stay caught up.

Finally, after what felt like hours, Davin turned around and called out to her. "We're almost there! Just over this hill."

She raised a hand in the air, unable to muster the breath to shout back. She paused momentarily and doubled over, putting her hands on her knees.

Davin trotted back to join her while the sheep continued to a spot they seemed to know well.

"Sorry, I sometimes forget how much climbing I normally do in a day," Davin said. He handed Charlotte a flask of water. "It's a lot when you start out."

Charlotte sipped at the water. After catching her breath, she took a few gulps. "You know, Jamroq has a mountain range of its own. We went through it once to get to the capital, Kinstun." Charlotte remembered her sisters' smiles on the way to the prize-giving ceremony. They had all been so confident in their plan to change the Imperial system—believing they would start by making a difference in Jamroq.

"And?" Davin raised an eyebrow.

"Sorry." Charlotte realized she had gotten lost in her thoughts. "That was the trip that led to my sisters' kidnapping." She frowned, then motioned for them to keep moving forward.

When they reached the top of the last hill, Charlotte's breath caught again, but this time for the beauty of the scene in front of her. A glimmering, blue lake filled a tiny valley between two mountaintops. White dots speckled the space around the lake where the sheep grazed and drank.

"Over that next hill…" Davin pointed to the other side of the lake. "It leads to the forest. This is as far as I ever take the sheep, though."

Charlotte allowed herself a moment to soak in the peaceful view.

"My dad always said that *El* has cattle and sheep on a thousand hills," Davin said, staring over the grazing sheep.

"Cattle and sheep?" Charlotte asked, confused.

"Meaning that he has resources all over the place," Davin answered.

Charlotte paused, thinking. Davin may be a boy, socially awkward, and focused on animals. But *El*'s truth and frequency were strong with him.

"I hope you're right." Charlotte's mind raced towards what might await her in the Sahemy's underground lair. "I'm going to need all the help I can get."

Down near the water's edge, a pair of robed figures emerged from seemingly nowhere, standing in the middle of the herd and gesticulating wildly.

"Perfect," Charlotte whispered. She now had the entrance marked.

The men looked around, then turned to where she and Davin stood.

Her heart jumped into her throat, but her hat and scarf were firmly in place. They couldn't know.

"Get these sheep out of here, shepherd! You've messed up our sensors!" one shouted.

Davin waved and trotted down the hill, calling out to his sheep.

The two Sahemy disappeared down a hatch that was now visible after the sheep had moved.

What kind of sensors do the Sahemy have set up? Charlotte wondered, adjusting the wide-brimmed hat on her head. *Is it just because of the lockdown? Davin said he's brought the sheep here before.*

The questions puzzled her, but she knew what she had to do. There was no sense delaying, and perhaps the sheep messing with the sensors was precisely what she needed.

She jogged down the hill and met up with Davin.

"Thank you for everything. But this is where we part ways." She got straight to the point.

Davin met her gaze, a hint of sadness in his frown. But he nodded. "I guess I knew this was the right place. I'm glad you found an entrance you could use."

Charlotte handed the staff back to him and shrugged off the cloak and hat.

"You sure you don't want to keep them?" Davin asked.

"I don't want anything to point back to you directly," Charlotte said. "You've helped more than enough."

"It wasn't much..." Davin half-shrugged.

"It was exactly the help I needed when I needed it," Charlotte assured him.

"I hope we meet again. But in case it's far from now..." Davin surprised her by pulling her into a spontaneous hug. "Be brave. *El* is ahead of you, behind you, and with you."

Charlotte returned the embrace, feeling a little closer to home. She let his words calm her buzzing mind. *Be strong and very courageous.*

Davin pulled away, called to his sheep, and led them up the hill back towards the palace.

Meanwhile, Charlotte knelt on the ground, feeling around for the hatch. What had Sonos looked for when he opened the entrance to the underground reservoir? It had been a stump with the Sahemy marking—a snake in the shape of a circle with a flame in the center. Then, he had pressed four buttons in a sequence.

Finally, her fingers found a short, wooden stump protruding from the tall grass. Sahemy tech was surprisingly rudimentary—using the same security protocols over and over. It was arrogance more than anything, Charlotte was convinced. But this was one aspect where she appreciated the unfettered pride held by the Sahemy.

She pressed the four buttons in the same sequence Sonos had taught her—East, West, South, North. A metal hatch clicked open.

Be brave. She replayed the words in her mind before slipping into the darkness.

Chapter 27

I NEED TO SAVE *Taine and Mani. I need to go to my brother. I need to get out of here.* The thoughts repeated themselves over and over in Sonos' mind. At times, panic swelled, but eventually, the panic gave focus to his plan.

"I'd start writing if I were you." Sal's voice broke Sonos' reverie.

Sonos looked up at the burly man who sat near the door, tinkering with his glowing orb.

But first, I need to get past him, Sonos thought.

"Those words you recited—or should I say, shouted—back in Grand Magus' office..." Sal let the orb settle above his head, pulsing a dim yellow. "Where did that come from?"

Sonos thought about what he should say. He was still trying to figure out why the head Sah could not read the notes he had made in the journal. "The unseen realm." He deliberately left the answer vague—it's not like Sal was likely to believe that a talking monkey handed the poem to Charlotte in a temporal portal.

Sal's mouth pulled tight. "I realize that. The words were not human."

"What did you hear?" Sonos asked, wondering if the words were confused like the handwritten journal.

"Oh, I understood the words you said. *'Your fight is futile...'*" Sal recited a line and raised his eyebrow. "But the power they held—I've never seen Grand Magus so angry."

Sonos cringed. He had been sure of the words and the necessity to speak them then, but the consequences of angering Grand Magus were playing themselves out now. And now is when he needed a little help. He needed to get to Taine and Taimani before sunrise.

Sonos folded the journal in his lap alongside the book Grand Magus had provided for the translation. Writing the words wouldn't work—he'd tried that already. He thought about writing nonsense, but Grand Magus seemed to recognize the power of the unseen realm. He couldn't take further risks because his friends' lives were on the line.

"I'm not trying to cause any trouble." Sonos swallowed hard, realizing that he needed to choose his words wisely. "If you just get me to my brother, I won't say anything about the past day or my capture. I'll even see if I can get Grand Magus an audience with the Emperor." He wasn't sure if playing nice would be of any help, but he thought he'd try that first.

"You're offering to help our cause? Changing sides so quickly?" Sal frowned, his eyes holding disappointment.

Sonos sat up straighter. His feet were bound, likely by some sorcery; otherwise, they wouldn't allow such freedom of movement with his upper body. He had no idea how far he was from the palace or how much time he had.

"I simply thought to offer an exchange. Take me to my brother, and there's supposed to be a reward—at least according to all the guards." His heart raced as he attempted to negotiate his way out of the situation.

"You assume we need a reward." Sal regarded Sonos with a skeptical look. "And you'd betray your beliefs just like that?"

"It's not about betrayal; it's about survival. Grand Magus has shown his true colors. He won't hesitate to use me as a pawn until he's finished with me. But I need to get to my brother before he has my friends killed."

Sal hesitated, and the glowing orb above his head flickered. "Focus on translating those words as you were instructed. That's your best hope of reaching Emperor Ade in time." Sal's voice was as flat as his stare. "I'll be back to check on your progress in an hour." He stood and stepped out of the room.

Sonos immediately tried pulling at the leather straps on his ankles, trying desperately to free his legs. There was no time to waste. But something unnatural seemed to hold them in place.

"Raph, you out there?" Sonos whispered. "Now would be a good time to help."

No response. Not even a flicker of movement.

Sonos grunted in frustration and pulled on the straps with all his might, his knuckles turning white. Escape felt so close, but yet impossible. He was sure if Taine or Taimani were in his shoes, they'd have found a way out already. Charlotte would have used tech to bypass whatever sorcery was in place.

But what do I have? Sonos lamented.

Stopping the negative string of thoughts, he forced himself to look around the room. His eyes locked onto the vials and chemicals organized on the table nearby. Hope ignited within him as he realized these vials might be the key to his escape.

With his upper body free, Sonos shifted his weight, trying to assess the distance to the table. He knew it was a long shot, but he had no other option. He scooted himself as best as he could across the slab he was strapped to. He could reach a chair to balance his upper body, even as his legs had to bend unnaturally because of the bonds on his ankles.

It was a painstaking effort, and the straps on his ankles chafed against his skin as he inched closer to the table.

He kept a running total of the time elapsing in the back of his mind. But he was also nervous that Sal would check in before the full hour had passed.

He lost focus momentarily, and the chair toppled from his grasp, causing Sonos to fall back against the slab. He cried out in pain as his legs stretched and he tried to pull himself fully back onto the slab. The straps cut into his ankles even further. He lifted his body as best as he could, eyes locked on the door, and ears tuned for any sound. Mercifully, there were no footsteps or creaking of doors.

The chair was still within reach, and Sonos managed to pull himself back up and angle his body again towards the table. Inch by grueling inch, he strained towards the edge of the table. Finally, his fingers brushed against the vials. He kept his core tight, trying to balance and inspect the labels. His fingers landed on one with dark blue liquid he thought he recognized.

"Dissolution." He gripped the vial with one hand and carefully pulled his upper body back to sit upright on the slab where his ankles were still trapped.

Sonos uncorked the vial with trembling hands and applied a drop of the liquid to the straps binding his ankles.

A faint sizzle and a puff of smoke emanated from the straps. The room filled with a faint, acrid odor, but he didn't care. He was focused on his goal: escaping and saving his friends.

Sonos felt a rush of hope, but then a drop landed on his skin. The surge of pain was instant. He kept from crying out, focused on ensuring that no more of the liquid fell on an exposed area.

Drop by drop, the straps weakened and loosened. Sonos worked quickly, his hands unsteady, applying more of the dissolving solution to the remaining straps until they finally gave way.

With his feet free, Sonos stood up. His legs were unsteady from being bound for so long. He grabbed his journal and made a beeline for the door. He'd done it! He had freed himself, and soon he'd save Taine and Taimni. Then, he could find Charlotte and her sisters.

He grabbed the door handle, pleased to find it unlocked, and swung it open.

To his horror, Sal stood blocking the way—arms crossed and eyes narrowed as the orb flickered above his head.

Sal shook his head as he spoke. "Wrong choice, Sonos."

CHAPTER 28

I SAAKO STEPPED THROUGH THE temporal portal in the Badlands and straight into mayhem.

A great mass of people was crammed into a town square. The Legacy Towers oriented him first, with their pointed red tops and evenly tiered levels. Only the highest floors were visible from where he stood, but they were unmistakable. He was in Pergamum.

"You must know who you are and who you are fighting for. That is your first battle." That's what Nissi said in the portal. The dragon lizard was nowhere in sight, but Isaako was used to being sent off on missions.

"No! Papa!" A little boy cried out nearby. He was being pulled back by his distraught mother, who glared at a man dressed in merchant clothes.

"I... I'm sorry... I can't." The man stuttered, but his head remained high, resolute.

"All those who renounce *El* and worship Emperor Ade, go this way!" An Imperial guard shouted, pointing his spear toward the mother and young boy. The mother spat on the ground and continued pulling her son. Only a fraction of the people in the square showed allegiance to Ade and were led to the exit.

Wait, did the guard just say Emperor Ade? Isaako thought in shock. Yes, he had seen the Emperor—Ade's father—transformed into a beast, but Nissi had said that it had only been a week since that had happened. Had Ade already taken his father's throne?

Isaako shielded his eyes against the high sun of midday.

As the crowd was sorted, families shouted at each other, and guards yelled at everyone. Isaako quickly looked down at his clothing. He didn't want to be mistaken for an Elite, and he was sure his old squad and other Elites would be looking for him.

Thankfully, Nissi had transformed his clothes when Isaako had stepped through the portal, and now he wore a simple cotton tunic, a scarf, soft leather pants, and boots. He could easily pass for the working class inside the city. His long, warrior hair was twisted into a bun high on his head.

"You! Make your choice!" A guard prodded Isaako in the back.

Isaako restrained his instinct to fight back and lowered his eyes to the ground. He stepped towards those who refused to give up their faith.

There was fear and uneasiness in the crowd, but also a deep determination. A young woman held onto the hand of a young man. Her blue eyes were fire, her jaw tight, her whole body tense as she tracked the guards. Isaako knew battle-ready warriors, and she was ready to pounce.

"Your faith is misplaced." An Elite addressed the crowd from an elevated place on a hovering flyer-board. He used tech that had been infused into his gazer to amplify his voice. When the Elite drew closer, Isaako recognized the scar that ran down his face—from his left eye to his jaw.

Isaako had stood next to Gamba when the sword from an instructor had sliced his face, and Gamba had almost been killed for defiance. They were two young men training for the Elite squad. Isaako had already been training with the guards for eight years—half his life—while Gamba had volunteered at sixteen. He was a citizen of K'Luma who wanted to serve the Empire he loved.

But little did Gamba realize that outright staring at the Emperor would be considered defiance.

Shaking himself back to the present, Isaako assessed his current predicament. Imperial guards stood at every exit to the square, spears upright. There was no escape or running away without being noticed.

"You have chosen to serve a god you cannot see with your eyes, and who has no power to save you," Gamba smirked as he scanned the crowd.

But El *transformed the Emperor into a wild beast and stopped Uzoma from defeating the Mountain Kingdom*, Isaako thought. *He has more power than you think.*

"Emperor Ade, may he live forever, is the only god K'Luma needs. You all will serve as an example that the Emperor's power is absolute and unquestionable." Gamba paused, his frown deepening. "Your heads will sit on spikes and line the roads to the Pergamum. Let all who see know who rules the great K'Luma Empire!"

A collective gasp went up from the crowd while the Imperial guards simultaneously banged their spears and shouted agreement with Gamba.

This is insane, even for an emperor, Isaako thought. There were at least a hundred people in this square.

Isaako may not know much about *El*, but he understood authority and was certain Nissi had not sent him to die. He was sent to this moment, to this place, for a purpose. He had to do something.

He took a breath and stepped forward from the crowd and toward Gamba.

A nearby Elite thrust out his blue-lit sword and held its point to Isaako's neck.

Isaako ignored the sword and kept his eyes trained on Gamba. "I am Isaako, and I stand to challenge Emperor Ade to a contest: a contest to show the true power of the unseen realm."

Those near him took a few steps back, distancing themselves further.

Gamba flew toward Isaako, his eyes wide with recognition as he drew closer, then narrowed. "Traitor," he hissed.

But Isaako raised his voice even louder. "If Emperor Ade's power is absolute, he will have his chance to prove it through his sorcerers." He wasn't entirely sure where the words he spoke were coming from. It was certainly nothing he had planned ahead of time. But the challenge came out of his mouth confident and strong. "However, if *El* prevails, he will let every last prisoner go free. Everyone in this square and anyone held on similar charges throughout the Empire." Isaako shocked himself with that last declaration, but the words seemed right.

Gamba's eyes went wide, and his whole body was tense. He looked ready to make Isaako the first example of a head on a spike.

But Isaako was all in. There was no backup plan and no turning back. He dropped his voice as he continued speaking to Gamba. "Using power to execute a group of defenseless people is one thing. But imagine the Emperor defeating a god." Isaako knew Ade and the sorcerers would be no match for *El*. They touched only a fraction of the unseen realm, a part which was corrupted and limited. However, *El* was the singular creator of all. Even with his limited interactions with followers of *El* over the years, and now his fractured memories from his childhood, Isaako somehow knew this at his core now.

Gamba sneered at Isaako's taunt, but the challenge had the desired effect. Gamba turned his back and used his gazer to make a call.

Isaako sucked in a breath when he saw the holographic image of who answered. Wylder. *Did they choose Wylder to be head of the Elites? Wylder? That dirty, greedy merchant?*

The sword still held to his neck pulsed with energy and gave him a slight but continuous shock, and Isaako fought the wave of nausea. All the Elites had undergone shock training to limit the effects of their specialized weapons should they be used against them. But it took tremendous restraint all the same.

Wylder's holographic image disappeared briefly, reappeared, and then he spoke to Gamba.

"Yes, sir, as the Emperor wishes, may he live forever," Gamba responded, cutting the connection. He turned and flew to hover right above Isaako. "Your challenge has been accepted, Diekolo-laoluwa. We will see you and your god defeated publicly." He pulled his sword off his back and raised it in the air, a signal to the others. Before speeding off, he fixed his eyes on Isaako once more and practically growled, "You may change your name, but it will never change who you are."

Isaako couldn't help the smile that played on his lips. He knew it was meant as a curse, but the statement was filled with more truth than Gamba realized. The Empire might have captured him and sought to redefine his identity for over two decades, but now, he knew who he was, and he knew who he served. He was already victorious.

Chapter 29

C HARLOTTE DESCENDED THE LADDER to the Sahemy underground base cautiously, feeling for each rung as she pulled the hatch shut above her head. She counted ten rungs to the ground—maybe Sonos and his attention to detail were starting to rub off. The floor was unyielding, hard as stone, and a cool draft whispered against her skin. The space was shrouded in inky darkness, and Charlotte hesitated to disrupt it with the bright glow of her gazer.

She retreated a few steps, her back pressing against the rough rock wall. Her fingertips brushed the wall near the ladder, searching for a hidden torch, but found nothing. As her eyes adjusted to the dark, the area began to take shape. She had a foreboding sense of the tunnel's walls closing in on her. She couldn't shake the sense that something was watching her—the underground lair buzzed with technology.

Charlotte calmed her racing heart and focused. She couldn't walk blind, so she pulled her hand deep into the sleeve of her jacket, trying to shroud the light from her gazer-ring as much as possible.

The tunnel lay empty, and Charlotte breathed a sigh of relief. Though, admittedly, she couldn't see very far in either direction.

A blinking red notification popped up on the dashboard. *Is it a message from Jax?* She dared to hope. Or maybe it was a notice that Sonos had been captured. While that would be an issue, at least he'd be with his brother, and Taine and Taimani would be okay until Ava and Lily could help devise a plan to save all of them.

But before she could open the message, heavy, echoing footsteps shattered the cavern's silence. Charlotte swiftly turned off the gazer, praying she hadn't been spotted. As light approached from around a distant corner, she retreated further into the shadows, wrapping Seena's scarf around her head and lowering face to blend into the darkness.

"I thought those sensors were fixed," a deep voice grumbled.

"How many times have we told that shepherd boy to keep those blasted sheep away from this part of the lake?" a woman replied. "We're stretched thin as it is having to watch over those prisoners."

Charlotte's ears perked up. Her sisters were likely with those prisoners. She crouched and moved closer to try and catch sight of what was happening. With any luck, maybe she could follow these two Sahs back to where the prisoners were being held.

A red-robed figure climbed the ladder. "The hatch is secure," the deep voice huffed, then descended back down the ladder. "We need to tell Joanie to test them again."

Charlotte tried to recall the significance of the red robe. She thought it was the tech group.

The other red-robed figure, smaller and more agile, turned in her direction, and Charlotte's heart jumped into her throat. She crouched even lower, ready to sprint away if they came any closer.

"Dee, come on. We don't have time to search," the deep voice called out. "The hatch is secure, and we must return to the prisoners."

Dee's face was shadowed, but she was still facing in Charlotte's direction, unmoving. Charlotte sensed that this Sah wanted to hunt rather than go back and guard the prisoners. But eventually,

Dee turned to her companion and headed back the way they had come.

Although it felt reckless, Charlotte knew she had to follow this pair back to the prisoners. She moved as stealthily as she could, following the Sahs. Her heart pounded in her chest, but her leather boots—a gift from the Mountain Kingdom—made no sound on the stone floor.

The Sah's light disappeared around a corner. Charlotte picked up speed, even in the pitch black. She couldn't lose them.

She kept her hand running along the stone wall, trying to keep her bearings. But as soon as she rounded the corner, she crashed straight into something—or rather, someone.

"I knew it!" Dee's voice sounded familiar as she grabbed Charlotte's arm. "I knew Joanie had fixed those sensors."

A blinding light pierced the darkness, and Charlotte tried to shield her eyes. Dee's grip was like iron.

Charlotte's heart went into panic mode, but her mind had a crystal-clear thought. *I must take her down before she alerts anyone else that I'm here.* With no hesitation, she threw her body against Dee's, slamming her into the wall—or at least where the wall should have been.

To Charlotte's shock, the wall gave way, and they tumbled onto the floor of another passageway or an inner room. She didn't have time to figure out what happened to the wall. She needed to focus on getting Dee's gazer.

Hand-to-hand combat was not Charlotte's thing, but adrenaline rushed through her veins. She recalled the minimal survival training that Jax had taught her from his days with the Freedom Fighters. And hopefully, she was fighting a Sah trained in technology, not fighting. She might have a chance.

Charlotte sprawled on top of Dee, who was taller but not much bigger.

Dee's eyes widened with recognition as she gazed at Charlotte whose scarf had come loose in their tussle.

Stop her before she screams or communicates through her gazer, Charlotte told herself and focused. She used her hips and legs to keep the woman pinned to the hard, stone floor. She made sure to keep a firm grip on Dee's wrists, and then Charlotte slammed her forehead into Dee's nose—as hard and fast as possible.

There was a sickening crack, and Dee gasped, her eyes rolling back as she slumped, blood streaming from her crooked nose.

Charlotte paused momentarily, catching her breath and rubbing her aching head. Pain throbbed from the impact, but it had done the trick. Dee's chest still rose and fell with a steady rhythm; she was out cold.

"Dee! Where are you?" a deep voice called out, though it was muffled.

Dee's gazer continued to emit a soft light. Charlotte glanced around, realizing they were in a new, smaller passageway, likely behind a false wall.

Charlotte grabbed Dee's gazer, swiftly accessed the holographic dashboard, and disabled all tracking and communication. Hopefully, it would buy her a little more time.

There was no option but to move forward, and Charlotte set off down the hidden passageway, determined to put as much distance as possible between her and Dee. She tried to control her breathing, but now she could feel the danger that lurked around every corner.

Then, she remembered the notification that had popped up on her gazer-ring. She crouched against the hard, smooth wall, trying to catch her breath as she flipped through the messages. She only hoped that Jax was having better luck. But the message wasn't from Jax.

CHAPTER 30

S AL TIGHTENED THE STRAPS on Sonos' ankles, pulling the leather tight against the open burn from where Dissolution had reached his skin.

Sonos bit his lip, determined not to cry out in pain or give Sal any satisfaction.

"Grand Magus will not be pleased, not at all," the big man muttered.

"I have to get to my brother," Sonos pleaded. "Lives are on the line." But it was his nerves talking. He knew that Sal would not go against Grand Magus.

Sal turned away from Sonos, moving the chair and all other furniture to the far side of the room, and ensuring nothing was within arm's reach of the slab. He then placed the stack of paper from Grand Magus and a writing instrument on the table where Sonos was strapped down. "I suggest you start writing. You don't want to anger Grand Magus further. He is known to have been the one who tutored Baku in the art of... finding information."

An involuntary shiver went down Sonos' spine. Baku had been notorious and rightly feared throughout Pergamum for his torture techniques. *Grand Magus had taught him?*

Sal sat against the far wall near the door and crossed his arms. He didn't take his eyes off Sonos, and his frown was pronounced even through the thick beard.

Sonos shifted his gaze to the blank paper before him, his heart pounding. Taine and Taimani's lives depended on him. He needed a plan. With hands trembling slightly, he pulled his journal from inside his cloak and flipped through the pages.

"Just start at the beginning," Sal commanded. The Sah's orb floated across the room to hover above Sonos' head.

The orb was unnerving. Sonos had never seen anything like it. But he refocused on the problem before him and pressed Grand Magus' pen to the paper provided. His thoughts were far from coherent.

Sonos began scribbling random characters on the paper, pretending to write something meaningful. He knew it was futile, but he had to maintain the illusion that he was cooperating. As he wrote, he tried to come up with a plan, a way to escape this dire situation and get to his brother before his friends were executed.

The door to the room creaked open.

Sonos' heart sank as Grand Magus entered, a malevolent smile playing on his lips.

"Ah, Sonos," Grand Magus sneered, his eyes filled with malice. "I hope you've been making progress on that translation."

Sonos swallowed hard—his throat dry. He couldn't afford to show weakness.

Grand Magus approached the table, his gaze fixed on the paper before Sonos, and a frown formed on his face. He leaned in close, his cold breath brushing against Sonos' ear as he whispered. "You see, time is a precious thing. And it's slipping away, second by second." He stepped back, his eyes boring into Sonos. "You have one last chance. Cooperate willingly, and you'll get to your brother before sunrise tomorrow. Refuse, and you'll watch your friends be executed, knowing it's all your fault."

Fresh guilt alongside panic coursed through Sonos. What could he possibly do?

In a rush of impulsiveness, Sonos flung the stack of papers at Grand Magus. The pages fluttered, causing just the distraction he had hoped for. He grabbed at the leather straps to pull them off. Sal had been muttering complaints at Sonos when pulling them tight, but from what Sonos had observed, there hadn't been any incantations or use of the dark realm.

His bet paid off, because the straps came loose, and he was able to roll off the table. Sal was already barreling towards him, but Sonos scrambled towards the table where the vials sat. His chemistry lessons had been limited, but he prayed they were enough.

Sonos desperately searched for anything he could use. His eyes fell on a shelf filled with strange concoctions and ingredients. He grabbed a handful of powdered herbs and tossed them into a nearby flame, creating a burst of smoke and sparks that quickly filled the room.

Blindly, Sonos stumbled towards the door, his breath ragged and his heart pounding in his chest. He couldn't see where he was going, but adrenaline fueled his movement to escape.

Just as he reached the door, Sal lunged from behind, his massive hand closing around Sonos' throat. Sonos gasped for air, his vision swimming as he fought to break free.

Grand Magus loomed in the smoky haze already fizzling out, his malevolent grin never fading.

"You can't escape, Sonos," Grand Magus hissed. "You're playing a dangerous game."

Desperation lent Sonos strength, and he elbowed Sal with all his might, forcing the big man to release his grip. Sal stumbled backward, gasping for breath, and Sonos made a break for it, grabbing the door's handle. This time, the door opened, and Sonos was thankful it wasn't sealed shut with sorcery.

"Enough!" Grand Magus shouted, and the door slammed shut before Sonos could squeeze through.

Sonos tried to tug it open, but it didn't budge. In frustration, he banged his fist against the hard wood, letting out a guttural cry. Why could he not get out of this room? For so long, he had evaded his brother. Now, all he wanted to do was reach him, which had become utterly impossible.

His anger transformed into raw fear when he noticed a shadow in the shape of a dragon slither up the door and reach out toward him. He spun around in a panic but ran straight into Sal, who blocked any retreat. His mind raced, searching for something from the journal to shout, but before the words could form, he felt a coldness tighten around his throat, making it hard to breathe.

"You chose this, Sonos." Grand Magus stood, eyes narrowed and sparking with pure hate. "Take him to the table and ensure it is *properly* secured this time," he instructed Sal.

"No..." Sonos tried to shout, but it came out as nothing more than a whisper.

Neither man paid him any mind.

Sal's rough hands strapped him by both the wrists and the ankles this time.

The shadow still constricted his throat, allowing Sonos to breathe, but making him unable to talk.

Grand Magus strode over to the slab, hands clasped behind his back. "It didn't have to be this way. But your decision not to follow simple instructions, and to try to run away at every turn, is beyond tiring. You will stay here until morning, and we'll see if you find any more motivation after the deaths of the Kimwaki warriors. Perhaps Charlotte, captured and with her life on the line, will do the trick..."

Sonos' eyes went wide with fear. How far was Grand Magus willing to take this? How many friends would he lose?

He struggled against the bonds, tried to shout, tried to do anything... but the shadow only squeezed harder, putting Sonos on
the verge of blacking out.

Grand Magus turned and calmly walked out through the door,
which opened for him.

CHAPTER 31

C HARLOTTE DREW IN A few ragged breaths as she crouched against the stone wall in the narrow passageway. Her fingers trembled slightly as she opened the notification from her gazer-ring. It was from Tuvo—King Mason's advisor from the Mountain Kingdom.

"If you're reading this, it means you are in the Sahemy underground base," the message read. *"Friends of the Mountain Kingdom put themselves at great risk in sharing this information, so this message is programmed to come through only if you find yourself in the Sahemy tunnels. If you're there, you'll most certainly need this map. Before you wonder, know that while we have friends inside their lair, most of the Sahemy you will meet will be allied with the Emperor, the Grand Magus, or any number of rising factions within the Empire. Give no one your trust easily. Be safe and listen carefully for the unseen realm to guide you. Be bold and courageous; do not be discouraged. El goes before you, always."*

Charlotte read the message twice to make sure she understood. The Sahemy had followers of *El* inside, though there were no clear instructions on how to find them. At least now she had a map.

Another nervous glance at her surroundings showed her she was still very much alone, so she removed the ring and placed it on the tunnel floor. Now, she had two hands free to use, even as she tried to continue blocking as much light as possible by hovering over the holographic dashboard.

Charlotte scanned through the file with the map, zooming in and out as needed. She then pulled up a command prompt and typed in some code to overlay her location on top of the map. A slight smile pulled at her lips as she entered her "zone," as Jax would call it.

At the thought of Jax, Charlotte's lips pulled tight. She pulled up their message thread. Still no replies to the message she had sent previously. She hastily typed a new one, "*WHEY YUH DEH?*" Asking where he was in Jamroq parlance.

Focusing again on the task at hand, Charlotte looked back at the map of the underground lair. Where could hundreds of prisoners, or any large group of people, fit? She didn't expect that the Sahemy underground base had been designed to house prisoners, based on what Seena had said. Moving them here seemed more like a rash decision from Ade.

She checked the time on the gazer—it was almost midnight. Sunrise was only hours away.

Had Sonos made it back to his brother? She only hoped so. Her stomach tightened into a ball of stress as she worried about Taine and Taimani... *You never should have turned yourself in!* Charlotte's anger simmered as she mentally scolded Taimani. But worrying wasn't helping. She pulled herself back to what she could control—finding her sisters. And she had to trust that Sonos would find a way to reach his brother in time.

"Oh, this looks promising," Charlotte whispered, zooming in on a room much larger than any other. It didn't seem far from where she was currently.

The passageway she was in ran parallel to the broader main tunnel. She wondered at the purpose of this smaller passageway.

Was it for emergencies? That didn't seem likely as, for the most part, it was only wide enough for one person, and most men would need to bend their heads and hunch their shoulders to walk through it. Were they spying on their own, then? Or maybe it was built by some nefarious group within the Sahemy?

At this moment, Charlotte was just thankful it existed. It was no small miracle that she had fallen into this hidden track. Charlotte smiled at the thought and mused on the last line of Tuvo's message. *"El goes before you, always."* She'd heard that numerous times over the journey, and yet again, it was proving true.

"Ade, you have no idea who you're messing with," Charlotte spoke to the air. He thought he was fighting her and Sonos, but really, his battle was against *El*. This knowledge was incredibly comforting.

Charlotte put the gazer on the dimmest light setting possible, slipped it back on her finger, and headed toward the large room.

In, out... in, out... Charlotte carefully controlled her breathing as she made her way through the cramped, darkened passageway.

I can do this, she told herself firmly. But her nerves still jangled with fear. This cramped tunnel was her only way forward, the only path that might lead to her sisters. She had to keep going, regardless of how her heart raced or her chest constricted.

The darkness seemed to swallow her meager light completely. She kept imagining things lurking just out of sight. Was the tech monitoring her somehow? Would a guard jump out at her around the next corner? What about living shadows like in the Badlands? And Rapha was no longer here to protect her...

Stop it! She admonished herself. It was just her imagination running wild.

The tunnel went on endlessly. How long had she been down here already? Surely, she had to be getting close to the large room on her map. But who knew what awaited her even if her sisters were in the big room?

Panic clutched at her chest again. No, she couldn't let the darkness and worry play tricks on her mind. She would not succumb to fear.

Drawing on every last reserve of courage, Charlotte forced herself to keep placing one foot in front of the other. Her sisters needed her. She would not be lost here forever.

Finally, when it seemed the passage might continue forever, her outstretched hands met smooth stone. She had reached the end. The door to the large room must be here. She checked the map on the gazer-ring, and the dot showing her location was blinking right outside where the room should be—but there was a literal stone wall in front of her.

Charlotte frantically ran her hands along the stone, searching for a way to open it. Her heart pounded with anticipation. Was she about to find her sisters? Or some new danger?

There! A tiny rivet just barely protruded from the wall. Holding her breath, Charlotte turned off her gazer-ring and pressed it. A soft click sounded, and part of the stone swung inward. She had found the door! The Sahemy must have devised a material that looked and felt like stone to the touch, or else they had powerful tech to move the stone door quietly and lightly. Charlotte was impressed but had little time to dwell on the door. Life was on the other side—she could hear the heavy breathing and shifting of many bodies.

She stuck her face to the crack in the door and peered through. The cavernous room was just as big as she expected but covered in darkness. Only a single torch—or some Sahemy-designed light source—on the far side of the room gave her a sense of the size.

And it was packed full of sleeping people. *The prisoners!* Charlotte thought excitedly. She had found them. Were her sisters right here in this very room?

Charlotte quietly eased herself through the crack and closed the secret door behind her. She crouched into a squat, trying to survey the room.

Where to start? She wondered to herself.

But before she could make a move, a hand reached out and grabbed her ankle.

CHAPTER 32

S ONOS HAD NEVER FELT such a deep sense of abject failure. Every single effort to escape from Grand Magus had landed him no further than the door. Now, he was strapped to the table with every bit of sorcery known to man—not to mention an unblinking, unwavering glare from Sal and his strange orb.

He had failed. Wholly and utterly failed. Taine and Taimani would be executed in mere hours, and there was nothing he could do about it.

He fought back a well of tears. They deserved better—more than his frustration.

In a moment of weakness, he had wanted to ask Sal to give him something to knock him out again. But even now, in the throes of exhaustion, he refused to close his eyes and accept sleep. If nothing else, he would stay these hours awake in solidarity with the warriors, even if they would never know.

The orb flew over the length of Sonos' body, hovering as if taking measurements or making some assessment. He was sure that whatever the Sah was looking for, Sonos had nothing to offer.

What more could he have done? Sonos wondered. He reviewed every escape effort, criticizing things he had done, and wondering what else he could have tried. Why hadn't he just run away from Sal when he had first encountered him in the hidden passage?

There are so many different decisions that he could have taken but hadn't.

With his wrists bound tight, he couldn't write out his thoughts, which meant that they just simmered and stewed endlessly in his mind.

He even thought back to the cave in the Badlands, where he had hesitated to jump, giving Wylder enough time to get through the barrier and immobilize Taine. Why had he abandoned his friend?

Voices sounded from the hallway—shouts.

Sonos turned his head groggily towards the door. Was he dreaming?

Sal frowned, calling the orb back to rest on his shoulder.

Moments later, the door banged open; two Elites entered with their swords drawn and glowing blue.

Sal stood, and the orb flickered, barely perceptible. The Elites' swords immediately stopped glowing. That was incredible. Sonos had never seen anything stop or jam the technology that infused the weapons. What kind of sorcery or tech were they developing down here?

The Elites looked at each other equally confused but kept focused. They scanned the room and then took up positions at the opposite ends of Sonos' table.

Two Sahs—one in a red robe and the other in purple—scrambled into the room, their backs to Sonos. They were trying to stop the man with a loud voice from entering.

"Please, sir, it'll be just a moment until Grand Magus can see you, and he can explain," one of the Sahs tried to say.

"I will not be delayed. Let me see your captive immediately," the man demanded.

Sonos' stomach dropped. He knew that voice. And it did not belong to a friend.

A floppy hat towered over the protesting Sah.

Wylder.

He pushed aside the two Sahs blocking the door, and his dark, narrow face broke into a mirthless grin as he locked eyes with Sonos. "It *is* you," he said, walking slowly to the table. "The whole Empire is searching for you in every nook and cranny, and here you are right under our nose."

Even though he hated Wylder with every fiber of his being, Sonos found a spark of hope igniting. Wylder was working with Ade. Maybe his nemesis could be the one who could break him out of this bondage.

Wylder spun around to face Sal. "I demand that this rebel be unbound and released to me."

Wylder labeling him a rebel was not a great sign—but at this point, anything to get him to his brother before sunrise.

Sal cleared his throat. "Grand Magus will—"

"Maybe I didn't make myself clear," Wylder interrupted, his voice lowering. "I come to you in the name of Emperor Ade, and I will take Sonos with me now." He turned to the Elites and motioned for them to cut Sonos bonds.

They used their swords to try and cut the straps, but nothing happened.

"What happened to your swords? Where's the tech?" Wylder snapped the questions out.

"They won't work against sorcery, I'm afraid." Grand Magus strode to the center of the room.

"Release the rebel to me now." Wylder's voice dripped with warning.

"He will most certainly be delivered to the Emperor, of course. But we are working to extract some valuable information for the Emperor." Grand Magus stood unmoving, his hands clasped behind his back. This was his domain, and he knew it.

The other two Sahs had scrambled to stand beside Sal near the doorway. Wylder held his ground near Sonos with the two Elites.

Sonos knew that Wylder could not overcome Grand Magus' sorcery.

"The Emperor will speak to his brother before any of your *extraction* takes place," Wylder said.

When the Sahs remained unmoving, Wylder continued. "Do you want me to call him now? Perhaps report about whatever technology you're hiding that disrupts his Elites?"

This is a power play—about who can prove themselves most valuable to the new Emperor, Sonos thought. And he was stuck in the middle as a pawn. For once, he was rooting for the wily merchant to succeed with his plans. Although a nagging thought came to his mind—what if Wylder decided to try and extract information from him on his own?

"That won't be necessary," Grand Magus answered after a long pause. He motioned to Sal, and the burly man went to work on Sonos' straps. "We were only trying to be of assistance to the Emperor."

Wylder scoffed in response.

Sonos sat up, rubbing his wrists and ankles, which were raw from the too-tight bonds.

"Let's go." Wylder wasted no time leading the Elites and Sonos out of the room.

"We will see you again, Sonos," Grand Magus said, barely above a whisper, as Sonos passed.

Sonos shivered involuntarily—he felt a truth to the sorcerer's words.

He still didn't trust Wylder's intent, but the priority was to get out of the Sahemy stronghold and get to his brother.

Chapter 33

C HARLOTTE FROZE AT THE sudden touch on her ankle. She nearly yelped but managed to cover her mouth and suck in a sharp breath instead. She tried to turn and face her attacker, but the grip on her ankle was unyielding, and in the process she lost her balance and tumbled to the ground.

She looked around in horror, wondering if the guards or anyone had heard, but no one came running or shouted out. Even the people sleeping nearby didn't stir.

Instead, two dark eyes reflected the low light, catching Charlotte's gaze.

"Who are you?" a female voice hissed, barely audible. But the question was enough for Charlotte to recognize the familiar accent that curled around the words.

"You're from Kimwaki?" Charlotte asked, trying to keep her voice low. She couldn't contain her excitement at having located the prisoners.

"I will not ask again," the warrior said with quiet force. "Who are you?"

Now that Charlotte's eyes had adjusted better to the room, she could see the warrior more clearly, especially considering their faces were practically touching in an effort to speak as low as possible. The warrior had the same charcoal around her eyes that Taimani favored, and the same dark hair put into two braids.

"I'm a friend." Charlotte pulled the scarf down from her face as a goodwill gesture.

"You have a way out for us?" the woman asked.

Did she have a way out? She didn't want to give away knowledge of the map so easily. *Don't underestimate these warriors*, Charlotte reminded herself.

"I... am here for my sisters first," Charlotte hoped that would be enough. She really should have thought this through and expected the mistrust of the warriors. Why couldn't she have found the Jamroq prisoners first?

"Sisters? They're from Kimwaki?"

"Jamroq," Charlotte corrected. She was giving a lot of information—more than she wanted, but she didn't see another way. "Are the Jamroq prisoners here?" she asked, trying to take control of the conversation.

"I'm the one asking the questions." The warrior leaned her face in even closer, almost touching Charlotte's nose. "Are you working with Sonos and the rebel girl?"

How should I answer that one? Charlotte wondered to herself. At least the warrior hadn't identified her as Charlotte yet... but would her working with Sonos be seen as favorable?

"Yes," Charlotte decided on the truth—though she omitted adding that *she* was the rebel girl.

The warrior held her gaze as if daring Charlotte to lie. After a moment, she motioned to the ground. "Keep low and follow me."

Charlotte's mind raced as she followed the warrior through the maze of straw mats and sleeping people. She sensed that some were awake and watchful, but no one moved. Was this warrior about to turn her over to the Sahemy? Or help her find her sisters?

The warrior stopped next to a large form lying on a mat in the dead center of the room. She leaned close and whispered in Kimwakian, and then there was some back and forth that Charlotte couldn't understand.

The large form moved and crawled toward another even more massive form nearby.

The warrior who had escorted her this far stayed with Charlotte, forcing her into a prostrate posture flat on the hard stone floor.

This is not good, Charlotte thought. She had a distinct feeling of being caught, not helped. She suddenly remembered Taimani recounting how the chief from the tower had betrayed Sonos and Taine to gain favor and leverage with the Emperor, Sonos' father. *This is definitely not good.*

A knot of worry grew inside Charlotte. Surely, she hadn't come this far just to get caught now. As her thoughts spun, she adjusted her posture on the mat and got ready to flee. But as soon as she lifted herself, a strong arm pushed her down from behind. She sucked in a breath as she hit the floor—this warrior-guard was equally as strong and quick as Taimani.

"Come." The one who had gone to talk to the enormous form had returned for her. He now beckoned her to follow him toward the large one, who Charlotte could only guess was the chief.

Maybe this will go better… Perhaps he feels bad about betraying Sonos before, and will help me now. After all, I'm trying to rescue some prisoners. Charlotte tried to stir up some hope inside herself, but it was fleeting.

As soon as she reached the chief, or the one she assumed was the chief, he sat up and slapped a meaty hand on her shoulder, and a bright red light shot straight up to the ceiling.

Shocked, Charlotte tried to cover the light with her hand—the guards would see it. But she was quickly pulled away, and her arms were locked behind her back.

Panic rose; this posture brought back memories of the night her sisters had been taken in Jamroq. *"No one fights the Empire and wins."* The haunting words replayed in her mind.

Had she come so far only to realize that truth now? That she could never win?

"What have you done?" Charlotte asked the chief, horrified. She hadn't even had a chance to talk, explain, or ask questions.

Others started stirring from their sleep, and whispers filled the room.

"A life for a life." The chief's deep voice was soft but slammed into her like a brick wall. "I was given this marker for if you or Sonos ever made contact. I am sorry, young one, but you all have made your choices. Though through your life, one of my own will be freed." He paused. "It may be enough to save Taine and Taimani—even if their capture was their own fault."

Anger boiled up in Charlotte. "You believe that monster? Do you think you'll be free? And who gives you the right to make that choice?" Charlotte spat out the questions. Tears of frustration welled in her eyes.

"Do you even know why I'm here?" Charlotte continued, staring at the dark form of the sitting chief. She had gotten so *close* to her sisters. So close!

Two robed figures with lights emitting from their gazers strode through the doorway on the far side of the hall. They started making their way towards the chief's beacon.

"My sisters were taken from Jamroq. They're here, too. I was going to set you *all* free." Charlotte's hands were balled into fists, and she squirmed against the warrior. She cursed Taimani's decision to run off. If she had been here, things may have gone very differently.

"No one can set us all free." The chief shook his head.

As the lights held by the Sahs grew closer, Charlotte thought she caught a look of remorse—or perhaps it was only pity—in the chief's eyes. Whatever it was, he did nothing to stop the Sahs from standing her up and taking her away. They half dragged her through the maze of mats. No one was sleeping now.

Charlotte searched the room desperately, hoping to at least spot her sisters. But everyone here had the long, soft curled hair and muscled bodies of those from Kimwaki. The prisoners must have been sorted by tower. Everyone here would be loyal to the chief. There was no one to save her.

"What about my trade?" the chief stood and called after the Sahs.

One of the robed men who looked like he hadn't seen the sun in years turned. "Trade?" he asked.

"For turning in one of the rebels, one of my own gets to go free." The chief crossed his arms.

The two Sahs exchanged a look.

"Uhm, sure. Yeah. We'll... uh, get back to you about that," the pale one said. They shifted nervously.

There was no way the Sahemy would be releasing any prisoner. Even Charlotte could tell.

A flash of anger crossed the chief's eyes. "*Au, 'ia e fa'atosina i latou!*" he called out, loud and clear.

Charlotte had no idea what the chief had commanded, but ten warriors jumped to their feet and surrounded Charlotte and the two Sahs that held her. Hope flared up within her. If she had all the prisoners from Kimwaki Tower with her, she'd be able to save her sisters.

"Stop!" the same pale one said. He held out his wrist, which showed a holographic red button. "This room is rigged with chemicals that can be triggered with a push of this button."

Charlotte immediately scanned the ceiling for any signs of where the chemical might come from. But it was too dark to tell. And, truthfully, she wasn't knowledgeable enough to know all the Sahemy's tools.

The threat seemed real enough to the warriors, though. They froze where they were. Unfortunately, chemical warfare is precisely what had defeated the great warrior nation decades before, so there were deep-rooted fears. Charlotte couldn't blame them.

She caught the chief's gaze and gave a brief nod. She'd go. She couldn't communicate that she would still help them if she could find a way, but she hoped the eye contact and nod of respect would at least signal that she wasn't resentful. Angry? Yes. But she couldn't hate the man for trying to protect his people.

The Sahs backed out of the room, Charlotte in tow. The pale one kept his arm extended with the red button visible, even as his arm trembled visibly.

She told herself that although they might have the upper hand at the moment, they were not infallible. She'd find her way back here one way or another.

Once outside the room and into the wide tunnel, the Sahs exhaled and barricaded the door.

"That was too close," the darker one who held Charlotte said.

"Savages," the pale one spat out. He shifted his gaze to Charlotte. "As for this one... It seems Sonos is already on his way to Emperor Ade, so they want her kept here as a high-stakes prisoner."

Charlotte closed her eyes in momentary relief. She was sad Sonos had been caught, and she wasn't happy to be a prisoner herself, but at least Taine and Taimani wouldn't be executed at sunrise.

The one holding her grunted. "I don't like all this prisoner guard stuff. We're scientists."

Charlotte opened her mouth, willing to take a risk and see if they might help her. Her sister, after all, had won an award for her brilliant math and science mind. Maybe if these scientists knew the value and capability of the prisoners, they'd be more willing to talk as equals. "I have an idea," she said brightly.

The pale guard seized that moment to tie a gag tight around her mouth.

Charlotte choked, taken aback by his sudden forceful action.

"We may not be guards, but we certainly don't need any chatter from you," he said, ensuring the gag wouldn't move.

Charlotte tried to take short breaths to calm her nerves. Her anxiety was on the rise again. The closer she got to her sisters, the further away she felt.

You have touched one who is unconquerable. The line from Rapha's poem broke through her spiraling worries. She repeated the words to herself, even though they felt far from her reality as the two Sahs led her through the maze of tunnels.

She was shoved into a small cell, and a metal door with vertical bars separated her from freedom. She wanted to cry.

Be strong and courageous; do not be discouraged. El *is with you wherever you go.* Charlotte repeated the words in her mind. She closed her eyes and rehearsed those promises despite what the physical environment told her.

At least her arms were free, and she removed the gag from her mouth.

The Sahs' footsteps faded down the long hallway, and along with them went the light. Charlotte sat in the otherwise empty cell in complete darkness.

"Did you see that gyal? Did you recognize her?" A very familiar voice in a very familiar accent asked from nearby.

It was muffled, but Charlotte would recognize her sister's voice anywhere.

CHAPTER 34

AFTER MORE TURNS THAN Sonos cared to make in an endless walk underground, Wylder finally led the way out of the mouth of a cave into the starlight.

Sonos breathed an immediate sigh of relief—it wasn't sunrise yet, even though his internal clock knew it was less than an hour away. He still had time to get to Ade.

A K'Luma carrier was waiting for them.

A bit extravagant, Sonos thought. But then again, who knew where Wylder had been searching for him? And at least it would get them to his brother fast.

One of the Elites prodded Sonos with the tip of his sword, which was back to glowing blue. A jolt of electricity shot through him—only for a moment, just long enough for a show of power, not to paralyze him.

Sonos grunted, then followed Wylder into the carrier.

They took off immediately and flew the short distance to the palace courtyard.

Ade was waiting when they disembarked. He walked forward and threw an arm around Sonos. "Welcome home, little brother."

Sonos pinched himself. Had Grand Magus drugged him with a new concoction, and this was all a dream? What was happening?

Ade led Sonos away from the courtyard. But not before turning his head around and shouting to Wylder. "You kept your word. I'm impressed. We'll talk later."

Sonos knew there had to be an ulterior motive with Wylder—thankfully, it aligned with Sonos' own goal this time.

"You've been gone so long, I was starting to worry," Ade continued when it was just the two of them. Despite the calm words, there was a sinister gleam in his eyes.

Fetu, Ade's Elite bodyguard, walked a few paces behind them.

"Where are my friends?" Sonos demanded, not wasting any time and not interested in playing whatever game this was.

Ade chuckled with a cruel edge to his voice and draped his arm around Sonos' shoulder. "They're all safe and sound. Don't worry."

He couldn't trust his brother. "I want to see them."

"Tsk, tsk," Ade cajoled. "You haven't been back more than a few minutes and already so demanding." His eyes softened. "But come, that crazy Sah has hurt you, and it's time to be refreshed."

Ade led the way to the Ti're River and the baths nestled beside it.

A line of attendants awaited them, even at this early hour.

"We have important matters to discuss," Ade said. "But first, you deserve a rest, and I have the best healers on hand." His brother wasted no time slipping out of his clothes and into the warm, scented water.

Sonos hesitated, remembering the last time he was here at the baths with Ade and their father. That was the day that Sibi had been mercilessly beaten, the day that everything had changed.

"Allow me, Highness," a gentle voice said, pulling back the edge of Sonos' cloak.

Sonos wanted to see his friends and ensure Taine and Taimani were safe. But Ade was already in the water, and Sonos *was* in desperate need of a bath. He allowed the servants to help him undress and ease into the pool. The scents of frankincense and myrrh filled his senses, reducing the pounding in his head.

He closed his eyes, taking a few deep breaths.

A young servant placed a tray nearby, filled with fruit and tea. One of the healers poured steaming water over a mix of herbs and handed the mug to Sonos. The scents of jasmine and mint wafted over him, and the tea warmed his insides as he sipped.

"I've missed you, brother." Ade's voice broke through Sonos' reverie. "It's been far too lonely in the palace with Father gone. And Mother and you both disappeared..." Ade's voice trailed off as he lounged at the edge of the pool, a servant massaging his shoulders.

"You seem to have plenty of company," Sonos said, cracking open his eyes. "And even some new alliances." Sonos wanted to understand his brother's choices.

Ade chuckled. "Who? The merchant? Wylder has his uses, to be sure. But you and I... *we* are meant to rule, little brother," Ade said softly, speaking to the pre-dawn sky, which was already beginning to lighten.

A strong breeze blew off the Ti're, and Sonos sank lower into the warm water. The cold air blowing on his face sharpened his senses. He had to tread carefully with his next question. "Why are you telling the Empire that Father turned into a shadow dragon?"

Ade snapped his gaze on Sonos, a dangerous glint in his eye, which quickly turned into something harder than anger.

Maybe asking was a bad idea after all.

"At the battlefield, when you cursed the Emperor, I was quite... upset," Ade said, his voice eerily calm. "But then I realized maybe you used this new power to get Father out of our way."

"Our way?" Sonos asked, not sure he had heard correctly.

"Did you ever think about it? We were raised our entire life to rule. What did you think our endgame could possibly be?"

A tiny seed becomes a mighty tree. Sonos thought of his mother and the values she sought to embed in him from early on.

Ade's eyes gleamed, perhaps mistaking Sonos' lack of argument for agreement. "Do you realize how many people had fought and tried to destroy the Emperor over the years? And then you come along and defeat him without touching a hair upon his head." Ade's tone held what sounded like genuine admiration.

Sonos was deeply confused. He had never received a compliment from his brother before.

"Everyone here wants something," Ade continued. "And soon enough, they all want the throne. Even Mother was only waiting for the chance to set her barbarians to rule over the Empire. I'm glad she fled."

Sonos cringed. "She was never—"

"You've always held a blind spot where she's concerned," Ade cut off Sonos. "It made you weak before. But that is exactly what makes you perfect for the role."

"The role?" Sonos chided himself for simply repeating the phrases that had him totally bewildered.

"As my advisor," Ade answered, as if it were the most obvious statement in the world.

Sonos rubbed the back of his neck and sat up straight. "I don't understand. You put a price on Charlotte's head, and on mine. You called us rebels. You almost executed Taine and Taimani. And now... you want me to be your advisor?"

What was Sonos missing? A part of him wanted to believe his brother—to believe that this had all been one big misunderstanding.

"All just measures to get you back here. I needed you. You were on the run. What was I supposed to do?" Ade waved his hand flippantly. "But you're here now. And I want you as my advisor.

You don't desire the throne—you never have, all your life, and you didn't try to take over when you cursed our Father."

Sonos hadn't even thought of trying to usurp the Emperor on the battlefield. And the curse hadn't even come from him. Yes, it was spoken through his mouth, but the words—and the power—had come from a different place.

"Baku was untrustworthy, and he believed that Father was still alive. Mother was too loyal to her people. Uzoma is fine, but he is meant for the battlefield." Ade made a point of ticking the names off on his fingers as he talked.

"I thought you made an alliance with Wylder and the merchant class?" Sonos locked eyes with his brother.

"Pfft," Ade shook his head. "That guy is the most ambitious of them all. But he did seem quite connected to you, or at least interested in you." Ade paused and raised his eyebrow. "Almost as much as you seem interested in him." The lines deepened around Ade's mouth.

Sonos shook his head. He didn't want to get distracted talking about Wylder.

"And if I were your advisor," Sonos decided to try another tactic, "what if I told you to stop killing the followers of *El*?" Sonos felt the anger welling again as he thought of Jamin's execution back in Harmony.

Something passed over Ade's eyes at the mention of *El*, but it faded quickly. "You have obviously found a source of great power, brother," he said. "I'd consider relenting on my decree regarding followers of *El*."

Sonos' jaw dropped. Was Ade being serious? Maybe *El* had changed his brother's heart, and this was the right choice to make.

"I want to see what you see." Ade's eyes were clear and focused.

Sonos was speechless, so Ade continued after he took a sip of his spiced wine. "You don't know how hard this past year has been." He gazed into the distance. "When you were in lockdown, the Emperor became even more focused on ensuring I would be strong enough to take the throne. The Empire doesn't know anything other than a strong hand. Even now, ever since we returned to Noiz, the nobles have been prowling and looking for an opportunity to seize power." He shifted his gaze to Sonos. "Father would be proud of my decision."

Something clicked in Sonos. "And what about Mother?"

Ade's voice became rock-hard. "What about her?"

Sonos needed to tread carefully. He didn't want Ade to find out that Sonos had seen her or knew where she was. "Would she be proud?"

Ade shrugged and took another sip of wine. "I've told you so many times. The Empress served as a trophy for Father, nothing more. Like everyone else, she only wanted an opportunity to put her people on the throne. But she's gone now, so all the better."

Sonos balled his fists under the water. His mind was made up. "No," he uttered the simple syllable in a low but firm tone. The sun had begun to rise behind the palace, and the sky was filled with lightening shades of red and purple.

"No, *what?*" Ade demanded, the wildness returning to his eyes.

"No to all of it," Sonos answered. He pulled himself out of the water and started to dry off. "No, I will not aid and abet you by being an advisor. No, you are not a god. And no, our mother is not a trophy. No matter how many times you repeat a lie, it doesn't make it true."

Ade's eyes narrowed, and his body shook as he stood.

Sonos wanted to curse Ade. He wanted to say something to stop the outrage that was about to boil over inside him, but no further words came. He closed his eyes, trying to concentrate and see with his heart, as Lenora had taught him. But nothing came. Not even a breeze.

Nothing except for a sharp punch to the jaw.

Sonos doubled over, stunned.

Ade was standing and shaking his hand, which was still balled in a fist.

Fetu ran over to Ade's side, sword drawn and pointed at Sonos.

"Seize him and throw him in the Emperor's prison!" Ade commanded. "Let him and his friends join Diekololaoluwa and *die* at the towers tomorrow!"

Chapter 35

— · —

"AVA?" CHARLOTTE WHISPERED THROUGH the darkness as loud as she dared, pressing her face against the bars. Given the total darkness she was in, she was scared to venture further back into the cell anyway.

"Charlotte?" Ava's voice made Charlotte's heart flip.

"Char!" Lily's softer lilt echoed from a little further away.

Charlotte wiped at the tears that started making streaks down her cheeks. It really was her sisters! After all this time, after such a long journey. Here at last. She tried to stick her arm through the bars and reach towards Ava who sounded the closest, but it was no use. She couldn't reach anything but air.

"Char, what... what are you doing here?" Ava was never one to beat around the bush.

A fleeting thought passed through Charlotte's mind that someone or some tech could be listening in the darkness. But she had difficulty holding back after waiting so long to see her sisters again.

"I came to rescue you," Charlotte said, trying to keep her voice as low as possible. The silence that followed gave her enough time to reflect on the absurdity of the situation. She had found her sisters, but now all three of them were stuck behind bars in total darkness.

"Don't get me wrong, it's great to see you—" Ava started.

222

"Hear her," Lily corrected from afar. Then added, "We can't see her."

Charlotte didn't have to stretch her imagination to know Ava was giving the biggest eye roll.

"It is so wonderful to hear your voice," Lily said. She had always been the peacemaker of the family. "Tell me, how are Mom, Dad, and Gran?"

The simple question felt like a punch to the gut. "Uhm..." Charlotte stalled. Should she tell them about their mom right now? She couldn't even see their faces. This is not how she imagined sharing the story.

"Something happened," Ava said when Charlotte hesitated for too long.

"Char?" Lily asked with a slight quiver in her voice.

Charlotte sighed. This was not going according to any plan. But she knew her sisters well enough to know they wouldn't let this go until she shared what had happened. "That first year after the Emperor kidnapped you was so hard... on all of us." She paused, trying to choose her words carefully. "We did everything we could to find a way to get to Pergamum, to link with people who could help, anything." Memories of that year flooded her mind—the pain, the tears, the frustration. She should have prepared for this moment with her sisters better. But she had been so focused on just finding them and bringing them home. She had held through so many impossibilities over three whole years that felt like an eternity.

"We tried," Charlotte continued. "But nothing would pan out. Every plan failed. Then, one night, Mom made a desperate decision on her own and convinced Jax's parents—"

"Jaxtyn? The fishing family with the big boat?" Ava interrupted.

"Yes, them. She didn't discuss it with us, but I guess she thought they could at least get her off Jamroq. A fierce storm blew on the night she left, and only pieces of the vessel were recovered over the next few days." Charlotte took a deep breath. "I'm so sorry," she added with a whisper.

One of her sisters sniffed from the other side of the wall.

"Jax went to live with Gran after that," Charlotte continued. "And Dad... he got really depressed."

"Oh, Char. I'm so sorry we weren't there for you and Dad." Lily's voice held no accusations or anger, only sadness and concern.

Charlotte held onto the bars of her cell, wishing she could be with her sisters, holding them close.

"Someone's coming," Ava whispered, breaking the silence.

Soft light spilled around the bend, and Charlotte scampered back to the far corner of her cell, trying to put distance between her and her sisters. She did not want to endanger them any further.

The walls and floor were stone—limestone, perhaps. She didn't know enough about the sciences to tell for sure. A red-robed Sah paused at the opening of her cell and peered in.

Charlotte sat on the floor with her back against the wall and her knees pulled up to her chest. She shielded her eyes, which had become accustomed to the darkness, but had the wherewithal to look around the cell in the dim light. A tattered straw mat was laid out in one corner, and a chamber pot was in the other corner a few feet away. Not a window, crack, or possibility of escape otherwise.

Great, she thought.

The Sah moved from her cell and paused at Ava's cell.

"Did you finally bring some food? Or why yuh passin' here?" Ava shouted at the Sah.

She has always been the brave one, Charlotte thought to herself—proud of her sister's courage.

"You know full well you're on one meal a day as part of your punishment, you ruffian," the Sah snapped back.

The Sah shuffled further down, likely to Lily's cell next. "You could teach your sister some manners; it would help you both."

"Yes, honored one," Lily mumbled.

Charlotte could imagine her sister's head bowed.

The Sah grunted in response, and the light grew dimmer as she moved down the corridor until, finally, it was pitch black again.

"Stop cowering before those fearmongers," Ava chided her sister.

"Stop kicking the beehive," Lily retorted.

Charlotte guessed it was likely an argument they'd had countless times.

"What did you both do to land in here?" Charlotte asked, trying to change the conversation.

"We got caught tampering with some Sahemy sensors, trying to escape with the other Jamroq prisoners down here," Ava said flatly.

"Unfortunately, we don't have your skills when it comes to tech," Lily added. "But you're here now! And surely you have a plan or some friends who can help, right?"

Charlotte's stomach turned at the hope in Lily's voice. She didn't want to disappoint them so quickly. But she hadn't planned to be stuck in a prison with them.

"We caught wind of some famous rebel that the new Emperor is looking for," Ava said. "Seems to be someone Prince Sonos is friends with. Are you working with her?"

Did her sisters know it was her? She didn't know if they had access to see the broadcasts. "Uhm... I am her," Charlotte answered tentatively.

"The rebel gyal?" Ava asked, allowing the Jamroq lilt to come through on certain words.

"You're working with Prince Sonos?" Lily added her question with awe spilling through her voice.

"I... I don't think of Sonos as a prince." Charlotte struggled to organize her thoughts. For some silly reason, she couldn't keep a smile from her face as she talked with her sisters about Sonos.

A low whistle sounded. "Char, it seems we have some catching up to do, you rebel." The pride in Ava's voice was unmistakable.

Charlotte exhaled with relief that her sisters weren't mad. "Yes, we do have a lot to catch up on." They still needed to talk through family stuff, though Charlotte did not want to pick up that thread in this damp, dark prison. "But first, we need to get out of here." Determination brought Charlotte's mind into focus once more.

"So, rebel gyal," Lily chuckled, echoing Ava's new name for Charlotte, "What do you need us to do?"

This moment was so different from what Charlotte had expected. Her whole plan—even from back in Jamroq—had been to get to her sisters and trust they would know what to do. She had even told Rapha as much when he first told her she had to save the Mountain Kingdom. But now she was here, in prison no less, and her sisters expected her to have the answers.

"How much time do we have before the Sah returns to do a prisoner check?" Charlotte asked as she tried to think about what to do next. *Why couldn't Rapha be here when I need him most?* She lamented.

Ava huffed. "About twenty-five minutes. They come every thirty minutes, more or less."

Charlotte tapped on her ring gazer, hiding it deep inside her jacket. The Sahemy wouldn't have known the simple band on her finger was technology. *The know-it-alls don't know everything.* Charlotte allowed the thought to give her courage.

"Hey! Is that light? They allowed you to keep the gazer?" Ava whispered.

Even though Charlotte shielded the gazer inside the flap of her jacket, even the smallest crack of light shone inside deep darkness.

"It's Mountain Kingdom tech," Charlotte answered. "I'll explain later."

Please answer, Jax. I need you... I need someone... Charlotte prayed as she tried to call Jax.

"Char!" An excited yelp came through the gazer.

"Shh," Charlotte tried to use the controls to keep his volume low, but his voice still came across loud.

"I'm not seeing anything, but is that you? You there?" Jax asked in softer tones.

"I... yes. It's me." Charlotte smiled, even though there was no video. "It's... it's so good to hear you. You okay?"

"You have perfect timing," Jax said. "It's been days, but I was just able to sneak away to get some signal. I've been worried sick about you."

"Who are you talking to?" Ava asked.

"I think that's Jaxtyn," Lily said from afar.

"Hey, was that Ava? Did you find your sisters?" Jax's voice perked up again.

"Uhm... kind of—" Charlotte started.

"Char! You did it. You got to your sisters. Your dad and Gran are going to be so happy!"

Charlotte instinctively turned to look behind her, seeing the metal bars. Her cheeks grew warm. She was embarrassed that she was stuck in prison and needed help. "It's a bit more complicated than that," she said. "I found the prisoners in the secret Sahemy headquarters, but then the Kimwaki Chief turned me in, and I got thrown into a prison cell, which happened to be the cell next to my sisters," Charlotte blurted everything out at once.

"Prison?" Jax asked, but he didn't wait for a response. "Char, listen to me. You found your sisters. That's huge. And I guess you're exactly where *El* needs you to be."

Jax's confidence never seemed to waver.

"Did he say *El?*" Ava asked.

Charlotte ignored her sister and kept focused on Jax. "Please tell me you're close to coming and can break us out of here. I could really use some help."

Jax practically growled. "I don't understand what we're waiting for. If I could fly one of their contraptions, I'd be there in a heartbeat."

"Maybe if you explain that we've all been caught..." Charlotte tried to think of what might convince King Mason to come—or at least allow a rescue mission.

"Your dear friend's mom..." Jax paused.

"Uh huh," Charlotte responded, knowing he was referring to the Empress.

"Well, she arrived and has been in deep conversations with the council here." Jax kept the details vague. "I believe they'll get to some consensus soon—it just feels like it's taking forever."

Charlotte let out a slow breath, trying to keep calm.

"I wish I could be there for you, but for now, just keep your eyes and ears open... and I don't mean just your physical eyes. As Sibi likes to say, *El* is always ten steps ahead of the guards."

Charlotte nodded, even though he couldn't see.

"Fight we must," Jax said the words with such confidence.

She knew he was trying to encourage her. "Win we shall," she said by faith, not by what she felt.

"Walk good, and I will see you soon. And big up your sisters for me," Jax said in familiar Jamroq terms, then clicked off the connection.

Silence hung in the darkness once more.

"Char, you have some explaining to do," Ava said.

A bright light flooded the cell from above, and Charlotte covered her eyes in pain.

Ava and Lily cried out as well.

"You *all* have some explaining to do." The same red-robed Sah rounded the corner, her mouth drawn tight into a frown. Her eyes were two different colors—the left was a deep brown, and the right was blue as ice—but they both blazed with anticipation.

CHAPTER 36

A DE'S BODYGUARD, FETU, PUSHED Sonos forward through the gardens and into the palace's open-air hallway while keeping his arms locked tightly behind his back.

He called out to an Imperial guard stationed nearby. Before the guard reached them, Fetu whispered in Sonos' ear, "Find a way to defeat your brother. More are with you than you may believe."

It took practiced restraint for Sonos not to turn his head or acknowledge Fetu's words.

The guard approached, and Fetu instructed Sonos to be taken to the Emperor's prison.

As Sonos was led away to the deepest, darkest, most secure place in the palace, a strange feeling washed over him—hope. He should have been feeling despair and a sense of failure. He had confronted his brother and had only provoked him further. No curse, no other words had come to stop Ade, and now he was being sent to prison. But there was a strong sense that since nothing was going according to Sonos' plan, things must be going according to *El*'s... and that brought Sonos comfort.

The guard led him down a set of winding stairs that acted as a reverse tower that led deep underground. The Emperor's prison was cut from stone, and there was only one way in and one way out—this staircase whose entry was in the heart of the palace.

Sonos wondered what level of paranoia caused his father to keep punishment of perceived dissidents so close to him in the palace. But now he was convinced from Ade's behavior that this palace had claimed another Emperor. He sighed.

Even though the Legacy Tower prisoners and the Sahemy had impressive and unexpected underground building skills, Sonos doubted anyone could infiltrate or form an escape from these cells.

When they reached the bottom of the stairs, he was handed over to the prison guards. These were not mere Imperial guards hoping to one day qualify as Elites. No, the Emperor's prison guards were a class all their own. They wore midnight black uniforms with no adornments.

"Well, now..." The prison guard smiled—an action that twisted the scar running down his right jawline. Sonos immediately recognized him.

Years ago, Ade had insisted that he and Sonos should visit the Emperor's prison. He had said they needed to know every inch of the palace since he would one day be ruling it. On that day, Ade had strode right up to the prison guard with the jawline scar, demanding a tour. The guard had laughed but conceded that this was one of the most important places in the palace, and had proceeded to give a tour that had scared even Ade.

"I'll take it from here," the scarred man said in a scratchy voice that matched his appearance.

"Right, then." The Imperial guard turned and practically ran back up the stairs.

"It's been years, *Highness*." Scarman circled Sonos, looking him up and down. "You boys never returned to visit after the first tour. But no worries, your visit will be a little longer this time."

Sonos kept his eyes fixed forward and his mouth in a tight line, but it didn't stop a shiver that ran down his back. He may have felt a surge of hope aboveground, but in this deep, dark dungeon, it was easy to feel forgotten and powerless.

"You can call me Scar."

Creative, Sonos thought sarcastically but wisely kept the thought to himself.

"For new guests, we like to give a special welcome. Please, follow me." Scar turned and walked deeper into the prison, not even glancing back to make sure Sonos was following.

Sonos briefly contemplated running back up the stairs and finding his brother to try and plead for reason once more… but no. *The only way through is forward*, Sonos thought. Plus, he had a feeling that Taine and Taimani were down here. He had no intention of leaving without them.

Scar tapped some buttons on the holographic image that projected from his gazer. Suddenly, the darkness turned into a painful, blinding light.

Sonos closed his eyes, giving them a moment to adjust. Thankfully, he hadn't been down here for days, weeks, months, or years like some of the other prisoners who cried out in pain at the sudden onslaught of light.

Three other prison guards in the black, unadorned uniforms sauntered over to Scar. They all wore shaded glasses to protect their eyes. Perhaps to even see in the dark, Sonos thought, looking closer at the lenses.

"The royal rebel has finally graced us with his presence." Scar gave a mock bow towards Sonos.

The other three laughed.

"Let's give the grand procession," one of the other guards said with a sneer, pushing Sonos forward down the wide hallway lined with barred cells.

Sonos cringed but bit his tongue to keep from saying anything.

"All hail the rebel, the outcast, the last remaining weakness of the K'Luma line!" The guards taunted Sonos past every cell.

Sonos kept his head down, but his eyes were anything but downcast. He used the opportunity to look for his friends in the light.

The first few cells held pale, emaciated strangers. It was hard to tell whether they were men or women, as their forms were obscured by their arms as they tried to shield their eyes.

Sonos held his breath, worried about how his brave friends might look after even a short time in complete darkness. It would explain the surge of pride he felt when he finally caught sight of Taimani.

She stood erect at the cell's door, unflinching, her hands gripping the bars. A large metal band was fastened tight around her neck and chained to the wall. She looked like a caged lioness. Her face was severely bruised, and her hair had been shorn, but her fierce eyes were unmistakable. She locked eyes with Sonos, presenting an unreadable expression.

He took a step toward her cell, but the prison guard walking behind didn't hesitate to strike him in the back, pushing him forward. "Keep moving!"

Sonos glanced back at Taimani, wanting to offer a word of hope, but he could think of nothing. How was he going to get all of them out of here?

You won't, the thought filled his mind. It was true. There was no plan. *El* was going to have to come through.

Sonos' stomach dropped at the next cell. Taine sat with his back against the stone wall, the same kind of metal band and chain attached to his neck. His bandaged hand was stained a dark red. He barely lifted his bruised and shaved head. There wasn't much fight compared to his sister, but his face was contorted with pain... or anger? Sonos couldn't blame his warrior friend for either.

They needed to get out of here.

The guards shoved Sonos into an empty cell next to Taine's.

Two guards followed Sonos into the cell, bringing it to near capacity. He was shoved against the back wall. He didn't bother fighting against the neck shackle—if both the warriors had to wear it, he couldn't expect any different.

The cold of the metal brought a deep sense of foreboding.

When the guards finished, they stepped out of the cell and slid the metal bars into place with finality.

"Welcome home!" Scar said with a big grin, then pushed a button on his gazer, and the whole place dropped into unnatural pitch darkness.

After a few excruciating minutes, Sonos tried to call out and keep his voice low at the same time. "Taine?"

"Not a word!" One of the prison guards growled, sounding like he stood right outside Sonos' door. He was probably looking at him through those special glasses.

Sonos cursed internally. He couldn't see his hand if he held it inches from his face.

So much for communication, but at least Taine and Taimani were alive, and they were all together. Sonos could take some measure of comfort in that thought. What now though? Even if—no, when—Charlotte got through and found her sisters, how on earth would they break into the palace, find these cells, and rescue everyone down here? The odds seemed impossible.

It might have been his imagination, but hours later—which Sonos measured through unconscious counting—he felt a little furball come up beside him in the darkness. He yelped, imagining rats, but then heard a familiar hum.

CHAPTER 37

C HARLOTTE AND HER SISTERS were taken to a dimly lit, claustrophobic room at the far end of the hall. If it weren't for the fact that the room had a door instead of bars, it could have easily passed for a small cell. A small orb floated in the corner of the room, casting a feeble light but keeping away the complete darkness.

Their captors had confiscated Charlotte's gazer-ring and emptied her pockets. Like her sisters, her wrists were clamped in cold, unforgiving shackles. But as soon as they were left alone, all three stood huddled together, shoulders pressed close, forming a tight circle. Charlotte felt the embrace despite the restraints that kept their arms firmly in front of them.

Warm silence covered them for a few moments; then, everyone started talking at once. Their tears seemed to start falling simultaneously without shame.

"I can't believe I'm here with you two..." Charlotte's voice trailed off, her emotions overwhelming her.

Ava cast a discerning gaze over Charlotte, approval evident in her eyes. "Look how big you've gotten!" Charlotte had been just thirteen when her sisters had been torn away from the family, and three years had wrought significant changes.

Ava's hair was uncharacteristically unruly. Her dark curls were usually tied up in a tight top bun, but now her hair was loosely tied at her neck. Hard lines were etched around her eyes, but the elder of the twins still missed nothing.

Lily, on the other hand, nestled closer to Charlotte, laying her head against Charlotte's shoulder. Her long, soft curls were loose, matching her carefree and loving personality. Charlotte was glad that kidnapping, followed by being locked in a tower and now an underground Sahemy prison, hadn't erased the softness of her sister.

"Is Mom really... gone?" Lily whispered, her head still resting on Charlotte's shoulder.

Charlotte couldn't hide the remorse in her voice. "I'm sorry." Guilt still gnawed at her for not discovering the plan sooner or paying more attention to their mother that fateful night. But she steeled herself and met her sisters' eyes. "But I will keep my promise to Dad and Gran and bring us all back home safely."

Lily stood straighter, and Ava nodded, looking expectantly at Charlotte.

The orb in the corner of the room was tech—Charlotte could practically hear frequencies emanating from it. It likely had a camera or other surveillance tech. She made a point of nudging her head towards it and alerting her sisters.

Ava and Lily caught the meaning immediately. They had been watched and eavesdropped on for a lifetime, even back in Jamroq—but here in the clutches of the Sahemy, the stakes were even higher.

Taking advantage of their precious moments together, Charlotte leaned in, ensuring their backs faced the cameras, and their faces remained inches apart. Though she didn't have a concrete plan, there was something her sisters needed to understand, above all else.

"I know you think *El* is just one of the old, banned deities—a fairy tale," Charlotte began.

Ava's mouth twitched downward, but she didn't interrupt.

Lily's eyes were simply curious.

"Trust me, there is an unseen realm. We've all seen the sorcerers and what they can do." Charlotte paused, waiting for her sisters' acknowledgment.

Finally, Ava nodded, though her skepticism remained in her narrowed eyes.

"What the sorcerers access is just a shadow of the unseen realm—the dark part. *El* is the source of it all."

Lily interjected before Ava could voice her doubts. "Char, you being here, coming all the way from Jamroq, ending up in the cell right next to us, deep in the heart of the Sahemy stronghold? It's enough for me to believe you."

That was a start, but Ava held out, her eyes unwavering and hard. She did not trust or believe in anything easily. She glanced towards the floating orb, then leaned closer to whisper in Charlotte's ear. "I may not see all the pieces, but I know enough to trust that there's *something* bigger at play—bigger than the Sahemy. I give *you* my trust. But I still have a thousand questions."

Charlotte exhaled. She could work with that—knowing that her sisters accepted there was more going on than met the eye. "I will explain everything in due time, but now—"

The door suddenly banged open, cutting off Charlotte's words. The red-robed Sah with the two-colored eyes walked in, a stern expression on her face. She was flanked by two equally determined men in matching robes.

Charlotte's heart pounded as she and her sisters remained huddled together, their shackled hands clinging to one another. She had only just found her sisters, and after a few hours, they were being ripped apart again. She knew it in her gut.

The female Sah pushed Charlotte against a wall, while the other two guards took Ava and Lily in the opposite direction toward the door.

"Where are you taking us?" Ava demanded. Her tongue was always as quick as her anger.

Frustration rose in Charlotte as she tried to figure out what to say. She knew that words had power. Sonos had proved that in the Badlands when he fought the shadow dragon and cursed his father. What was the phrase he had repeated from the commander of *El's* army?

"Those who are with us are greater than the darkness!" Charlotte blurted out, the words coming to her in a sudden rush.

All eyes, including her sisters', fixed on her.

Ava's surprise was palpable, for Charlotte had always been a tinkering techie wallflower in the shadows of her sisters.

Lily was curious, as always, but she spoke first. "Yeah! What she said."

Charlotte allowed herself the slightest of smiles, proud that her sisters were backing her up. Maybe the Sahemy would shrink back in fear like the shadows had done for Sonos.

However, the Sah holding Charlotte only tightened her grip on her shoulders. "What did you say?"

Taking a deep breath, Charlotte repeated the words with unwavering conviction. "Those who are with us are greater than the darkness."

The Sah's lips curled into a tight, sardonic smile. "We'll see about that," she hissed.

That was not the response Charlotte was expecting. She tried to pull away from the brown and blue-eyed Sah, but a sudden shock jolted through the shackles on her wrist. Charlotte cried out in surprise as much as pain.

"What are you doing to her?" Ava's cry rang out.

As her sisters were forcibly dragged from the room, Charlotte struggled to show a glimmer of hope or strength, but her voice was silenced before she could respond.

CHAPTER 38

"**R**APH! IS THAT REALLY you?" Sonos dared to whisper as he reached out his hand in the darkness.

The humming sound drew closer, and Sonos smiled, tuning his heart to the frequency of calm and peace emanating from Rapha.

Soon, the little monkey had found its way to his lap.

Sonos took a deep breath and exhaled slowly. "Thank you for coming, and I'm glad you're okay." He kept his voice as low as possible and rubbed Rapha's head. "You can't imagine what I've gone through to get here. Don't tell me, did you just walk through a portal?" Sonos chuckled softly at the thought. "It's just great to see you," he said again.

Rapha chittered a response.

Even if Sonos couldn't understand the sounds, Rapha's presence brought assurance that Sonos was in the right place at the right time. All of the doubt, the pressure, the adversity, and his multiple failures on this mission, melted from his heart. Here, in the utter darkness, in the deepest, most secure prison, Rapha had come. Sonos knew that *El* was with them.

"Have you been with Taine and Mani?" Sonos asked, hopeful that his friends had been receiving a measure of comfort and strength.

Rapha nuzzled Sonos' hand.

The shackles clanked with even the slightest movements. The metal chafed his neck.

"I don't suppose you have a lock pick or some other way to get me out of these chains?" Sonos muttered.

Rapha just continued humming. He seemed in no hurry to move from his lap, so Sonos closed his eyes to fend off the darkness and waited.

Hours might have passed, or even minutes—Sonos' internal tracking systems were failing in this dark, still place, so he had difficulty counting time and orienting himself.

At one point, he heard faint whispers of conversation. He imagined it was Charlotte's voice, but that was impossible. She couldn't be down here. She had to be safe. *Please let her be safe.*

The lights blared on without warning, and Sonos cried out as the brightness assaulted his senses.

"It's a day of conquest and victory for Emperor Ade; may he be blessed and live forever!" A prison guard shouted.

Sonos cringed at the exact phrase they used to use for his father not so long ago. *Well, he's cursed and certainly will not live forever*, Sonos thought.

In a moment of panic, Sonos thought of Rapha, worried he'd be caught inside the cell, but the monkey was nowhere to be seen.

"O le a le mea o fai e lenei tagata malaia iinei?" Taimani's voice rang out clear and strong.

Sonos wasn't fluent in his mother's tongue, but knew enough to pick up that Taimani was questioning why the new prisoner was down there.

Taine uttered a faint response that Sonos couldn't make out. He worried about his friend. Had his hand become infected? The urgent need to escape from this dark hole grew.

"The former captive, turned captain, turned captive once more is here!" The prison guards continued to call out taunts and mockery.

Could it be...? Sonos shuffled towards the bars of his cell, ignoring the pull and heaviness of the shackle around his neck.

Scar walked slowly by Sonos' cell, a sinister smile playing on his lips. "It is a day of victory for Emperor Ade, indeed!"

Sonos gasped as the new prisoner came into view. "Uncle Die..." His mouth hung open. *What is he doing here?* The last time Sonos had seen his uncle was during a shouting match in the Badlands, and he had shamed Die and had left him to fall on his sword, presumably. Sonos remembered Miss Gemma's words that Die was alive, but seeing him here in the prison...

What had his mother said Die's true name was? *Isaako*, Sonos remembered.

His uncle locked eyes with Sonos for a brief moment as he passed, and something was different. There was no anger or ruthlessness... no malice or bitterness. Instead, there was a spark of knowing—as if they were on the same side.

Sonos ran a hand through his hair, which had grown out significantly since he had shorn it in defiance of his father.

The procession passed, and the bars of the cell beside Sonos' made a grinding sound of metal scraping upon stone.

"Where's your sword and captain's cloak now, Diekololaoluwa?" The prison guards continued mocking his uncle.

"Where's your honor?" They broke out in raucous laughter.

Sonos winced, feeling partly responsible. He had cut his uncle's cloak, knowingly taking his honor, but Sonos had only wanted to escape and get his friends to safety—not to hurt him.

He heard the click of the shackles and instinctively rubbed the metal band around his neck.

"Fight. We. Must!" The words rang out deep, loud, and clear—enunciated with precision and force. It took Sonos a moment to realize they had come from his uncle... from Isaako. Was he with *El* now?

"Win we shall!" Taimani's unmistakable voice shouted the response.

Sonos' chest filled with pride and hope. He remembered the line from his journal. *You have touched one who is Unconquerable.* "Win we shall." He didn't shout it, but the words held weight he could almost feel.

Moments later a tremendous shock jolted through the metal cuff on Sonos' neck. His whole body felt like it was on fire. He gasped, almost blacking out from the instant onset of pain.

The shock lasted only a few seconds, and the prison guards walked up and down the corridor.

"Consider yourselves lucky that we have more guests coming soon," Scar said, stopping momentarily to stare at Sonos. "But have no fear; you will pay for this little insurrection."

Sonos focused on steadying his breath. The metal on his skin seemed to grow heavier, now that he knew the pain and not just the restraint they represented.

He focused his mind on what Scar had said. *Guests?* He wondered. Were there more prisoners to come? He worried again about Charlotte and her sisters. *Please let them be safe...* Maybe his brother was coming down to gloat?

He didn't have long to wait. Two red-robed Sahs raced past Sonos' cell. *Technologists*, Sonos thought. Their hoods were drawn up, and they moved as if they didn't want to spend a second more down in the Emperor's prison than necessary.

He could hear scuffling from Isaako's cell. *What in the Empire is going on?*

One of the prison guards stepped in front of Sonos' cell. He placed a small device on the floor in the hallway. "We wouldn't want anyone to miss the show," he said with a wink.

Sonos' stomach was tied in a tight knot.

"Everything is in place," a voice said from Isaako's cell.

A holographic screen projected from the device the prison guard had placed in the corridor. Ade was front and center on the screen, seated on the Emperor's throne with a smug look on his face—but Sonos also saw the deep lines etched around his mouth and the dark circles under his eyes. The shadow of a dragon slithered down from the ceiling to make constant figure eights along the wall behind the throne.

Sonos frowned. He didn't know where his father was, but he was convinced the Emperor hadn't turned into some silly shadow. It fit Ade's narrative, though.

"Citizens and servants of K'Luma," Ade began. His voice held an edge that matched the hard lines on his face. "It is a day of great victory for K'Luma!" He paused and allowed applause to erupt around him in the throne room.

"Our little problem of the rebels has been solved. Sonos is captured and secured." Ade's mouth pulled together in a tight line.

Sonos knew his brother was upset with Sonos' decision not to serve as his advisor. *But what use is giving advice to fools?* Sonos thought.

"I am the ultimate and unquestioned ruler of the K'Luma Empire."

Is he trying to convince himself?

"But we continue to discover and uproot followers of *El.* Yesterday, right here in Pergamum, an unexpected champion stepped forward on behalf of *El.* One who once served this great Empire but has fallen from favor and now seeks to lead a ragtag, hopeless group."

The pieces started to fall into place.

"See your great champion of *El!*" Ade taunted.

The screen shifted to the Emperor's prison and the cell next to Sonos'.

Isaako was chained at the neck, wrists, and ankles, and his mouth was gagged. Perhaps this last measure was due to Taimani's outburst during the last broadcast. Sonos smiled at the thought.

Despite all the restraints, his uncle held his head high, and his eyes were fixed, staring right into the camera. There was no fear, no worry. Only blazing determination shone through.

Sonos had to blink, thinking he saw an actual flame in his uncle's eyes.

Perhaps Ade was disappointed that he didn't get the defeated champion he had hoped to showcase, because the screen switched back to his brother on the throne. This time, a purple-robed figure with golden cuffs stood beside the elevated throne.

Grand Magus. Sonos' jaw dropped open.

The wizened man looked taller than he had in the underground office. He stood with his hands clasped behind his back and a smug look on his face.

Ade sat up straighter. "It is my decision to accept this prisoner's challenge, and to once and for all demonstrate the ultimate power and authority vested in me by my father, by the dark realm, and by all who serve K'Luma."

"I hope my uncle knows what he's getting into," Sonos whispered to the empty cell, still wondering when and how Isaako got connected to *El.*

Then a thought struck him—it sounded like something Charlotte or Rapha had said before—that Ade had no idea who he was really fighting. Sure, he knew a little about the dark arts through the sorcerers, but that was just a shadow—a tendril of the true unseen realm and the one who created it all. Ade thought he was after Sonos and Charlotte, and fighting rebels. But really, Ade was picking a fight with *El*.

"Tomorrow morning at sunrise, we will gather the power of K'Luma at the Legacy Towers to prove the filth and futility of this religion." Ade paused, and the holographic screen split to show Ade on one side, and his gagged and chained uncle on the other.

"The display will be broadcast to every town square throughout the Empire, and all will know the truth."

The video ended, and the holograph disappeared.

A strange peace washed over Sonos. Even though he understood the dominance Ade was trying to show, Sonos saw through the facade. *El*'s victory was already assured—he could feel it in his bones.

The two robed Sahs passed Sonos' cell, practically running to the stairs. As soon as the sound of their footsteps dissipated, the prison went into dark-out mode once more.

"Emperor Ade, in his wisdom, has declared it our duty to ensure all of you newcomers are fully ready for tomorrow morning." Scar bellowed the words into the darkness. "It'll be quite the show, and all of you will have a front-row seat. You will share in Diekololaoluwa's fate."

Something in the way Scar was talking caused a shiver to run down Sonos' back.

"Your anthem seems to be a call to fight—" Scar continued.

"Fight we must!" A guard chimed in, punctuating the words with laughter.

"Well, let the fighting begin!"

The lights came on again in a flash, and outside Sonos' cell stood an Elite, sword drawn and blue light sparking to life.

It's going to be a very long night. Sonos' heart filled with dread.

CHAPTER 39

"**N**O INTERRUPTIONS!" THE TWO colored-eyed Sah called after the men dragging Charlotte's sisters away.

"Yes, Cap," one of the men replied.

After the men and her sisters disappeared, Charlotte was left alone with Cap. She wasn't sure if the name was short for captain—which would be strange if these Sahs were part of the technology-focused faction of the Sahemy, not the army or guards.

A small table with two chairs was set against one of the walls.

Cap practically growled and told Charlotte to take a seat.

Charlotte complied, her previous surge of courage fading by the moment. She interlocked her fingers and placed her shackled hands in her lap. She tapped her foot, trying to release some of the nervous energy that had built up to overflowing.

Cap eased into the chair across from Charlotte, placing her elbows on the table and leaning close.

Charlotte tried not to shift her gaze between the two colored eyes—she didn't want to anger this woman any further.

"Who are you working with? How many rebels are there? What were you planning with Sonos?" Cap barely allowed a moment's pause after every question.

Charlotte bit her lip, not sure what to say or do. Based on the litany of questions, it didn't seem like Cap expected an answer—yet.

"Who are you?" Cap's voice dropped, and she narrowed her good eye.

Charlotte furrowed her brow. Of all the questions, that seemed the most obvious. Cap had overheard her talking to her sisters and with Jax.

But Cap fixed her gaze on Charlotte, waiting for an answer.

"Uhm, Charlotte," she answered, shifting in her seat.

Cap pounded a fist on the table in an explosive burst of energy. "Who are you?" She practically shouted the question.

Charlotte recoiled in confusion and fear, but she was wise enough to understand that something else was being asked below the surface of the question.

Cap stood and paced the room. "Who are you to threaten the Emperor, to corrupt a high prince, and to spout vicious *lies* about a dead religion?"

Oh. The pieces started to fall into place.

"Silence? That's all you have? You had plenty of chat earlier."

Charlotte swallowed. There was no correct answer—not one that Cap would accept. *I hope Ava and Lily are faring okay*, she thought. Thankfully, they were not part of any plans to stop Ade and would have no intel to offer.

Cap tapped the gazer on her wrist and projected a holographic dashboard.

Charlotte couldn't quite make out the commands Cap entered, but a sudden and fierce shock jolted her entire body out of nowhere. She cried out in pain, her eyes wide with surprise. Just as suddenly as it had started, it stopped.

Charlotte heaved in great gulps of air, trying to reorient her senses. *What was that?*

The electricity had come from her shackles. Her wrists and arms were still convulsing slightly with lingering tremors.

"That was just a taste." Cap's voice was deadly calm. "You will answer my questions, rebel girl." Her eyes sparked with malice. "Who are you?"

"Charlotte King," she whispered. The whole Empire knew this already, so there was no harm in sharing.

Another jolt of electricity.

Charlotte cried out again, the pain intensifying.

"Are you a rebel looking to usurp the Emperor?"

"I..." How could she possibly answer that question?

In her hesitation, another shock.

This time, tears overflowed and ran down Charlotte's cheeks. She would not say anything to implicate her friends, and Cap would not believe anything she said about *El*. But her body was quickly betraying her.

Is this where I die? In this empty cell? Worries came unbidden to Charlotte's mind with every impossible question and every new jolt.

It seemed that Cap knew the science surrounding how much shock to send and how often, because it was painful, but never enough to cause Charlotte to black out—like what the Elites had done to her parents when Ava and Lily were taken.

Thoughts of her parents, Gran, her sisters, Jax, and Sonos ran through her mind. The questions were of no consequence any-more.

How long the interrogation went on, Charlotte couldn't say. Her wrists were raw and bleeding. Her body was numb. The tears streamed as though they had an unending water source—making silent tracks down her cheeks.

At some point in time, the wicked Sah left the room, and Charlotte collapsed face down on the table, shackled hands hanging limp in her lap. She couldn't even muster the energy to whimper. But she did think about her sisters. Were they going through this same horrible interrogation? A part of her hoped that she was being given the hardest time because of her association with Sonos, and the fact that Ade had labeled them as the Empire's most wanted rebels. But another part of her knew they would be considered guilty, even if by association.

The door squeaked on its hinges as it was opened, but Charlotte just shut her eyes. She didn't know if she could take another round of electricity and pain.

A cool breeze ruffled her hair, a hint of jasmine on its breath. Memories of Rapha in the samaan tree, in the cellar of her home, and on the ship to Portemore filled her mind.

The moment of peace didn't last long. Cap strode into the room. "Sit up!" she demanded.

Charlotte tried to place Cap's accent in an effort to keep her anxiety at bay. The woman spoke with a perfect Pergamum clip—almost too perfect, like she was trying to hide her native accent.

"Every living, breathing human in K'Luma is required to watch the Emperor's upcoming broadcast." Cap slapped a small, round device on the table, then sat opposite Charlotte.

Is this some game? Charlotte wondered.

A holographic image sprung up from the small device, and Ade's face filled the screen.

Charlotte half-listened to his words, not wanting to see any more videos of what they were doing to Taine or Taimani. But Sonos had been caught, she reminded herself. Or was it their execution? Panic coursed through her veins.

Ade spoke, and the screen split to show a beat-up Captain Die in some prison cell.

Charlotte gasped. *He's alive?* Then she remembered the Empress and Miss Gemma talking about Die. What did they say his name was? Isaako? He's fighting against Ade? Does Sonos know?

The questions swam around in Charlotte's mind, but she sat up straighter and forced herself to pay attention to what Ade was saying.

"It is my decision to accept this prisoner's challenge, and to once and for all demonstrate the ultimate power and authority vested in me by my father, by the dark realm, and by all who serve K'Luma." Ade's voice was dark and erratic—almost crazed. The shadow dragon he claimed was his father circled the wall behind him. "Tomorrow morning at sunrise, we will gather the power of K'Luma at the Legacy Towers to prove the filth and futility of this religion."

The broadcast shut down, and the device went dark once more.

The corners of Cap's mouth were turned up, but her eyes held no mirth.

An idea had popped into Charlotte's mind unbidden. "I want to be there tomorrow... with *El*'s champion." She might not know how Sonos' uncle had come to follow *El*, but he was standing against Ade in the name of *El*. That was enough.

Cap cocked her head to the side, perhaps wondering if Charlotte's mind had been fried. But then her whole face contorted with a grin. "Yes... Grand Magus always loves a show. Having you, Sonos, and the warriors there might be just the thing." A sinister chuckle left her lips.

Charlotte knew she should be scared, but something else was at work inside her. Yes, she had started this journey in search of her sisters. Yes, she and Sonos had played a key role in saving the Mountain Kingdom. And yet, it felt like everything had been leading up to this moment—this confrontation between *El* and the dark realm.

Followers of *El* had been ridiculed and forced into hiding for as long as she could remember. Gran, Sonos' mom, Miss Gemma, Seena, and many others. The Emperor had been cursed, though only a few had witnessed it. Now was the time for *El*'s power to be shown so all may know the truth.

Cap exited the room in a flurry.

The ending words from the poem Rapha had handed her in the Badlands rang in Charlotte's mind. She had memorized the words by this time...

Your fight is futile,
You come against eternity with time,
Your roar is harmless,
You come against truth with lies,
Your mammoth shows of power are no more than whisps,
for
You come against El *with humanness.*
So fight on, my giants,
Make your show, my foes,
Plan your ways,
Mark your path,
Set your sights.
But hear this—
Hear it loud,
Ringing clear,
The shout of a king is among us!
Hear the mighty thunder of Noiz,
See the numbers who stand in Truth,
Feel the tremble as El *arises,*
You have touched one who is unconquerable.

CHAPTER 40

"**R**ISE!" THE ELITE STANDING outside of Sonos' cell commanded.

Sonos blinked, his eyes still adjusting to the harsh light.

The shackle around his neck unclasped on its own accord and fell to the cold stone floor with a resounding *CLACK*.

Similar sounds echoed from the nearby cells.

Blue electricity sparked from the Elite's drawn sword, and Sonos hesitated.

His heart raced, and thoughts flew through his mind. *What is going on?* Surely, Ade wouldn't have them all killed right before the decisive showdown... would he?

Taimani's trill battle cry pierced the silence, and suddenly, everything shifted into high gear.

Whatever his attacker's intention—whether to kill, maim, or hurt—when the Elite lunged forward, it was pure survival instincts that kicked in. Sonos swiftly sidestepped the Elite's attack and spun around, landing a punch to the Elite's back. It wouldn't do much damage, but it was enough to momentarily knock the Elite off balance.

He quickly regained his composure and turned to face Sonos once again. They locked eyes and shifted warily, each waiting for an opening.

Locked in a tense standoff, they were surrounded by the cacophony of metal clashing against stone as others fought nearby.

Sonos wished he were more skilled in fighting, considering using the chain as a weapon. But all he could think of was the electricity from the sword surging through the metal. There were no other options.

Time was running out. Sonos needed to escape, and this might be his only chance, with his back against the bars and the Elite inside his cell.

The Elite seemed to sense his intention and lunged forward once more.

This time, Sonos turned and bolted through the cell door, attempting to slide the bars shut behind him. But the bars wouldn't budge. Those seconds cost him dearly as the tip of the Elite's sword touched his hand.

Electricity coursed through Sonos, causing him to yelp in pain.

Surprisingly, the Elite didn't try to knock Sonos out, but waited for him to recover before delivering another painful blow to his shoulder.

He yelped again as the second bolt of electricity shot through him. The Elite simply waited again for Sonos to recover. The power must have been set on low. Another blow came, this time to his arm.

They're only seeking to hurt, not kill, Sonos confirmed, scanning the corridor for his friends.

His Uncle Isaako and Taine ran into the corridor moments later, each locked in combat with their own Elite guard.

Perhaps sensing more of a challenge, the Elite, who had been facing Sonos, turned to double-team Isaako.

It took Sonos only a moment to decide his next move. With a fierce shout, he charged forward toward Taine's attacker. Taine was hampered by his maimed hand and seemed in greater need.

Sonos was able to land a kick squarely in the Elite's back, causing the burly man to double over for a brief moment. It was all Taine needed to move and grab the Elite's sword with his good hand.

Taine and Sonos shared a look. It was only a moment, but it was enough for Sonos to see loyalty and determination—no malice or anger. He breathed a sigh of relief. Seeing his friend moving and fighting, not cowering in fear and pain, was good.

"Behind me!" Taine's eyes darted to the regrouping Elites.

Sonos hesitated a moment; he was part of this fight now, not just a royal who needed protection. He hurried to stand beside Taine, wishing again he had a weapon or something other than his fists to fight with.

Taine's eyes went wide with surprise, but only for a moment. He gave a nod of respect, then turned his gaze to Isaako, who rolled under the blue glow of a sword and ran to stand on Taine's other side. The breadth of the three of them spanned the width of the corridor.

"*Fa'atau le Atua, fa'atau foi le toa!*" Taimani's strong call echoed through the prison.

Call upon El. Call upon the warrior. Sonos thought he had the words right.

She burst out through her prison door, dragging an unconscious, dark-haired Elite by the collar.

Sonos shook his head in amazement. Taimani was unstoppable.

"*Ua matou sauni!*" Taine responded to his sister's battle cry. *We are ready.*

Taimani grinned in his direction.

"*Fa'atau le Atua, fa'atau foi le toa!*" Isaako's voice gained confidence as he repeated the same cry from Taimani. *Call upon El. Call upon the warrior.*

Taimani ran to join Taine, Sonos, and Isaako. She pulled Sonos backward to stand behind the wall that she, Taine, and Isaako now formed.

Sonos frowned at being pushed away from the fight once more.

Isaako mumbled something to Taine, taking his glowing sword and shifting Taine back next to Sonos.

Sonos glanced towards the stairs, wondering where the prison guards had gone. Why were only Elites in the fight? Then, he spotted Scar, a smug look on his face, sitting casually on the steps.

"They're just playing with us," Taine spat, his gaze following Sonos'.

"Let them play. We will fight," Taimani said, facing the three Elites in the other direction.

The two groups stood locked in battle-ready stances, forming a tense standoff, while the prison guards watched, amused.

A quick glance at the other cells showed them to be securely locked. The other prisoners were not part of this battle.

"We're not getting out of here," Isaako said firmly, sparing a quick glance at Taimani.

Taimani's eyes blazed with anger. "Surely, we can take on a few guards—even if some of them are Elites."

"That's not the point," Sonos said. He understood what his uncle was thinking.

"Tomorrow's confrontation will allow the entire Empire to see the power of *El*." Isaako stood to his full height, his jaw set. "I called for the challenge, and I'm not backing down or running away," he continued. "It's my purpose."

"It's *our* purpose." Sonos laid a hand on his uncle's shoulder. 'This is not your fight alone. Each of us has journeyed here, for this moment, this time."

"*Fight* we must," Taimani didn't shout it, but her words were fierce.

"Win we shall," Taine practically commanded it.

That was the spark that shifted the Elites into full attack mode.

CHAPTER 41

"T HEY'RE GONE," TAIMANI SPOKE softly, but the sound was enough to jolt Sonos awake.

He was exhausted and stretched out his sore limbs as best he could in the cramped cell. Last night had been an endless barrage from the Elites. The remnants of the jolts and jabs still throbbed through his body. But they were alive.

The Elites had never set out to kill them. Sonos was sure his brother wanted Isaako to be weak and tired before the contest against Grand Magus. *But what Ade doesn't realize is that he's not fighting us... It's not my uncle's power he has to worry about*, he thought. It was the power of someone who could create temporal portals and turn the Emperor into a wild beast.

Sonos squinted his eyes in the dark, trying to make out shapes in the blue glow of the swords Taimani and Taine held at the prison cell door.

At some point during the night, the prison guards had turned off all the lights, assuming it would give the Elites an advantage. Each Elite and prison guard had special Sahemy-made glasses that allowed them to see in the dark. But when this happened, their group crammed into one cell. It was tight, but it had allowed them to fight at only one small entry point, which two people could easily cover. They took turns, allowing each person small moments of respite.

Even with only one good hand, Taine had insisted that he and his sister cover the last few hours so that Isaako and Sonos could rest, for they would lead the biggest fight in the morning at the Legacy Towers.

Isaako stirred from his corner of the cell. He had slept like a rock, perhaps for the first time in days, Sonos guessed. Ever since he had challenged Ade, he'd been beaten and weakened, he'd admitted during the night. But his resolve was unshaken, Sonos noted. Isaako was a man—a warrior—on a mission.

"What time is it?" Isaako asked.

"We're not sure, but something is happening. The Elites just disappeared," Taine answered, his voice as soft as his sister's. The darkness created a foreboding atmosphere.

The showdown against Ade and Grand Magus was supposed to be at sunrise. It must be coming up soon. Sonos tried to run a clock backward in his mind, but he was too disoriented.

The lights flashed on without warning. Sonos groaned, covering his eyes against the sudden brightness.

"They need to stop doing that," Taimani muttered.

"Rise and shine, rebels." Scar sauntered to stand at the front of the cell, arms akimbo. "Today, you will experience the full might and power of K'Luma." He fixed his eyes on Isaako.

Scar's arrogance didn't faze his uncle one bit. If anything, it made him stand taller.

And to Taine and Taimani's credit, they stood unflinching, battle-ready. But Isaako laid a hand on each of their shoulders, stepped forward, and addressed the head prison guard. "I am ready."

Taine and Taimani lowered their swords but kept their grips strong as they made way to allow Isaako to pass.

"Oh! Don't feel left out," Scar chuckled and shifted his gaze to Sonos and the warriors. "You are all coming."

Taine's sword raised again in defense. But Taimani laid hers on the floor and stood beside Isaako. She exchanged a few hand signals with Taine, who clearly disagreed.

Sonos moved from within the cell to stand on Isaako's other side. "We stand with you, Uncle, and with *El*."

The minute Sonos came forward, Taine's sword clattered to the floor. Loyalty ran deep.

"Fools," Scar spat, but then a glint returned to his eyes. "But by all means, come peaceably to your deaths. It takes some of the fun out of it... but I will still enjoy your very public defeat."

CHAPTER 42

"WHERE ARE YOU TAKING me?" Ava's voice was muffled but demanding. It wafted through the still-closed door of Charlotte's torture room. At least, that's what she had named it.

"Ava?" Charlotte's voice croaked as she tried to call out. Despite the pain, she lumbered over to the solid door of the room, straining to hear what was going on or where her sisters were. She prayed they had been spared the same fate as her.

Cap had yet to reappear since Charlotte had declared that she wanted to stand with *El*'s champion for the showdown.

"Cover her head and bring her!" The Sah, whose voice might forever haunt her nightmares, threw open the door and pointed to Charlotte.

Instinctively, Charlotte cowered in a defensive posture. She wasn't ready to be shocked again. But a different robed Sah threw a linen sack over her head and grabbed her shackled wrists roughly.

"This way," he pulled her towards the door.

Charlotte winced at the pain—the skin around her wrists was raw and bruised. But as she stumbled forward, she wondered why the Sahs were protecting their hideout by blinding her, if they expected her to die alongside Isaako.

"Where are my sisters?" Charlotte dared to ask, no longer hearing Ava's voice nearby.

"Quiet!" Cap's familiar voice demanded. "Just keep walking. No questions."

Worry gnawed at Charlotte's stomach. She couldn't lose her sisters now—not when she had gotten so close, not when she had actually seen them.

A door creaked ahead, and a cool breeze touched Charlotte's skin.

Gruff arms pushed her forward into the chill air. There wasn't much light seeping through the sack on her head. The showdown was supposed to be at dawn, so it must still be dark outside.

She forced herself to pay more attention to her surroundings. It felt like hard, packed earth beneath them, no clicking of heels on stone. But the muffled sounds from their movements echoed as if they were in an enclosed place or tunnel. Were they still in the Sahemy underground lair?

"Where are we?" Charlotte asked.

"I said, no questions," Cap retorted, emphasizing the point with a hard push to Charlotte's back.

After stumbling and bumping around blindly for what seemed like an eternity, the sack covering Charlotte's head was finally pulled off. She took a few deep breaths and looked around. They stood before a wooden ladder in a dimly lit tunnel.

But there was no tech here like in the Sahemy tunnels. This tunnel was fresher, the ladder more rudimentary. The earthen and rough tunnels were unlike those in the Sahemy's underground fortress.

"Get climbing!" Cap barked at Charlotte.

She hesitated. This felt like a trap. But Cap's eyes were ready to bore holes into her, so Charlotte placed her shackled hands on the ladder and started climbing.

It was only a short way until the ladder led through the tunnel's ceiling and into a small room above—a closet, really. Another robed Sah stood guard as Charlotte struggled to her feet.

Cap was right behind, and she prodded Charlotte through the door of the closet into a more expansive, open room. A group of purple-robed Sahs were gathered there.

Sorcerers, Charlotte judged by the color. She scanned the room for signs of Grand Magus, worry sinking into her chest.

"Do you know where you are?" Cap stepped close to Charlotte, a smug look on her face.

Charlotte's mind raced to piece together a puzzle that she should know. She scanned the room: it was circular, with a large staircase going through the center of the... *tower*! The realization struck her with brute force. She was in one of the Legacy Towers.

Cap chuckled. "I see you finally worked it out. And it's the Jamroq Tower, in case you were wondering."

Charlotte covered her mouth with her hand as she spun around and took in the prison that had held her sisters captive for three years—and decades for other prisoners.

"It seemed appropriate for it to be the last place you'll ever visit. Too bad there isn't time for a grand tour before the towers are destroyed," Cap said.

Destroyed? Charlotte repeated the word in her mind.

Just then, a pair of red-robed Sahs raced by, carrying a large bundle up the stairs.

"Be careful with that!" A blue-robed Sah called out after them. "We don't want anything to go off before time."

Blue... blue is for science. Science, tech, and sorcerer Sahs all working together? Charlotte wondered. Ade was definitely up to something, and whatever Isaako had planned, it wouldn't be a fair fight.

Cap checked her gazer while Sahs from every discipline scurried about. She grunted and tapped her foot impatiently.

Charlotte pressed her fear down deep inside and decided to ask something. After all, what did she have to lose? "Why did Emperor Ade empty the towers? I thought these were the pride and joy—"

"Did you think Emperor Ade wouldn't have figured out how Sonos escaped last time?" Cap cut her off.

Charlotte recalled how Sonos, Taine, and Sibi escaped the inner city with Taimani's help through the hidden tunnels connecting the towers to Pergamum. Of course, Ade would have dealt with any security breach.

"You should have learned by now that the Empire always wins."

Charlotte felt dizzy for a moment, her heart beating fast as she remembered. *No one fights the Empire and wins.* Those words had haunted her for three years, playing in her mind on repeat during her weakest moments.

A large door that led to the outside swung open.

Cap grabbed Charlotte's shackles and pulled her forward. "Let's go."

Charlotte squared her shoulders, determined to enter the courtyard with a different mantra on her heart. "Fight we must... no matter the cost. But win we shall. Those who are with us are greater than the darkness." She mumbled the words softly to herself. It was enough to restore calm to her mind.

But nothing could have prepared her for what lay ahead.

CHAPTER 43

L OUD JEERS FROM THE crowd of nobles caused Isaako to lift his head from where he stood in the middle of the courtyard at the Legacy Towers. The shackles on his wrists, ankles, and neck clanged with his movement and rubbed his skin in all the wrong places.

The sky had finally begun to lighten with the pre-dawn glow.

After leading them out of the Emperor's prison, Scar had taken them to a large room somewhere in the palace. There, Isaako and the rest had been shocked, burned, and shouted at before finally being brought to the courtyard of the Legacy Towers.

"Ade is scared," Sonos had said earlier through labored breaths, trying to encourage the others in the large and open torture room. That comment had only earned them more pain.

There had been moments when Isaako had wished that the others—the warriors and his nephew—had somehow been allowed to be innocent bystanders. He had never doubted his own calling that had led him to this confrontation. He was sure of the command and power of the one who had sent him. But did the others have to be in this same fight? Wasn't he enough?

The courtyard of the Legacy Towers had been set up like an ancient stadium—Isaako in the center with the towers behind him. In a semi-circle before him, a royal platform was erected with a stand for the nobles on one side and a stand filled with robed

Sahs on the other. The prisoner's box was situated further off to one side, on the edge of the towers. That is where Sonos, Taine, and Taimani had been chained to several benches.

Isaako took a deep breath and closed his eyes as the nobles and Sahs continued to fill the stands. He may not have gotten much rest, and his heart was beating fast, but in his core, he knew *El* would prevail. This wasn't about showing off or embarrassing Ade or Grand Magus—this was about sending out a rallying cry and encouragement to all the followers of *El*. This was about erasing any doubt about who held the true authority over the Empire.

Movement behind him caused a new round of jeers and shouts to erupt from the gathered crowd.

Isaako turned his head to see a group of red-robed Sahs leading a petite, wild-haired young lady across the courtyard.

"Charlotte," he gasped in recognition.

There hadn't been much conversation last night, but Taimani had asked Sonos about what had happened to their friend. Sonos had hoped that she was safe and sound with her sisters. But it appeared she had been caught in the melee as well.

Something scampered across Isaako's feet. He caught the slithering movement of a dragon lizard. "Nissi?" he whispered under his breath.

The lizard made a small track of movement in the few weeds that sprouted up through the stone of the courtyard as it scampered towards where Sonos and the others were being held—to where Charlotte was being led.

"Go figure," Isaako muttered, watching the familiar lizard leave him. But he quickly chastised himself. Nissi was here. That meant resource was here, and he'd have what he needed when he needed it. That knowledge was enough.

The prisoner's box was a small thing with two benches. Taine and Sonos were chained to the top row, and Charlotte was locked into a place next to Taimani.

Isaako was too far away to hear any words exchanged, but there was a mix of joy and worry on the faces of the friends reunited.

More nobles filled the stands than Isaako would have expected. It was early morning, and the nobles were a fickle lot. They either expected a good show, or perhaps they were still navigating relationships with the new Emperor.

A few vendors had set up booths around the periphery of the courtyard. The smells of roasting meats and fresh-baked pastries snaked into Isaako's nostrils, stirring a pang in his stomach.

He closed his eyes and took a deep breath. It was time for focus, not distraction.

Trumpets blared, announcing the arrival of the Emperor and his entourage. Right on cue, the sky turned shades of red, purple, and orange with the sunrise.

The entire courtyard shifted with the blare of the trumpets. Depending on their station or class, some prostrated themselves fully, and others took a knee with bowed heads.

Isaako fought a lifetime of training and kept his back straight, and his knees unbent. Even if Ade held the throne, it did not seem like a moment for bowing to another power.

Then the pain came. Greater force than had been used the entire previous night coursed through Isaako's body. He cried out and unconsciously doubled over, trying to force the electricity out of his body. He dropped to his knees. How long the shock lasted, he wasn't sure. He wasn't even sure if he had managed to keep from blacking out. But as quickly as it had started, the surge finally stopped.

Isaako took a few steadying breaths to regain his composure, then stood again and raised his head. Ade was staring straight at him, his chin lifted and a smile playing on his lips.

How could Sonos and Ade turn out so differently? The thought struck Isaako as he looked at his older nephew. But the Emperor had groomed Ade towards the lust for power from his first breath. Meanwhile, Isaako's sister, the Empress, had sought to plant seeds of *El* and a different way of life into her second son. Sonos had the right soil for those seeds to take root.

Isaako could feel the anger mixed with pride emanating from Ade. He was a tall and imposing figure, having grown into the full height of his Kimwaki roots.

A camera crew made up of red-robed Sahs was set up in front of the platform where Ade's throne had been erected. Holographic screens sprang to life, ensuring everyone in the stands had a clear view of the proceedings, which would also be broadcast throughout the Empire.

"It is time," Ade began, looking into the camera, his voice booming across the courtyard. "The champion of *El* stands battered and bruised, accompanied by the rebels who would defy the power of the Empire."

Jeers rose from the stands of the nobles as the camera panned across Isaako and then to the prisoner's box.

Isaako gritted his teeth and clenched his fists. He needed his wits about him, and he didn't need any more bursts of electricity frying his insides.

Grand Magus stepped onto the platform with Ade, followed by Wylder, who wore a long, black coat that reached the ground. Both men looked equally pleased with themselves.

"Let the contest begin!" Ade shouted, his voice amplified and filling the courtyard.

CHAPTER 44

"DO NOT MAKE ME regret restoring this alliance, Sah." Ade's eyes flashed as he spoke under his breath.

Grand Magus did his best to keep his face impassive, despite Ade's deliberate refusal to use his proper title. He only clenched the hands clasped behind his back a little tighter. Did Ade not realize that it was the power wielded by the Sahemy that kept the entire Empire afloat? He glanced at the giant shadow dragon that emerged from behind Ade's throne.

Gasps went up from the nobles—of course, they'd believe any lie that helped to perpetuate their privileged lives. Even within the Sahemy, it was only the Order of the Sorcerers, within which Grand Magus had been trained, who understood how to control the dark realm.

"I want them defeated... and shamed." Ade enunciated each word. "No mercy."

"There is no doubt, Emperor. They will not walk out of this courtyard alive." Grand Magus watched closely for Ade's response, ensuring he was committed to what this showdown would entail—the finality of it all.

Ade did not flinch. He only clenched his jaw and nodded once.

Grand Magus took that as his dismissal—and permission—and he turned to exit.

Wylder caught him before he stepped off the platform and leaned in close. "We have a lot of money backing you, magician. I hope you know what you're doing."

Grand Magus narrowed his eyes but paused a moment to compose his response. He despised the merchants. Before the day was done, Grand Magus hoped to ride Ade's favor and convince the Emperor to push the merchant class back down to where they belonged—certainly not on equal footing with the nobles or the Sahemy, as Wylder saw himself now.

"Enjoy the show, merchant." Grand Magus returned the insult with a sniff and left the platform.

Sal's bulky figure joined him as soon as he stepped off the stage. "Everything's in place, Eternal One."

Grand Magus smiled at the name. It spoke to the significance of their work—especially in the dark arts. The sciences and tech disciplines were useful enough but were... limited. The dark arts held the real power, and there would be no doubt after today. He glanced at the stands filled with Sahs and the deep purple, red, and blue robes. The purple robes filled the back rows of the stand, but after today, they'd be given a proper place of preeminence.

Those most faithful to Grand Magus had been working all night on the preparations. "Go triple-check that everything is in place," he instructed Sal.

Sal walked off towards Jamroq Tower, while Grand Magus walked decisively towards the chained and pathetic Diekolo-laoluwa. The disgraced captain may have taken a new name, but he'd meet his destiny this day—to *die*.

When Grand Magus had first heard that the Emperor had agreed to a confrontation with a champion for *El*—none other than the former captain of the Elites—he had been thrilled. Finally, a chance to show, beyond doubt, the power of the dark realm. But when the broadcast had flashed to the Emperor's prison and showed the image of a chained and beaten man, Grand Magus' excitement had dwindled. What kind of show would be possible against someone who was already broken?

Against Grand Magus' counsel, the Emperor had insisted that the Elites harass the prisoners all night long. He wanted to take no chances that the champion would win.

Such little faith in me... Grand Magus lamented. But no matter. Today's victory was just the beginning.

To his surprise, life sparked in Die's eyes as Grand Magus drew nearer to him. Despite everything, and regardless of the chains, the former captain looked determined... and even confident.

The corners of Grand Magus' mouth lifted. Perhaps it would be a good show, after all. But one thing was certain: the whole notion of *El* would be eradicated after today.

As Grand Magus took his place near Die, he turned and faced the stage where the Emperor was seated.

"You should have fallen on your sword in the Badlands, Captain. It would have saved you from the public shame of today." He spoke under his breath, barely moving his lips but loud enough for Die's ears.

To his consternation, Die didn't react. Not even a frown. He just fixed his eyes forward.

Wylder walked to the edge of the stage where the Emperor sat on his throne. The floppy hat was finally gone, but he still wore the long midnight-black cloak that looked to be infused with some sort of tech. It didn't move like natural material. Wylder was insufferably tight-lipped when Grand Magus asked him about it. But it was no matter—Grand Magus would get to the bottom of it with the tech-Sahs when his authority was restored once more.

"May the Emperor be blessed and live forever!" Wylder intoned into a microphone.

Agreement echoed from the nobles and Sahs alike.

"The rebels have been captured!" Wylder continued, gesticulating towards the prisoner's box.

Another cheer.

Wylder shifted his gaze to the cameras. "Emperor Ade has agreed to a demonstration which will once and for all show the unbreakable might and power of the K'Luma Empire. No person, no god, no power stands above the Emperor."

Hoots and hollers erupted from the stands. Grand Magus thought it was a little over the top, but since the proceedings were being broadcast, he supposed the masses would appreciate the show.

"Grand Magus, leader of the Sahemy and head of all sorcerers, has been chosen to represent the Emperor."

Cheers went up but were not as strong as Grand Magus expected, given the buildup. He frowned.

"The champion of *El* is the disgraced former captain of the Elites, Diekololaoluwa of Kimwaki."

Boos and jeers erupted from the stands.

"Fight we must!" A singular voice broke out above the rest.

Grand Magus glared at the prisoner's box. It was the upstart rebel girl who had been on the run with Sonos—Charlotte.

"Win we shall!" The others in the box called out, strong.

Die raised a cuffed fist in the air and shouted the cry again. "Win we shall!"

Suddenly, the rebels, including Die, quieted. In Die's case, he doubled over, grabbing his wrists.

Finally, Grand Magus thought. It had taken the Sah in control of the prisoners' shackles far too long to send the shocks through the cuffs. He'd have to address that later.

Wylder cleared his throat from the stage. "The challenge is to bring down one of the Legacy Towers through words alone."

There was a stirring among the crowd. It was impossible to destroy a physically imposing structure with words alone. However, Grand Magus had left nothing to chance. Sal and the others would make sure of that.

"Standing on behalf of the blessed Emperor Ade, Grand Magus will go first," Wylder completed the announcement.

"Everything is ready and all the people are in position," Sal's voice whispered through a device in Grand Magus' ear.

It was show time.

CHAPTER 45

— · —

Hours passed, and nothing happened. The sorcerers had produced plenty of frenetic activity, but no tower had fallen.

"This is getting awkward," Taimani said under her breath.

"Ent?" Charlotte echoed her agreement.

Sonos chuckled to himself, listening to the girls' exchange in the row in front of them in the prisoner's box. The tenseness of the morning had begun to wear off from everyone as boredom and restlessness set in. The crowd had come expecting a show, and instead were being treated to an embarrassing display of futility and frustration.

"Why doesn't he just give up?" Taine muttered from beside Sonos, rubbing at the shackles on his ankles.

An undercurrent of worry flowed through Sonos. He could see how badly Grand Magus wanted his plan to work. The wizened man was red-faced with effort, sweat dripping and forming dark spots on his robe.

Other purple-robed Sahs had joined Grand Magus throughout the morning, shouting incantations towards the tower. They had started a large fire and had attempted to make a smoke dragon. Poor Charlotte had panicked when the smoke dragon had begun to take shape—recalling the one that attacked her in Portemore. But it had fizzled out almost as soon as it had formed.

So far, all of the Sahs' efforts had been in vain.

"I'm telling you," Charlotte said in a low voice, "a whole group of Sahs was trying to rig that tower with explosives. I saw them working when they brought me up."

"Well, something's stopping them," Taimani said. Her eyes were fixed on Isaako, who sat cross-legged in the middle of the courtyard. He was still shackled at the ankles, wrists, and neck, but his back was straight, and his head unbowed.

"I hope not one stone falls off that tower," Charlotte said.

Taine jerked his head up. "You don't want them destroyed?"

"Of course she does," Taimani interjected. "But *we* should be the ones to bring them down—not Ade."

Charlotte nodded. "Exactly."

Taine's stomach rumbled loudly, and he shifted in his seat. "How long do you think this will go on for?"

Sonos couldn't remember the last time he'd eaten.

"Those meat pies from the merchants are smelling perfect right about now." Charlotte sighed deeply.

Grand Magus was huddled together with other sorcerers outside of Jamroq Tower.

"You have to admit that the longer this takes, the more foolish Grand Magus and his sorcerers look," Sonos said, trying to divert the focus from everyone's hunger. His own stomach was feeling hollow, but he did everything possible to sit up straight and keep his chin high. He would not allow Ade a modicum of satisfaction at his discomfort.

But he did wonder how long Ade would let the embarrassment of the Sahemy continue.

"I hope my sisters are okay." Charlotte wrung her hands.

Sonos' shoulders sagged just a bit. There was no guarantee of anyone's safety right now.

"Do you think *Tina* is watching the broadcast?" Taimani turned to ask her brother, running a hand over her shorn hair. *Tina* was the Kimwaki word for mother, Sonos remembered.

"I am sure that Ade has every town and village watching this broadcast, based on what was announced." Taine sat up a little taller and glanced at where the cameras were set up.

"I wonder what Dad and Gran think, seeing me in the prisoner's box," Charlotte said. "They must have seen when I was listed as a rebel, too." She cringed a little.

"They should be proud," Taimani nudged Charlotte gently, then she looked at her brother with a mischievous grin. "Hey, what's happening?" she shouted towards Grand Magus. "Maybe the dragons are sleeping?"

Charlotte gasped, and hissed at Taimani, "What are you doing?"

But Taine squeezed his sister's shoulder and chuckled.

"What more can they do to us?" Taimani shrugged. "Besides, the people need to see Grand Magus and the sorcerers for the fools they are."

Isaako smiled from where he sat in the middle of the courtyard, then turned to shout his own taunt. "I guess the dark realm doesn't work in the daytime. Maybe you need to chant louder!"

A few chuckles rose from the stand of nobles.

Sonos glanced at his brother, who was deep in conversation with Wylder. Neither man looked pleased. There was no way Ade would let Isaako come out on top today. He worried about what the two were plotting.

Wylder moved to the edge of the platform and cleared his throat. "Emperor Ade, may he be blessed and live forever, has decreed a pause for refreshments. Engaging the unseen realm is no small matter. We will resume in one hour when the champion for *El* will make his attempt on Kimwaki Tower."

Isaako stood and lifted his eyes to the sky. A small lizard kicked up a tiny cloud of dust as it scampered away from Sonos' uncle and toward the prisoner's box.

This lizard looked similar to the one who had been making laps around the prisoner's box earlier. Dragon lizards were not common in Pergamum. There was something strange about it... Could it be that Rapha had morphed into another animal?

He was about to lean forward and ask Charlotte what she thought, but as the lizard made its way to the prisoner's box, a glowing blue streak flew through the air, pinning the creature's tail to the ground.

—•—

CHAPTER 46

CHARLOTTE'S HEART HAMMERED IN her chest as the dragon lizard thrashed violently, trying to wrench itself free from the savage hold of the tech-infused knife.

When the creature had slithered by the prisoner's box earlier, its intelligent eyes and lack of fear around humans reminded her eerily of Rapha. It didn't speak or say anything. It didn't even hum. But there was a frequency—Jax and others had described it as a feeling, but she thought in terms of technology—that seemed to resonate from the creature.

Wylder approached the trapped lizard, his harsh eyes glinting cruelly. He pulled out his knife and scooped the lizard up, studying it with an intensity that made Charlotte's blood run cold.

Taimani gasped.

"Let it go!" Isaako called out—the first he had spoken in hours. "It's done you no harm."

Wylder only sneered in response and carried the writhing, bleeding lizard to the Emperor's platform.

Ade barked a chilling laugh, then stood and spoke loudly enough for those around to hear. "What is this? *El*'s champion is a disgraced man in chains, and he sends a lizard as some kind of... what? A token of power? Get that vile thing off my stage."

To his credit, Wylder was reluctant to release it, as if sensing its power. But eventually, he sauntered back to the center of the courtyard and made a show of dropping the lizard onto Isaako's shoulder. "Behold the champion of the great *El*!" he mocked, eliciting a few jeers from the noble and Sahemy stands. Most of the crowd had either flooded the merchant booths or stepped away for a break from the blazing sun.

The lizard crawled around Isaako's shoulders, its tail no longer bleeding. Charlotte swore it stuck out its pointed tongue at Wylder's back.

She glanced up at the Emperor's stage, but it was vacant. It seemed even Ade needed a break from the sun and a lack of entertainment.

The air shifted, and a breeze blew through the courtyard.

Charlotte closed her eyes and took a deep breath. Opening her eyes again, she noticed a dark cloud the size of a man's fist in the sky. It looked out of place in an otherwise blue and cloudless sky.

Grand Magus paid the sky no attention as he gesticulated frantically while conferring with his sorcerers. It seemed he was still planning something.

No one else in the stands seemed to notice the cloud either. But everyone in the prisoner's box sat up a bit straighter.

Isaako didn't take his gaze from the cloud, and the lizard remained perched on his shoulder.

"Something stirs," Taimani whispered. She looked between the sky and Isaako.

Taine looked at his sister. "Those who are with us are greater than the darkness."

Taimani cocked an eyebrow, a hopeful look playing in her eyes. "With *us*? Does that mean... you're now connected to *El*?"

Even Sonos adjusted his body to look at his friend.

"Rapha came to me in the prison," Taine answered.

"I thought you didn't believe in children's stories?" Taimani chided him, but only half-heartedly. Her face was beaming.

The corners of Taine's mouth turned up ever so slightly. "I have a feeling that after today, it's not going to be a matter of belief or disbelief. But rather, whose side we choose. And I'm with you—with *El*."

It was a day of battle, but the victory was already won. They were unconquerable. Hope surged in Charlotte.

Then Taimani cried out suddenly, a look of horror on her face, as she looked at the center of the courtyard.

Dread clenched Charlotte's heart.

Isaako, who had been staring at the sky, crumpled to the ground, unmoving.

CHAPTER 47

I SAAKO BLINKED HIS EYES against the brightness.

One moment, he stood, staring at the unnatural, singular dark cloud in the sky. The next thing he knew, the world had gone black. There had been no pain or electric shock, so he doubted it was the Sahemy.

"What in the Empire?" Isaako spoke slowly in disbelief as he stood and looked at his body sprawled out in the courtyard. He held his hands out before him; he was no longer shackled—well, this version of himself was no longer shackled.

He could vaguely hear shouts coming from the prisoner's box.

"Am I dead?" He voiced the question aloud, if for nothing else, to hear his own voice.

"You are far from dead, warrior," a deep voice rumbled.

Isaako turned and faced a tall soldier who had materialized next to him and stood a head above him. The dark, muscled man emitted a soft light.

Isaako wondered briefly if it was a hologram, but no. The entire environment had changed. The towers and crowds were still there, but dim and muffled.

"I am the commander of *El*'s army," the man continued. He was dressed in a midnight black uniform with multi-colored stripes running down the sleeves of his jacket.

Isaako dropped to a knee and bowed his head. He knew authority, and this was no random vision.

"Stand, Isaako. You do not submit to me."

Isaako stood and clasped his hands behind his back, slightly confused but ready to receive his orders. This may be the unseen realm, but he understood authority and chain of command.

"I am here to tell you this fight is not yours." There was no censure in the commander's voice. He spoke the words with unquestionable power. "You will say the words given to you at the right time. Say no more, no less. This battle belongs to *El*, and it has already been won."

Something felt familiar about those words.

Isaako nodded his head and tapped his fist to his heart twice. It was the gesture of a Kimwaki warrior, and he didn't know a better way to show respect and honor.

The world went black again. A cacophony of sounds pummeled Isaako awake.

"Uncle!"

"Isaako!"

"Wake up!"

"Someone help him!"

Isaako coughed and sputtered as he sat up on the dusty ground. He took a deep breath, trying to orient himself back to the courtyard and the chaos forming around him.

Wylder marched toward the center of the courtyard.

Isaako glanced towards the prisoner's box, hoping to assure Sonos and the others that he was okay. He was more than okay. He had just met the commander of *El*'s army, and the victory was assured. What was the saying? *Fight we must. Win we shall.* He smiled.

"Well, you are looking fine to me," Wylder said, arms crossed. "What was that? A play for some excitement?" He raised an eyebrow. "I certainly hope it wasn't an attempt to gain sympathy because—"

"It wasn't." Isaako cut him off and stood to his feet, feeling stronger than he had in years.

Nissi was nowhere in sight. But the little dragon lizard had a habit of disappearing and reappearing. Isaako wasn't concerned. He had his orders and was confident in whom he followed.

Wylder looked at Isaako with a mixture of shock and confusion. "What?"

"How'd you do that?" Wylder asked, circling him now.

"Do what?"

"You're unshackled."

Isaako looked down at his wrists and ankles, which were indeed free from the cursed Sahemy chains. Even the cuff around his neck was gone. His smile widened.

"No matter," Wylder said. "It's your turn now anyway." He tapped a button on the gazer on his wrist.

"Welcome back, citizens and servants of the great K'Luma Empire!" Wylder's voice boomed through the courtyard. The camera crew ran closer.

The nobles were slowly trickling back to their seats. The Sahemy stands were full of expectant faces. Ade sat on this throne, leaning forward, elbows on his knees. The shadow dragon had disappeared sometime that morning—likely affected by whatever was interfering with Grand Magus' powers.

Isaako caught Sonos' gaze and nodded. He glanced at the others in the prisoners' box. Each person sitting there was significant. Representatives from Kimwaki, Jamroq, Salan—considering Charlotte's maternal heritage—and even the royal family. A thought struck him.

"I want the prisoners with me," Isaako said, more like a command.

Wylder cast him a side-eye but tapped his gazer again, turning the amplifier off. "What did you say?" he hissed.

"Grand Magus had his sorcerers with him. I want the prisoners to stand with me." As Isaako spoke the words, a confidence built within him. Yes, this seemed fitting.

Wylder gazed around at the bored audience. The crowd had barely responded to his greeting. But Ade still wanted a show, Isaako knew.

"Fine." He tapped his gazer and walked to pace in front of the stands. "This afternoon, the Champion of *El* will be joined by the Emperor's prisoners as they attempt to bring down Kimwaki Tower."

Ade sat up straighter, but had a smile on his face. It worried Isaako how easily Wylder and Ade had agreed to have the prisoners join him. It almost felt like he was leading the others into a trap. And why did they shift to the Kimwaki Tower instead of Jamroq's?

Yes, the commander of *El*'s army had promised that the victory was already won. But Isaako knew how battles worked well enough. Victory never came without a cost.

CHAPTER 48

A RED-ROBED SAH UNLOCKED the shackles from Sonos' ankles. Between Grand Magus' lair and the prison, it felt like an eternity since Sonos had been free.

Taine grunted, rubbing his raw ankles, which had been bound much longer.

Charlotte had passed Taine some herbs earlier—remnants from Jax's medicinal repertoire that had been untouched in a hidden pocket of Charlotte's jacket, she had explained. Some color had returned to Taine's face, and even though his mutilated hand still looked the worse for wear, the warrior looked ready for battle.

A Sah with two colored eyes, one brown, and one blue, walked over to lead them toward the towers.

Charlotte gasped and tensed as soon she caught sight of the woman.

Sonos thought he heard her whisper, "Cap." Whatever it was, the look on Charlotte's face was one of sheer terror.

Sonos stepped closer and intertwined his fingers with hers. It was a gesture of friendship and encouragement more than anything, but his pulse still raced when she squeezed his hand in return.

Cap led the way across the courtyard. Taine and Taimani walked a few steps behind Sonos and Charlotte.

The Legacy Towers stood tall and menacing. Each was a six-story tiered building with sharp roofing structures that turned upwards at each level. Each represented a conquered land, and the Emperor had erected them all with fondness and pride. They had been called living temples, filled with the best and brightest from the lands. Sonos scowled. They were, in fact, a ploy to imprison any hope that could arise from these places. Were they genuinely conquered if the Emperor executed common folk every chance he got?

Isaako stood ramrod straight, staring at Kimwaki Tower.

Cap chuckled once they reached where Isaako stood. "You're not going to break it apart by just staring at it," she taunted. "But don't worry, soon you'll eat its dust." She motioned for the other Sahs to follow her, and they retreated to Jamroq Tower, where Grand Magus was huddled with his forces.

"What's the plan, Uncle?" Sonos asked Isaako when their little group had been left alone.

Charlotte still held Sonos' hand. Taine and Taimani stood at their backs, facing outward toward the crowds in a warrior stance, protective against any threats that might arise. They trusted Isaako and *El* to do what was needed to bring the tower down and would do their part to protect the group.

Isaako said nothing but shifted his gaze from the tower back to the sky.

The small storm cloud that had appeared earlier had grown massive in size, and it now created an overcast sky obscuring the blazing sun.

Charlotte broke the silence. "Isaako?"

Isaako's lips twitched as he spared a glance at her. He hesitated, then explained. "When I blacked out earlier, I had a vision. The commander of *El*'s army came to me—"

"Big, dark guy, with an immaculate black uniform and colored stripes on his sleeves?" Sonos interrupted, raising an eyebrow.

Isaako's eyes widened. "How do you...?" the question trailed off.

"We've met him twice," Sonos explained. "First, when we entered the Badlands—he told us to stay close to the river when you were... uh... chasing us."

Isaako frowned, his eyes softening. But he didn't say anything.

"And again, when we escaped Wylder." Sonos glanced behind him towards Taine, feeling guilt, but slowly realizing that everything had led them to this place.

Isaako placed a hand on Sonos' shoulder. "We can't carry the weight of the past. However, I am sorry for the blind obedience I once gave to the Emperor. Let us both focus on the next right step."

A weight lifted from Sonos' shoulders—one he hadn't realized had been resting there and growing all this time. He pulled his uncle into a quick embrace.

Suddenly, a deep voice boomed from the entrance to Kimwaki Tower. "You fight against power you cannot even fathom."

A stirring went through the stands.

Sonos clenched his jaw and looked around the courtyard. Grand Magus and the other Sahs had disappeared. This was some trick of the Sahemy; he could feel it in his gut.

Charlotte crossed her arms. "You can't tell me anyone thinks this is the dark realm actually talking."

Murmurs rose throughout the stands of nobles.

"Bow to Emperor Ade, and you will be given a merciful death," the deep voice continued.

Isaako tensed, his tanned cheeks turning a shade of red. He turned away from the tower and took a few steps toward Ade. His whole body was tense and determined. He passed his gaze over the stands of nobles and Sahs. Then he looked at the camera, which would have been broadcasting to the rest of the Empire.

"People of K'Luma, hear this truth. *El* will not be mocked, and this is *his* battle." Isaako's voice was calm and projected outward strongly.

The whole courtyard was silent, listening to his words, even though he wasn't using a Sahemy amplifier.

Sonos stepped closer to Charlotte. The words coming from Isaako held power—Sonos recognized their force and frequency, as Charlotte would have described it, similar to when Sonos had cursed his father, the Emperor.

Isaako looked at the sky full of dark clouds and raised his hands. "*El*, the one who was, who is, and who is to come. Let it be known today that you are God, and I am your servant and have done these things at your command. Answer me, so that all in K'Luma will know that you are *El*, and you are turning their hearts back to you once more."

A few angry shouts came from across the courtyard. Ade stood red-faced near the throne. But any other sounds were quickly drowned out by loud *CRACKS* of thunder in quick succession.

Lightning split the sky, blindingly bright. Four bolts simultaneously struck each of the four towers—Kimwaki, Jamroq, Salan, and Portemore. The thick stone began to crumble, rocks crashing down onto the courtyard below.

"Everyone hold steady, and don't run," Isaako instructed.

Sonos instinctively wrapped an arm around Charlotte. She held a hand over her mouth, eyes wide as she looked at the crumbling towers.

People scrambled in all directions, screaming and panicking as chaos erupted around them.

But Isaako and those around him stood steadfast in their semi-circle, unmoving. The dust swirled around them, but an invisible cocoon shielded them.

Amid the shaking, Ade hung on to the side of his throne, eyes narrowed, and he was shouting. But his voice was indiscernible as every single tower crumbled and was destroyed.

El's power was unstoppable.

Another *CRACK* of thunder, and a lightning bolt flashed behind them.

Sonos gasped, realizing it had hit the throne where his brother had stood moments before.

When the dust finally settled, all that remained of the Legacy Towers was a pile of rubble, and the throne had been spectacularly split in two.

Grand Magus and some red-robed sorcerers lay motionless on the ground just beyond where Jamroq Tower had stood. It looked like they had tried to escape and failed.

"Are they… dead?" Charlotte whispered the question, holding tightly to Sonos' hand.

Taimani ran over to check while Taine held his warrior pose, continuing to scan the courtyard.

Taimani moved from body to body, then came back to rejoin the group. "No one lives," she stated, mouth pulled tight, and rejoined her brother in standing guard over their small group.

There was movement on the stage, and Wylder's tall form helped Ade stand. Ade must have jumped from where he had been standing next to the throne at the last moment. Sonos was relieved that his brother hadn't been killed. There was still hope.

Ade stared at the rubble heaps that the towers had become, eyes wild and his face covered in dust.

Sonos glanced toward the camera and wondered what the people watching this broadcast must think. Were they amazed, fearful, or confused? *El* had brought down four towers and the throne, with his power alone, and in a heartbeat—no weapons or magic necessary.

The crowd in the stands had noticeably thinned—many must have run for their lives. But a few nobles remained, and they knelt and bowed their heads, looking towards Isaako and the group that stood unscathed. Sonos realized that no one in their group had a speck of dust on them.

The atmosphere was charged with emotion—Sonos felt it too, a deep sense of awe at what had just happened before their eyes.

Isaako cleared his throat and took a step toward the stands. "Fight we must!" His voice rang loud and clear.

"Win we shall!" The loud cry responded. Even a few Sahs added their voices.

"*El* is the one true power—the one true God," Isaako continued.

Cheers scattered across the courtyard, but the cameras and screens projecting the whole affair went dark.

Then, a voice cried out. "Arrest them!" Ade was pointing at Isaako and those around him.

What? Was his brother so foolish? Had he not just seen the power of *El* for himself?

The dragon lizard scampered up Isaako's leg and perched on his shoulder. He flicked out his pointed tongue. No words came, but Isaako nodded as if understanding something unspoken.

"*El* is not finished," Isaako said loud enough for the small group around him to hear. "We must not fight the arrest."

Taine and Taimani turned to Isaako with equal looks of disbelief.

Inwardly, Sonos cringed at the thought of being sent back to the prison cell and enduring more torture. But he wouldn't argue with his uncle at this moment. Something bigger was at work... he hoped so, too.

The Elites approached hesitantly, unwilling to touch any of them.

"Follow us," the leader commanded. His voice was firm but harbored no tone of malice or anger.

Sonos followed his uncle, along with the others.

It was time to see what else *El* had planned.

CHAPTER 49

C HARLOTTE FOLLOWED ISAAKO, KEEPING close by Sonos' side, as the Elites led them towards the Emperor's prison. From the little Sonos had shared, it was one of the last places they wanted to go.

"But we just won!" Taimani grumbled under her breath from where she walked behind. "And this is the reward? Back to the prison?"

Taine walked up front, looking ready to lash out at anyone who tried to raise a hand against Isaako.

Charlotte shook her head. "This can't be the end." *It can't*, she repeated in her mind. "I still need to get Ava and Lily out of that Sahemy prison."

Sonos grimaced. "My brother has never taken defeat well. But I thought—"

An Elite jogged up beside them, commanding them to be silent.

Tears of frustration threatened to spill from Charlotte's eyes.

As they were escorted out of the courtyard and through the palace, she was acutely aware of all eyes on their group—nobles, Sahs, servants. She felt exposed in a way she had not expected. Some glances held mocking taunts. More than a few people who passed by were surprised or even wary. A precious few were brave and bold enough to offer an encouraging smile.

A young servant girl with blond curls that reminded Charlotte of Sibi even whispered the words, "Fight we must!"

The Elites led them to a staircase in the middle of the palace.

Charlotte shuddered as they were led down the winding steps. Cold, damp air seeped into her bones. Once again, she was hit with an overwhelming longing for the sunshine and warm air of Jamroq. Would she ever get to see her home and family again?

Isaako had been insistent that they did not resist arrest. But it was so unfair! *El* had overwhelmingly shown his power in destroying the towers. Was that not enough?

An eerie silence in the prison made the darkness even more oppressive.

"Does this place not believe in lights?" she mumbled.

Sonos slowed his pace and let her come closer.

"Where are the prison guards, Gamba?" Isaako asked loudly as they reached the bottom of the stairs.

Light flared to life overhead, and Charlotte had to cover her eyes from the sudden brightness.

"Sorry," Gamba answered. He was the only Elite near Isaako. "It's a little hard to figure out this place. The prison guards, they were..." he hesitated. "They were trying to help Grand Magus in Jamroq Tower and took all the other prisoners with them when everything and everyone was... destroyed." He eyed Isaako with... was it admiration? *Fear?*

Gamba cleared his throat, looking at the two other Elites who stood behind Taimani. "We are under orders from Emperor Ade. I'm sure you can appreciate that, Captain." He looked nervously at Isaako.

Isaako narrowed his eyes. "I am not your captain. Do what you must. But know that *El* is not finished with this day."

Gamba shifted his weight.

Will he let us go? Charlotte hoped.

"It's just until we sort things out... please. Otherwise, the Emperor would have killed us on the spot." Gamba was pleading.

Isaako turned to look at Sonos, Charlotte, and the warriors. "I can't say what will happen down here. And I'm sorry we have to return to these bars so quickly. All I know is that the battle is not over."

"Those who are with us are greater than the darkness," Taine said, tapping a fist twice over his heart.

Taimani would never leave her brother again—she also tapped her heart twice.

Sonos glanced at Charlotte, concern in his eyes. "I know you want to find your sisters."

Her heart fluttered, thankful for his response and concern. He'd stick by her side; she knew it in her gut. But she didn't want to separate the group again. "We'll stick together," she said.

Sonos nodded and mouthed the words *Thank you.*

Isaako turned back to the Elite. "Do as you must, Gamba. But keep us together." He spoke the words as if he was in charge.

Gamba bowed his head with deference and opened the door to the first cell.

Isaako stepped in first. Taine followed on his heels into the same cell.

Gamba's eyes opened wide in confusion, but he didn't protest.

"I'm coming in, too," Taimani said, joining her brother and Isaako.

Sonos again looked at Charlotte, allowing her to lead.

"Together it is," she said. It would be crowded, but at least she wouldn't be in a cell alone.

"What about the chains?" One of the other Elites asked Gamba.

Gamba's eyes flitted over the group.

Charlotte's whole body stiffened, and she instinctively rubbed her wrists which were still raw from the night with Cap.

"Leave them," Gamba said. "The locked door will be enough." He slid the bars into place.

Charlotte exhaled. She could take imprisonment. But she could not handle being shocked anymore. She sank to the floor, pulling her knees to her chest. There wasn't much room.

Thankfully, the lights stayed on, and the prison wasn't cast into darkness.

Sonos slipped down next to her. He leaned close, his breath warm. "I agree with Isaako. This isn't the end. We'll get Ava and Lily back."

Charlotte looked into the deep, blue-grey eyes that focused on her. She believed him. "Thank you."

"I was really worried about you," he added.

Charlotte leaned her head back against the stone wall and sighed. She knew he was being kind, but she was exhausted, angry, and worried—quite simply a ball of emotions. At this point, she just wanted to be reunited with her sisters and be on the way back to Jamroq together.

Gamba and the other Elites disappeared. But the bars of the cell remained resoundingly locked. They were stuck here.

Soft humming broke through her reverie.

Charlotte's eyes snapped open; she was half-expecting a small ball of fur to be running toward her.

But Rapha was nowhere in sight.

Nor was Nissi.

"Did you hear that?" she asked.

"Hear what?" Sonos responded, worry creasing his mouth.

Charlotte hummed the soft sound she was hearing.

Sonos shook his head. "I hear you... but—"

He paused as Charlotte continued.

Isaako knelt in front of her. "I recognize that sound." He started humming with her.

Charlotte couldn't explain it, but as Isaako joined, the sound grew stronger.

Sonos relaxed beside her, closing his eyes. After a few moments, he also joined in.

Soon, Taine and Taimani added their sound to the growing frequency.

The sound vibrated off the cell walls—growing stronger and stronger. So strong that the floor started shaking.

Everyone stopped humming, but the shaking only increased.

Chapter 50

"WHAT IS ADE UP to now?" Sonos cursed under his breath, offering a hand to help Charlotte stand.

More shaking threw them to the ground.

The lights flickered off and on, messing with Sonos' vision.

"I'm not so sure this is Ade," Isaako said.

Charlotte covered her mouth, coughing.

Dust began to fill the cell from where the stones were grinding against each other. His mind flashed to the earthquake that had happened when they first stepped foot in the Badlands.

Taine shouted when a chunk of the back wall collapsed.

Everyone pressed toward the bars that locked them in the cell.

"Let us out of here!" Taimani shouted. "Someone, open this door!"

But no one came.

Is this something that Ade or the Sahemy could have caused? Sonos wondered. But with Grand Magus and the mightiest of his sorcerers dead, how?

Isaako and Taine crouched against the barred door, trying to open it, as Taimani continued shouting.

A cool draft of air wafted against Sonos' skin. He scanned the cell and inched towards the back wall. There was a visible crack in the stones.

Charlotte leaned over his shoulder. "A way out?"

Sonos stuck his fingers into the crack, praying the stone would give way.

Charlotte joined in the effort, picking another point in the crack.

At long last, the first section of the wall moved.

Another tremor and more shaking of the ground sent them back to huddle together in the center of the cell.

"This place is going to crumble at any moment," Taine grumbled.

The latest tremor had further eroded the structure of the stone wall, and it looked ready to cave in and crush them in the cell.

"I think the bar is moving," Isaako grunted, pulling at one of the bars.

Sonos moved in beside Isaako, squeezing Taine out. Sonos had two hands intact, and now was not the time for arguing. He put two hands on a different bar and pulled with all his might. Sweat dripped down his forehead. He hoped it wasn't his imagination that the bar was starting to give way.

Suddenly, Isaako cried out, falling backward, but with a triumphant smile and one of the bars in his hand.

Taine used the freed bar as leverage against the door.

Taimani joined her brother to help, and finally! The barred door came off its hinges, providing enough space to squeeze through.

Isaako ushered everyone out.

They huddled for a moment under the flickering light in the hallway.

"Our first priority needs to be finding my sisters," Charlotte declared.

"Our first priority needs to be staying alive..." Taine muttered, glancing around. "But we will also get your sisters," he quickly added.

If anyone understood the bond of siblings, Taine and Taimani knew it well.

Sonos felt disappointed as he thought of his own brother, who seemed intent on keeping his pride and power, even if it meant killing his own blood.

Isaako studied Charlotte with a new light in his eyes. He nodded slightly. "Let's go find your sisters." He led the way up the steps.

Even though Sonos had grown up in the palace, his uncle, the former head of the Elites, would know the hidden and safe corridors. Most importantly, he should know how to get to the Sahs who were holding Charlotte's sisters hostage. Sonos didn't want to voice the worry that her sisters might have been caught up in the destruction of the towers.

They emerged from the staircase into a world of chaos. The earthquake hadn't just been in the prison. Some pillars on the ground floor of the palace had crumbled or were leaning precariously against each other, while bits of plaster rained down from the ceiling.

"Sonos, you okay?" Charlotte laid a hand on his arm.

He didn't realize he had stopped.

Taine walked up to his other side, holding the bar from the prison in his hand as a weapon. "I made an oath to protect you, and I intend to keep it. Always."

Sonos cast him a thankful gaze.

"Focus! Keep a tight formation and follow me," Isaako commanded. "We do not rest until the battle is finished."

Nissi was once again perched on Isaako's shoulders. *When did he appear?* Sonos wondered, horrified. Had he been so distracted that he was no longer reflexively cataloging details?

There was no sign of Rapha, however.

"You said they're in the Sahemy prison," Isaako cast a backward glance at Charlotte. "There's a secret entrance to the Sahemy underground base in the throne room. We'll head there."

Taimani moved to the group's rear, leaving Taine to stick close to Sonos. Isaako led from the front. He led them through the palace, sprinting down hallways and leaping over crumbled walls as they made their way to the throne room.

To everyone's credit, no one complained, and they all stuck together.

The rubble and broken walls spoke of chaos and violence. Every step they took seemed to echo off into eternity. A crash of thunder shook the ground again, and lightning zigzagged through the skies above them.

It feels like the whole Empire is breaking apart, Sonos thought. But he kept focused on moving forward and keeping the group together.

When they reached the grand threshold of the throne room, Isaako stopped short. Stationed outside were half a dozen Elites with swords drawn, glowing blue, and ready for battle.

Even though they were outnumbered two to one, after a few hand signals, Isaako, Taine, and Taimani surged forward in a united wave of determination and power.

Taine shouted a battle cry and raised the broken bar from the prison above his head. He swung it at the nearest Elite, connecting with a sickening thud and sending the soldier sprawling backward. He picked up the fallen man's sword and tossed the bar to Isaako.

The Elites charged, but Isaako was too fast. He deflected the first blow and ducked beneath another. Taine and Taimani flanked him on either side.

Charlotte stepped forward, but Sonos held out a hand to stop her. It was not for fear, but there was a rhythm and a dance that the warriors had.

The siblings and Isaako fought as one, taking out the Elites with precision and strength.

Once the last of them was defeated—Sonos hoped they were only unconscious; death had a way of haunting him—he stepped forward with Charlotte.

Isaako pushed open the large wooden doors that led into the throne room.

A chill ran down Sonos' back as he stepped over the threshold.

Ade sat wild-eyed on the throne, and Wylder shifted nervously beside him.

"Does Wylder look scared to you?" Sonos whispered to Charlotte. He wondered if the merchant had finally realized that there was something stronger than tech.

The air seemed to still around Sonos as he surveyed the silent figures of a few red-clad Sahs—technologists. His mind flashed to the Sahs who had lain unmoving in the Legacy Towers courtyard.

Ade looked up and locked eyes with Sonos. There was a moment when Sonos wondered if his brother was finally out from under the influence of the darkness. The shadow dragon was noticeably missing. But then Ade raised his hand and called, "Bring them out!"

Wylder motioned to two Elites in the corner and walked to meet them in the middle of the throne room. They roughly pulled two young women along with them.

Charlotte gasped. She instantly moved towards the girls, whom Sonos assumed were her sisters, but Taimani stepped in front of her, eyes locked on Wylder. Even though Wylder eyed their group warily instead of arrogantly, Taimani, like Sonos, knew better than to trust anything in this place.

One sister was tall and slender, her dark hair pulled back, and her mouth drawn tight. The other had loose curls that fell past her shoulders. They both held a familiar ferocity in their eyes.

Sonos' heart pounded as he looked from the sisters to Wylder, and to his brother on the throne. He wanted to protect and fight for his friends—but he had to be careful.

Ade's face split into a manic grin as he stood up from the throne. "I knew you'd come looking for them... Wylder made the connection to your rebel girlfriend."

Charlotte was breathing hard now.

Sonos balled his hands into fists and stepped toward his brother.

Ade's eyes narrowed. "Come any closer, and they'll be killed."

Chapter 51

"Char... Charlotte! You gotta breathe."

Sonos' voice broke through her panic.

Charlotte was on the floor. She didn't remember falling...

"What did you do to her?" Ava's shout filled the room.

Ava and Lily... they were here. They were here! Charlotte sat up more quickly than she intended, and the world spun.

A tiny lizard crawled onto her hand—*Nissi.*

Sonos put a hand on her shoulder as he knelt next to her. "Stay with us, Char. It's okay." His voice was low and steady.

But her focus had returned across the room to the sisters she had sought for so long. They were here. They were still alive. The Sahemy hadn't put them in the towers before the destruction.

Wylder shifted on his feet from where he stood next to the Elites guarding her sisters, casting a wary glance between Charlotte and Sonos.

Charlotte's pulse raced, and her chest tightened again. She thought she had worked through these panic attacks, but the sight of her sisters in danger once more...

She shifted her gaze away from Ava and Lily and their worried looks, and tried to focus on Sonos' face... his voice. His grey-blue eyes spilled equal amounts of calm and concern, reminding her of a storm over the ocean. She closed her eyes and thought about the ocean waves back home in Jamroq. She took a few deep breaths. She couldn't fail everyone now.

She grabbed onto Sonos' arm and stood slowly. She squared her shoulders, Nissi scrambling up to perch where Rapha used to sit.

Taine, Taimani, and Isaako spread out in a semicircle around Charlotte and Sonos.

A little ball of fur scurried from behind the throne toward Charlotte.

Ade shouted in surprise.

But Charlotte smiled.

Rapha scurried up to her other shoulder.

A deep urge to speak rumbled in her core. She looked between Nissi and Rapha, but neither made any noise, and this wasn't the hum of technology. It was like a pot about to boil over.

"Are the rebels in the business of starting a menagerie with wild animals now?" Ade asked in a mocking tone from his throne.

His tone was loud, but Charlotte could sense that there was fear and something even deranged behind the bravado.

Isaako turned and looked expectantly at Charlotte, seeming to acknowledge that it was up to her now.

What was she supposed to say?

Words spoken by Princess Lenora on the eve of the attack against the Mountain Kingdom flooded her mind... *The heart has eyes that the mind cannot see.*

Charlotte took a step forward.

Sonos kept pace alongside Charlotte as she approached the throne.

"Stop walking! I'll have you killed!" Ade shrieked the closer they got.

But the Elites in the room held back—or at least hesitated. It was almost as if they could sense that the balance of power was shifting, even as the slight tremors of the earth continued.

"I'll have *them* killed!" Ade pointed towards Ava and Lily.

Charlotte stopped. She tilted her head, listening for any indication from Nissi and Rapha, but they simply sat calmly on her shoulders. Sonos also gave her space and didn't try to take the lead against his brother.

The swell of words and emotions boiling inside her erupted in an icy calm. She faced Ade with a stony gaze, like a warrior from Kimwaki. "No, you won't. You will not kill my sisters, nor anyone else." She stepped closer yet, narrowing the distance to the throne, raising her voice as she continued to speak. "*El*'s power was broadcast for all of K'Luma to see when he brought down the Legacy Towers with a breath."

The words spilled from her mouth but came from somewhere beyond her conscious thought. Her voice was strong and clear—no fear, only the sound of absolute authority. "You have been blinded by pride and arrogance, just like your father. But this day, I command that you open your eyes and see!"

Ade began to sputter a response but stopped abruptly as if an unseen force had struck him.

Nissi and Rapha scampered from her shoulders to dart to opposite sides of the room, but nothing more happened.

Was that it? For a moment, Charlotte began to doubt herself.

Then the air began to vibrate—not the earth this time. It was as if the room shimmered and transformed.

The collective gasp that followed was deafening.

The commander of *El*'s army appeared, standing at attention by Charlotte's side, a sword in his hand. Dozens of other warriors, wearing the same midnight uniform with multi-colored stripes, assumed battle-ready positions throughout the throne room.

Where did they come from? Were they always here? Was it my command that made them visible? The questions spun through Charlotte's mind.

"How did you do that?" Sonos leaned in and whispered.

"I..." Charlotte scanned for Nissi and Rapha, but the room was too packed to see the small animals.

"We are here, sent by *El*," the commander declared loudly.

"You have no right to be here! This is my Empire!" Ade shouted from the throne, his voice shrilly like a defiant boy.

Did he not realize that the Elites were outnumbered at least two to one? "What is he doing? Trying to sentence everyone in service to him to death?" Charlotte whispered to Sonos.

"Wrong," the commander responded to Ade. "The Empire belongs to the one who created it. *El* has chosen a new steward, and you will step aside... or be forcibly removed." The commander walked towards the throne.

Ade tried desperately to call his Elites to arms, but the warriors had all dropped to a knee and laid their swords before them. Most of them were from Kimwaki, and even if Kimwakians served a Great Chieftain, they also had a deep respect and fear of beings from the unseen realm—Taine and Taimani had shown that in the Badlands, even before believing in *El*.

"Do we... uh..." Charlotte started to ask Sonos. But the question stopped in her throat. Wylder had managed to slink away, and her sisters were now surrounded by kneeling Elites.

No questioning was required. Charlotte ran straight towards them.

Taimani was on her heels and used a sword to cut the bonds from Ava and Lily. In a blink, the three of them were hugging each other, squeezing tightly. Tears streamed freely down Charlotte's cheeks. She had no intention of letting go, but the door to the throne room banged open, and a familiar voice filled the hall.

"We're here!" Jax called out, slightly breathless, a mischievous grin plastered on his face. Lenora helped him walk, and they were

flanked by Sibi and Dayo, who led the way proudly before the
Empress.

CHAPTER 52

S ONOS STOOD FROZEN IN place, his gaze fixed upon his mother. The throne room fell into an eerie silence, every eye tracking her deliberate steps toward the throne.

The commander of El's army and all the warriors shifted and, without speaking, created a passage to the throne for the Empress.

Her attire—a striking blend of a long, verdant gown adorned with intricate golden patterns mirroring her tattoos—displayed the pride of her heritage. The markings worn by all Kimwakians of age were unique to each person and represented their community, heritage, personality, responsibilities, and even their future. Sonos also didn't miss the K'Luma crown sitting on her head above her intricate braid.

As she passed Sonos, a faint nod and a fleeting smile acknowledged him, but her focus swiftly redirected towards Ade, still defiantly seated upon the throne.

Jax and Lenora paused to stand near Sonos, while Sibi and Dayo walked proudly before the Empress, serving as her honor guard.

Ade rose, a glimmer of lucidity returning to his eyes. He threw his arms open wide. "Mother, you have returned safely."

Sonos grappled with his brother's erratic behavior—one moment deranged, the next almost composed.

"Yes," the Empress replied icily, "but I'm not here for you, Ade. I am here to claim the throne as *El* has commanded."

His mother had never shown interest in power before. But something was different... *El* commanded, she'd said. This wasn't lust for power like what Ade had displayed—their mother was operating in authority under someone else's command.

Something caught Sonos' attention from the corner of his eye.

A sudden shout erupted near the Empress.

Isaako stood before his sister, a dagger in hand—caught just in time.

Shock gripped Sibi and Dayo; they were frozen in disbelief. Sonos was, too. Ade had just tried to kill their mother.

Sonos' heart raced. Ade had just tried to kill their mother—the realization repeated again and again in his mind.

Fetu, Ade's bodyguard, wrestled Ade to the ground, restraining him as he thrashed between threats and pleas, wild eyes scanning for aid.

"I am the Emporer! No one else!" Ade's shouts fell flat.

The other Elites in the room remained on bent knees while the commander of *El*'s army and his warriors stood watchful but unmoving.

The Empress stepped onto the platform and sat on the throne, Isaako standing on one side, and Sibi and Dayo on the other. A sliver of light shone through a crack in the ceiling, casting a soft glow on the throne.

All tremors had stopped.

The commander of *El*'s army sheathed his sword. "As *El* has decreed, until the curse upon the Emperor is completed in seven years, Ali'tasi will reign as Empress of K'Luma." The authority with which he spoke was unquestionable, and he did not wait for a response. He signaled to his warriors, and in a blink, the air shimmered, and they were gone.

Rapha and Nissi were the first to move, scampering to the throne in their own ways.

Charlotte, her sisters, and Taimani joined Sonos and Taine in the middle of the room.

"That was abrupt. I thought the commander could have stuck around a bit longer," murmured Sonos, still reeling from the shock.

"They don't serve your mother," Charlotte said as gently as she could.

Sonos shot her a look—did she have a new plan now that she was with her sisters?

"They're part of the unseen realm," Charlotte quickly added. "But I'm guessing they'll be here if *El* thinks we need the help."

Sonos' eyes softened, apologetic. Things were changing rapidly, and he needed to get control of his emotions.

"Ade, you have one chance." The Empress sat tall on the throne and fixed her gaze on Ade, whom Fetu still restrained. Her eyes were not cold, but held great determination. "Step aside peaceably and recognize *El*'s decision, or you will be banished from K'Luma immediately."

"I will not serve something that doesn't exist!" Ade shouted.

How can he deny what happened to the Legacy Towers? Sonos was dumbfounded.

The Empress didn't argue; she was full of decisive action. "A K'Luma carrier is waiting in the palace courtyard. It will carry you to the lands beyond the Mountain Kingdom." The Empress' voice resonated as if she had been on that throne all her life.

Two Elites stepped forward to escort Ade to the waiting carrier.

The Empress scanned the room as if looking for someone. She rested her gaze on Wylder, that slippery fellow. He hovered just behind where the sisters had been held, trying silently to shuffle away.

Sonos scowled and balled his hands into fists.

Isaako leaned down to whisper something in his sister's ear.

"You!" The Empress pointed towards Wylder. "You will continue to attend Ade in his banishment, just as you saw fit to serve him during his quest for power."

Wylder opened his mouth to protest, but two Elites pointed their glowing swords at him.

It took half a breath, and Wylder dropped something from his hand. A cloud of smoke erupted. He cast Sonos a wink before flaring his tech-infused cloak and disappearing.

The hairs stood up on the back of Sonos' neck. He was sure it was a trick of the Sahemy. Even though Grand Magus and the other advanced sorcerers were dead, the Sahemy held other power. *And it doesn't mean the dark realm is dead*, Sonos chided himself for being naive.

The two Elites who had been closest to Wylder looked to the Empress. She gave a slight shake of her head. "Let him go." She sighed but turned her attention to her brother.

"With immediate effect, Isaako is reinstated as captain of the Elites," the Empress declared.

Isaako bowed to his sister, and then turned to face the room.

As one, the Elites tapped a fist to their hearts twice and then stood.

Nissi flicked his tongue from where he now perched atop Isaako's shoulder.

The Empress nodded, a pleased smile on her lips. She turned and beckoned Sonos forward. "Bring Charlotte with you."

Charlotte glanced at each of her sisters, hesitating to put any distance between them.

"You can all approach." The Empress offered a gentle smile, much more at ease with the open threats having been removed.

Sonos placed his hand on the small of Charlotte's back and led her to the edge of the platform.

Rapha sat calmly next to the throne in front of Sibi and Dayo, who tried their best to appear stoic and serious. But Sibi gave Sonos his signature wide grin and looked ready to jump down from the platform and hug him.

"You all have been on a long journey, but have done everything required. Well done," the Empress said looking around at the group.

Sonos' heart filled with the praise. With the Emperor, his mother had never been allowed to offer anything but quiet subservience.

The Empress fixed her gaze on Charlotte and her sisters. "I understand your last name is King, is that correct?"

Charlotte glanced at Sonos, but he shrugged. He didn't know what his mother was thinking.

"It is." Charlotte nodded slowly.

"While I was with King Mason and his leadership council at the Mountain Kingdom, we discussed the best course of action for the immediate future. I want to appoint local governors to lead in each of the territories." She paused for a moment. "Tell me, do you know much about your father's background?"

Charlotte and her sisters looked at each other, but they looked genuinely confused.

"He didn't speak much about his history before Jamroq was conquered," Ava said pointedly.

Charlotte's eyes widened in realization. "Seena Sweethand said something about surnames being linked to a person's profession or identity. Are you saying...?" Her question trailed off, and she grasped Sonos' hand.

The Empress shook her head. "He was not the king, as sadly the Emperor ensured no member of the immediate family lived." Pain flashed across her eyes. "However, there is reason to believe there may be a link. We'll need to speak with your father to confirm the details."

"That would explain so much," Charlotte whispered, turning to her sisters.

"I know this is much to process, but I hope you'll understand my need for alacrity." The Empress paused and shared a look with her brother. Things were moving at speed. "I would like for both you and Sonos to serve as my advisors and foreign emissaries."

Charlotte turned a questioning face to Sonos. But he was just as surprised. Nothing was going according to anything he had planned, though somehow it all felt right.

His mother was making the same request Ade had made, but this time, Sonos was being asked to build, not break, and he'd be serving *El*. He slowly nodded at Charlotte, wanting to give her the chance to speak first.

Charlotte stiffened her arms at her sides and bowed toward his mother. "I appreciate the honor of your request, Empress Ali'tasi. But I actually wanted to spend some time at home, with my family." She glanced at her sisters and smiled. "I have a promise to keep."

Sonos restrained himself from feeling disappointment; Charlotte's joy was contagious, and he couldn't ask her to stay away from her family. He would just need to spend as much time as possible in Jamroq.

"Of course." The Empress inclined her head, but then shifted her gaze to Sonos, awaiting his response.

He realized he also had a duty to family, his mother. "A tiny seed can bear much fruit. I am at your service." He bowed.

Pride shone through the Empress' eyes.

"M-may I offer th-the Mountain Kingdom as the f-first alliance." Princess Lenora stepped away from Jax and approached the Empress with bowed head.

The Empress stood and stepped down to face Lenora. "It is my honor to accept King Mason's right hand of fellowship. We stand together." She placed her hand on Lenora's shoulder and touched their foreheads together. It was the ultimate form of trust and allegiance. "I look forward to seeing your father and Prince Malachi once I can call Uzoma off the attack."

Lenora bowed her head and returned to Jax's side while the Empress returned to the throne.

"Speaking of Uzoma, please send one of your men to find Elisa," the Empress told Issako. "I want to ensure she doesn't need to follow Ade into exile."

Isaako nodded and called one of the Elites over to confer with them.

"Ava, Lily, come forward, please," the Empress turned her attention to Charlotte's sisters. "I think it goes without saying that there will be no more prisoners for the Legacy Towers. There will also be no sorcerers; no one who practices the dark arts will be welcome. However, the Sahemy plays a vital role. I would love for you to join the Order of the Sciences, and perhaps start a creative discipline, as we look not just to rebuild the Sahemy, but also to expand it and take knowledge to every corner of the Empire—not just Pergamum."

Lily gasped and placed a hand over her mouth. "It's exactly what our dad has wished for all along."

Ava furrowed her brow and straightened her shoulders. "With respect, it's been over three years since our kidnapping. I want to return home to Jamroq first, then give you our decision... if it is a choice."

Charlotte cleared her throat, but Ava paid her no mind.

Sonos couldn't blame her—the Emperor and Ade had torn many a wounded family apart.

"Of course, I understand," the Empress said gracefully. "And yes, you will always have a choice."

Ava nodded, and pulled Lily and Charlotte close.

Taimani stepped forward, not waiting to be called. "I would like to return to Kimwaki to finish the training I was pulled from."

"I have heard that you and your brother were the top of your class," the Empress replied. "I would love to attend your graduation when you have finished."

Taimani beamed in response.

Sonos leaned towards Taine, knowing the deep stubbornness in his bodyguard and friend. "You have more than fulfilled your vows to me. You should return with Mani."

Taine's eyes flared wide momentarily, but then he wrapped his arms around Sonos in an unexpected bear hug. "You were worth every sacrifice, my friend."

When Taine pulled away, Sonos tapped his heart twice, giving honor and respect to the friend who had followed him through every peak and valley of the journey.

Taine took his place next to his sister, communicating with hand signals. It didn't take long for her smile to grow even wider.

Sonos didn't miss the way his mother's eyes lingered on Taine, deep in thought. Perhaps she was thinking the same thing: Taine would be excellent as part of the Kimwaki leadership. Surely, she would not allow the chief from the Kimwaki Tower to govern; he was far too quick to blindly betray. He would speak to his mother about it.

"Last but not least, Jaxtyn, what is your desire?" the Empress asked.

Jax glanced at Charlotte, who nodded in understanding at her friend.

"I'd like to join the healer quadrant at Noiz," he said. "I know I'm older than most, but they've offered to allow me to study in an exchange program with Jamroq."

"A perfect way to begin the rebuilding, and to open the lines of communication once again." The Empress nodded her approval.

She then scanned the rest of the room, with the scattering of Elites who remained. "Thank you for your service, which is first and foremost to *El*. We have much to rebuild over the next seven years. But to start, I have an Empire to address and nobles to meet."

Isaako directed some nearby Elites, who then half jogged through the exit. Others took up inconspicuous positions around the throne room. It was like a great weight had been lifted from the room since Ade and Wylder had left and the Empress had taken power.

Nissi continued to perch on Isaako's shoulder, looking quite at home.

Rapha jumped down from the platform and made his way to Charlotte. She nuzzled him, holding him close.

The Empress walked toward Sonos, her face more relaxed and eyes full of unabashed love.

Sonos stepped into his mother's embrace, the last vestiges of angst and worry seeping off his chest.

"No longer a seed. You, my dear Sonos, are a tree planted by streams of water," the Empress spoke for his ears alone. "The next seven years before your father returns will not be easy. I'm glad to have you and Isaako by my side."

"I've always been with you," he answered, "Even when I didn't understand, you helped ensure my heart was tethered away from the Emperor. Thank you."

She gave him one last squeeze. "You have been through a lot. Isaako and I will work to settle the capital, but your first assignment will be to visit and assess Jamroq. You'll have a K'Luma carrier available to you at all times. Take her and her sisters home."

CHAPTER 53

"**D**ID SHE JUST SAY we get to go home?" Charlotte asked, barely able to contain her excitement.

The Empress had departed with Isaako, Sibi, and Dayo by her side.

"You're going home," Sonos confirmed, his eyes twinkling.

Overwhelmed with joy, Charlotte pulled everyone nearby close—Sonos, her sisters, and Jax—into a tight group hug.

"We're going home! We're going home!" She couldn't help but keep repeating the words.

Ava and Lily, wearing genuine smiles, exuded a sense of relaxation unseen since their arrival.

Jax pulled Lenora into their circle, and Taine and Taimani draped their arms over the group.

Charlotte relished the moment. This is what they had fought for—what *El* had promised.

Rapha swung to each person, humming a happy tune.

"There's more to that monkey... than just being an animal, right?" Ava asked Charlotte.

"We have much to catch up on," Charlotte answered. Where would she begin?

Rapha, saving Charlotte for last, wrapped his small arms around her neck. In that embrace, she understood he wouldn't return to

Jamroq with her. But as she had assured Sonos regarding the commander, she knew Rapha would always be there when needed.

He glanced at Charlotte, winked, and left the room.

Her heart dropped just a bit, watching him leave.

"H-he's like th-the wind." Lenora stood next to her, looking in the direction Rapha had disappeared. "You n-never know where it'll b-blow."

"I think you're right," Charlotte said. "But he kept his promise. And I have a feeling it's not the last we'll see of the little furball."

"True dat," Jax said while leaning on Taine.

"You're looking so much better!" Charlotte looked at Jax's ankle. It was wrapped in something that looked like stiff, crusty, white cloth. But he was moving on his own, albeit with the help of a long stick. It hadn't been much more than a week since he'd been in a wheelchair.

"The Mountain Kingdom healers in Noiz are amazing," Jax said.

Lenora blushed beside him.

"Sorry that I didn't talk to you before telling the Empress where I wanted to go," Jax continued. "But now that everyone is safe, I want to return to Noiz, finish getting better, and study with their healers. I know I've learned a lot of herbal medicine on my own, but they use tech on top of everything." His deep brown eyes grew more and more excited as he talked.

Charlotte threw her arms around his neck, almost toppling him over. "Of course!"

"Please tell Gran and your dad how much I appreciate everything, and sorry I didn't bring you back myself. But... you do have the crown prince for an escort now." He grinned his mischievous side grin.

Charlotte felt her cheeks heat at the mention of Sonos. But more than anything, she was glad their initial awkwardness, stemming from Jax's fleeting crush, had dissipated. He was her best friend once more. "You're right. The Crown Prince of K'Luma is taking me and my sisters back home. Can you believe it?" she said with a soft laugh. "But seriously, you need to come and visit as soon as your foot is healed."

Jax nodded. "Walk good, Char."

"Walk good." She echoed the familiar salutation from Jamroq.

Taimani came over, stepping in front of Sonos. "My turn next." She winked.

"Taine and I will be returning to Kimwaki to see our family and finish our warrior training," she said. "But I was thinking we could take a small diversion if you let us come on the K'Luma carrier with you. I remember a promise of roast fish on a beach somewhere..."

Charlotte inhaled deeply, thinking about the salt water and fresh fish over a fire with a smile on her face. "Homeward bound, then!"

Sonos came over and wrapped an arm around her. "Shall we?"

"Fight we must!" Charlotte gave one last cry, filling the throne room with her voice.

"We win shall!" The resounding answer reverberated off the walls.

"We win shall," she repeated, a single tear of joy making a track down her cheek. "Win we shall."

—·—

EPILOGUE

S ONOS STRETCHED HIS LEGS on the warm sand, breathing in the
salty air. He closed his eyes for a moment and listened to his
friends' banter.

Over the last six years, their core group—Sonos, Charlotte,
Taine, Taimani, and Jax—had formed an unspoken agreement
that they'd celebrate the Feast of the Broken Towers together.

This year, they were all gathered in Jamroq, and oddly enough,
it was even starting to feel like home—or at least a very familiar
place. Truth be told, Sonos tried to visit Jamroq as often as possible.

"Hey, you." Charlotte slipped down next to him and nudged him
softly with her shoulder. "You're looking quite pensive."

Sonos turned with a smile and slowly opened his eyes.

Charlotte's green eyes danced, her curls swaying gently with the
ocean breeze.

He reached out and tucked a loose strand behind her ear. "I was
just thinking how I'm the luckiest man alive."

Her eyes softened, but the moment was interrupted when Jax
squatted behind them. "I might have to disagree with you there,
Sonny."

Sonos cringed at the nickname, which he knew only fueled Jax's
joy in pushing his buttons. But Lenora was on a video call.

Her hologram projected from the gazer on Jax's finger.

"Hi, Char! Hi, S-Sonos!" She waved cheerfully. "S-sorry I couldn't be t-there this year."

Charlotte turned on her knees, facing Lenora's hologram. "Nonsense! I already told Jax he has to bring you back some food and ensure it's enough for that little one on the way."

Lenora smiled and rubbed her bulging belly.

"Make sure the *smallie* doesn't decide to make an entrance before I get there next month," Charlotte said.

"Yes, I've already scheduled an extended visit with the Mountain Kingdom to ensure I'm there for the birth, too," Sonos added.

After four years of Jax studying with the healers in Noiz, he and Lenora had tied the knot two years ago and were expecting their first baby. The first of a whole tribe, if anyone listened to Jax.

Sonos and Charlotte had only had vague conversations about the future. So much effort had been focused on rebuilding the K'Luma Empire and supporting the Empress. He was constantly traveling, and meeting with emissaries and leaders inside and outside K'Luma. Charlotte was relentlessly focused on building the tech order of the Sahemy inside of Jamroq. She had already made significant strides in improving the storage of power for tech. The Empress was always trying to recruit her to Pergamum, but the King sisters were all intent on building at home, first.

The women continued chatting about the baby and life in Noiz.

Sonos gave his regards to Lenora, then excused himself for a little walk.

He didn't get far before Taine jogged up next to him. For once, Taine was out of uniform, relaxing in a sleeveless top that showed off the tattoos that ran from his right earlobe down his neck, shoulders, chest, and back. A few new markings had been added recently. Sonos guessed they were related to Taine's continued rise through the ranks of Kimwaki's leadership. The Isles were still a part of K'Luma, but tensions were rising as the Emperor's expected return drew closer. Only one year remained in the curse.

Taine started talking first. "So, when are you going to pop the question?"

Sonos wasn't ready to take the bait, especially given the growing knot in his stomach. "I already know when Charlotte wants her roast fish. I can tell Robbie without asking her first."

Taine scoffed and jogged in front of Sonos, stopping him in his tracks. "You know that's not what I was referring to. You two have been smitten for over six years... and still, no union yet?"

Sonos sighed. How could he explain? "You know that we only have seven years with my mother ruling before the Emperor returns. Next year is going to change everything."

He hated feeling fearful. He knew the strength of his mother and, more importantly, of El. Things would never go back to the way they were before. But still... he didn't trust his father. Nor his brother, who had not been seen in K'Luma since his banishment. However, if intelligence was to be believed, Ade was amassing his private army in the lands beyond the Mountain Kingdom. Wylder and Elisa Wumi had disappeared, and Uzuma had been locked away for war crimes. Too much was brewing to feel comfortable.

Taine laid a hand on Sonos' shoulder. "Though the future is unknown, we know that when the dust settles, we will always win."

"Well said, brother."

Sonos jumped at the sound of Taimani's voice directly behind him.

She laughed at his surprise.

"I swear, ever since graduation, you have only become more stealthy. I'm surprised the commander of *El*'s army hasn't recruited you yet," Sonos muttered.

"Who says he hasn't?" she retorted with a grin. "But it's not me we're talking about," she pivoted the conversation. "Stop delaying and worrying about the Emperor. If anything, the journey has proved that we are only stronger when we're together." She glanced down the beach to where Charlotte was still sitting, talking to Jax and Lenora. "And she is someone you need in your corner... forever."

"Unless he's too scared to talk to her father." Taine winked. "Josiah King is a force to be reckoned with."

It was true. Sonos had seen firsthand the strength of resolve Josiah brought to any negotiation, especially when it came to talks about establishing the autonomy each isle would have within the Empire. But it was less about Charlotte's dad, and more that Sonos was more and more worried about the overall stability of the Empire and the growing threats they faced. He knew Taimani was part of top secret missions and worked to secure the borders of K'Luma and the Mountain Kingdom. The reports he received were more than enough to justify his worry.

"You, of all people, should know how precarious things are in K'Luma right now," Sonos said, fixing his gaze on Taimani.

Her mouth drew into a tight line. "I do. In fact, I'm heading out again as soon as the meal finishes." She cast an apologetic glance at her brother. "But as I said, we're stronger together. Hope and commitment to the future are the bravest choices we can make in the face of danger."

Charlotte let out a deep laugh that carried on the breeze. She was still deep in conversation with Jax as they video-chatted with Lenora.

Sonos let his anxiety recede and attuned to Charlotte. She was brilliant, beautiful, full of joy... there was nothing more he could ask for—no one else he wanted. The warriors spoke truth; it was only his fear holding him back at this point.

"You're right," he said eventually. "Of course, you're both right. And that is why I have this." He pulled a gold band from a hidden pocket near his chest. He'd been carrying the band around for the better part of the last two years. He was always distracted by something or someone whenever he got close to asking Charlotte the big question.

But this day, on this beach, surrounded by friends, everything would change. He was going to ask Charlotte King to marry him, and by *El*, he knew their future was secure.

Fight we must, but win we shall. We are unconquerable.

ACKNOWLEDGEMENTS

My first thanks go to you, dear reader. Stories only find meaning when they reach the hearts and minds of others—so thank you for helping to bring this to life!

I hope you found uplift, encouragement, and hope in the midst of this journey.

Mosaic, you have already received the dedication of this book, but I will expand on my love and thanks here, too. This book would not exist without your weekly diligence, encouragement, and feedback from the first draft to the final round of edits. Having fellow writers share in the journey of each other's stories is invaluable. Whether you were there at the start, the finish, or every word in between, this is your story, too. Ntebogeng Archer, Elizabeth Peters, Naomi Kitcher, Tawjna Williams, Miles Mungo, Dario Shields, Richard Ince, and my beloved Gordon Alert.

Gordon, you are my husband, my alpha reader, my beta reader, my developmental editor, my proofreader, and my best friend.

Zhaun and Zakyla, you will always be at the heart of every endeavor.

Kevin Khelawan, thank you for beta-reading both books and being a force of encouragement every step of the way. A special shout-out to Zakyla and Anaba Henry for your input on the beta stage as well. Ruth Rudden, you were my first-ever gamma reader, and I appreciate the effort to find all those pesky and sneaky typos!

Grayson and Shala (and your tribe of Alerts in Trinidad & Tobago), I am incredibly thankful for helping to bring this book to a final, polished state. Shala, you are an editor extraordinaire! Grayson, the cover is perfect, and I love Koen, Ruel, and Raena's input. The towers absolutely needed to look like a prison.

My Gilliland and Takosky crew in PA... thank you for being my biggest cheerleaders and champions! For every time you handed out or gifted Fight We Must, for every picture you've sent of where it turned up on a library shelf, for every word of encouragement: thank you! You are what inspires every scene of the power of a family's love.

To my Elijah Centre family and Congress-WBN global community, this book is built upon the life and journey we share. I truly hope that the words, phrases, wisdom, and truth are recognizable from what we've heard over years... it's been a joy to bring them to life through a story!

Last but not least, I want to thank every person who has taken the time to write a review, engage in social media, or send a direct message after reading book one. Each word spoke life and encouragement into the journey to keep moving forward. Thank you!

About the Author

Heidi Alert spends her days in the corporate world, but the midnight oil burns brightly with stories that need to be told.

Originally from Harmony, PA, a country suburb of Pittsburgh, a winding journey led across the U.S. and eventually to Trinidad & Tobago in the Caribbean for eleven years. She now calls Atlanta, Georgia, home, together with her Jamaican husband, two teenagers, and rescue pets.

She holds a bachelor's in marketing from the University of Pittsburgh and her MBA from Georgetown.

Connect on IG @heidialert or visit www.heidialert.com